WESTERNS 3:
BROTHER OF
THE WOLF!

ED GARRON

WILDCARD WESTERNS

Other books by ED GARRON...

WESTERNS: WARPATHS & PEACEMAKERS

WESTERNS 2: WILD AS THE WIND

WESTERNS 4: YARNS OF THE OPEN RANGE

www.edgarron.com

WESTERNS 3:
BROTHER OF THE WOLF!

WILDCARD WESTERNS
PUBLISHED BY THE DERNFORD PRESS

ISBN: 9781976963131
Set in US English/Constantia by JM Services
Cover illustration by kind permission of KH reproductions

WESTERNS 3:-
BROTHER OF THE WOLF!

SIX NOVELLAS:

BOOK ONE...

MURDER BY
LOST SOULS' MESA

'Advise persons never to engage in killing.'
-Billy the Kid

MURDER BY
LOST SOULS' MESA

CHAPTER ONE:
A KILLING IN SILVER COUNTRY.

Billy Gillespie had no choice but to see an innocent man shot dead. Once he'd decided to put a gun on that prospector, and rob him his goods and money, his cards were dealt. After that, there was nothing for it but to play the hand through to the end.

Billy and his accomplice had found the man on a trail by Lost Souls' Mesa. At first they had exchanged friendly words, and even walked a distance together; but then the young outlaw made his fateful decision. He had weighed up the other man, and found him vulnerable and weak. The fellow wore no gun-belt, carried no rifle, didn't even have a hunting knife close at hand; but he did have a buckskin gelding that Billy coveted badly. Furthermore, by his own admission, the man was heading back to town to exchange his silver for real currency. All in all, there seemed plenty to gain from relieving that stranger of his possessions, and very little risk attached.

Billy was relying on the man giving him no trouble and meekly surrendering his heavy poke of silver, and his sleek buckskin horse. There were other goods too, as Billy was soon to discover, including a roll of notes, a gold pocket watch, and even a concealed pistol – fully loaded.

As might be expected, it was the gun that upset Billy's calculations, that and his intended victim's over-confidence in his own prowess. Furthermore, the fellow, who happened to be married and the father of two children, was rather determined to hang on to his hard-won treasures. So, when turning out his jacket pockets, and slowly producing an old but serviceable .44 Colt revolver brought back from the war, the miner had suddenly tried the trick of throwing the gun from left to right hand and fanning it. He'd even managed to get off a shot. Perhaps he'd been practising it on those long, lonely nights by his camp fire. Perhaps it was something he'd rehearsed, and believed he could pull off.

He almost succeeded too; but though his gun threw out a single bullet, he received two back in quick succession – and so the pot went to the other man.

"Oh, Billy!" cried Amy, who'd accompanied young Billy Gillespie on this ill-starred errand, "My God, we've killed him!"

"The fool went for his gun," said Billy. "You saw it; he left me with no damn choice. I had to drop him."

He wasn't so bothered he'd shot a man – he'd done that a dozen times before – but only that Amy had seen him do it. Moreover, he'd made Amy his accomplice; and Amy was the only one in the world he cared about, the only one whose criticisms cut him to his very core. He had dragged her into his world of shame, and now she would never forgive him for it.

She looked at him, a look that made him wish he'd never been born. He looked back at her, and knew her life would never be the same again.

"Oh Billy!" she said, with tears on her cheeks, "You promised me, you promised me!"

"I shouldn't have promised," he said sullenly; "But sayin' we'd rob a man without harming a hair on his head – that relied on him playin' fair an' square an' not attemptin' no fool tricks – but you saw what he did."

"I saw a man killed for trying to hold on to his own property," she wept, "an innocent man – who was mindin' his own affairs – a man we should have let alone!"

"We had to do it Amy," said Billy; "After your horse broke down, we had to get another, come what may. There's men in these hills would kill their own mother to get at a girl like you; it was him or us, Amy; an' God knows I'd do anything for you."

"Don't say that, Billy," she wept, "I told you already I'd rather starve, or take my chances trying to walk back to town, than have somebody else die out here in my place."

"Yeah," said Billy, "you said it – but I couldn't let you do it. Now you think I'm the devil – an' I guess you're right."

"I don't think it-" she began.

"Listen," he said, "If it makes you feel any better, that man has evened the score – he's repaid a bad man in kind."

"Don't talk foolish," she said, "How has he repaid you?"

"By giving me one back," said Billy, slumping to the ground, "right in my gut... just as I deserve."

Hearing her cry of anguish, and watching her feeble attempts to help him, were part of the punishment for a dying man.

"Oh Billy," she wept, "Don't leave me all alone, out here in the middle of nowhere!"

"Can't be helped," smiled Billy grimly; "But one thing you can do for me – go get Stevie Fitzpatrick. Tell him to come out here. I'll get him to help you. He still owes me that favor. Tell him Billy got shot by a man he robbed – be sure to tell him that. You understand me?"

"What if he won't come?" she said.

"Oh he'll come," said Billy, wincing in pain; "Them

9

Fitzpatricks have a funny sense of honor about these sort o' things. Tell him Billy Gillespie's callin' in that favor he owes. Tell him to follow you back to Dead Man's Pass, an' he'll find me by Lost Souls' Mesa."

"That favor is from way, way, back," she said, "an' a lot of water has flowed under the bridge since the day you saved his life from Alvarez..."

Billy, now resigned to his fate, only smiled at her lack of faith. He *knew* Fitzpatrick would come.

"If he don't rustle, tell him he's a cowardly dog for not coming, an' leavin' a woman in trouble. Remind him he's the county sheriff. You'll see, he'll follow meekly as a dog – 'cos there's one thing will always turn the head of men like Stevie Fitzpatrick – an' that's puttin' in their brain the notion – they got no sand for the job!"

CHAPTER TWO:
LOST SOULS MESA

Stevie Fitzpatrick was quite aware of the well-defined local custom of speaking to a man when one comes upon him in the dark – providing, of course, he is of friendly intent. He was also aware of an old wound in his shoulder, from a strict observance of this courtesy, when the other man, contrary to custom, had drawn and shot – then apologised. So Stevie waited for the figure to step clear of the shadow of the corral bar before he spoke.

"State your purpose," said Fitzpatrick, drawing away from the light that streamed from the open bunk-house window.

The small stranger stopped.

"Stephen Fitzpatrick?" asked the figure.

"Yeah," he answered, his hand quickly slipping away from the concealed Remington in its shoulder-holster, for it was the voice of a woman.

"I want to speak with you," she returned quickly.

"Come into the house, then," he said.

"No," she said, stepping closer to him, "we can talk here."

As he advanced to meet her he saw that a handkerchief hid the lower part of her face, and the broad brim of a hat concealed the upper. A gray shirt and brown chaps completed the resemblance to a puncher – or an outlaw.

"Well, miss," he said, as he extended his hand, "you're takin' a long chance in that outfit. You look as near like Billy Gillespie as twin calves. He's your height and the same hat. I thought I was just about goin' to attend to a little official business as sheriff of the county."

"It's not too late yet, and that's why I came," she replied.

"It was Billy Gillespie sent me. He's badly wounded, and I came to get you to go him."

"Billy sent *you?*" he breathed; "I don't understand..."

"I'm wearing his hat and coat," she said, "And it's true he's about my height. I've been trying to change his ways; but I failed. He robbed a man and got shot. He has important stuff to tell you."

"I see," said Fitzpatrick; "And who are you?"

"Never mind that – will you go?" she said.

"I'll have to think about it," he replied.

"Then you're a coward," she interrupted hotly.

"Well, maybe I am – or maybe I don't like being shot in the dark. Billy must have thought I was losin' my mind if he expected I was goin' to fall for a game like this. But, miss, I wasn't born yesterday – I know there are men who'd dearly like to put me under the ground, an' Billy Gillespie, he's at the front of the queue!"

"You don't believe me, then – you think I'm not telling the truth? I'm telling you, Billy is shot, real bad. Look, there's blood all over this coat."

Fitzpatrick examined the coat, but still looked dubious.

"Listen," she said, "he told me to remind you of the time – if you refused to come – when he came upon you while you were standing off Pancho Alvarez and his men, and that you told him, if ever he wanted a friend, to call on you. That was before he went wrong and took that strong box from the stage – you understand?"

"Yeah," said Fitzpatrick, "I understand."

Four years before, on one of his regular hunts for the legendary Lost Souls Mine, he had been caught in a little rock-strewn dip by Alvarez and his gang. They were outlaws from

12

way south who'd taken a liking for the Utah badlands. They'd waylaid Stevie Fitzpatrick, neither knowing nor caring he was a county sheriff. They simply wanted his horse, his money, his guns. Through the blistering heat of the day he had stood them off; until his ammunition got so low he had made up his mind to end it all by coming into the open and making them kill him – rather than endure the torture. It was then, from a pile of drift in front, that a Winchester opened up on the outlaws from their rear, and drove them from the rocks into the open, where they dropped one by one before Fitzpatrick's pair of Remington .36's. Only Alvarez and one other man escaped that day, both of them wounded. That episode made history, and gave Stevie Fitzpatrick an even loftier reputation as sheriff of the county.

That famous victory, however, was only made possible by Billy Gillespie. Fitzpatrick had told the boy, when he came out from behind the drift that day, if ever he wanted a friend, to call upon him. He told him he would not forget to return the favor; and now the call had come.

The complication was that Billy had gone wrong since then, and Fitzpatrick had been looking for him for months. He had vowed to let the law make of him what it would. But there were those who said that he did not want to get him, because of the affair on the Lost Souls' trail. The simple truth, however, was that the sheriff had hunted him, time after time. From desert to water-hole, from sun-blinding sands to chaparral, and missed him always in the drift-littered beds of Dry River Canyon, or up in the rocks beside Lost Souls' Mesa, where the chase invariably led.

"Will you come?" the girl was repeating. "Will you come – or must I go back and say you were afraid?"

"No, I'm goin', miss," he said. "Where's your horse?"

"Tied to the corral gate," she answered.

"You wait for me down by the cottonwoods. I'll be there as soon as I can saddle and pick up a few things. You say he is badly shot up – what about a doctor, then?" he asked.

"It's too late for that. He knows there's no use," she muttered, moving toward the gate.

"You sure?" he asked.

"I'm sure," she said; "Now hurry."

Fitzpatrick went into the house and took up his Winchester, and his gun-belt with the pair of pistols, and a sack of stuff for the trail; then he returned to the corral. He saddled the big gray that came up in response to his whistle.

At the foot of the little hill, the girl was waiting.

"Now then," he said softly, "lead the way; and remember, I ain't takin' any chances, an' I ain't hostile. I'm just keepin' my word to Billy, so I'm dependin' on you. You understand me?"

She did not answer, but turned her pony's head to the west, and led him away from the trees, into the shadow of the hill. Soon they had left the Bar Z ranch way behind them; they entered the semi-desert that formed its western boundary. They were only a two day ride from the town of One Dog Creek, but the weird sandy landscape and the blackness of the huge Mesa ahead against the stars gave the impression of an even more remote and forlorn quarter of the world.

In silence they rode for an hour. Then they began to climb the steep narrow trail that led into a series of high, broken cliffs that overlooked the Bar Z ranch on one side, and a whole lot of dry desert on the other. On and on, through the winding path that clung to the side of one towering range they rode. Farther and farther they climbed, among the dull blanketed

14

columns that reared their tops to the starlit sky.

"How far?" asked Fitzpatrick, as he trotted up to her side, when the trail was wide enough to permit it.

"Another six miles, or so," she answered. Then her pony stumbled and for a moment it seemed he would go down on his knees. Stevie Fitzpatrick quickly reached over, and made as if to lift her from the saddle. She seemed to shrink from him, and he loosened his hold, just as the buckskin recovered himself. Fitzpatrick breathed a sigh of relief, then drew the big gray in behind. She turned, their eyes met for a second, and Fitzpatrick saw in them a terrible sorrow. He realized then, he had been lured out onto that dark trail not only by the story of Billy lying wounded and needing his help, but also by something in those lost and hopeless eyes. He told himself that he wouldn't allow himself to be taken in or won over by the owner of those eyes – a promise he was by no means sure he could keep.

Again they were climbing. They traveled until the moon came up and lighted the trail, just as she turned sharply to the right, into a narrow path that shone like a painted strip on the dull rocks. Fitzpatrick recognized the trail; it led to Lost Souls' Mesa, where he had long ago looked for the old silver mine old timers said was hidden there. But he, just like all the others, had failed to discover the legendary source of treasure, and assumed the stories to be nothing more than travelers' tales.

"Just a minute," he said, for he knew that the trail ahead was blind, unused, and ended squarely against the face of a great rock.

"Come on," she urged, "This way – or are you afraid?"

"No," said Fitzpatrick, "but haven't you missed the trail?

This is Dead Man's Pass, which is a dead end for sure; and down there is Dry River Canyon."

He pointed into the great abyss below, where the moon's rays had not reached.

"I know where we are," she answered, now several feet in advance and still moving on; "Come on, this is the way, you'll soon find out I'm right."

"Very well – but you're wrong," he replied, for he knew the place, and that they would soon be stopped by the wall of rock beyond.

So they were; the rock was there, closing the way. The girl slipped from the pony's back, went over to the rock and fumbled for a match, lit it and then led her pony through the rock – or so it seemed. There was a fissure in the cliff just wide enough for a horse to squeeze through, while brushing either stirrup on the stone. The vertical faults in the rock-face had given the illusion of there being no way through, even at a few steps' distance.

Fitzpatrick dismounted and, leading his horse, followed slowly, suspiciously, until he could look into the trail beyond.

"This way," she commanded. He walked through, too surprised to question. When he had cleared the gap, he turned and looked back, as if not believing what they had just done.

"Come on, come on," she cried, as she mounted and spurred on. Fitzpatrick's eyes raised in wonder at the black holes in the cliffs towering above them. Almost reluctantly he followed, closely observing the piles of old drift that lined the trail. Beyond was a moonlit space, a square. Around its edge were low, rock-walled houses. Their roofs had long since fallen in, but the stone walls were good as ever. Fitzpatrick stared in awe. He had heard the descriptions of it, a silver mine on the site of an ancient Indian settlement in the mountains. The story, oft repeated, was that a group of miners had found the place already deserted, and partially emptied the hills of silver; later, bandits struck and killed them, every one, in order to take their treasure and keep the secret of its origin. But that was thirty, forty, fifty years before – or so the story went.

Fitzpatrick thought it likely that the easily-gotten silver had already been mined and removed. There was no evidence of machinery or workings of a proper, large-scale mining operation, only heaps of spoil and rock dumped seemingly at random around the empty village, close to the face of the mesa. Dark tunnel-mouths led into the cliffs. Fitzpatrick guessed that endless hours of toil had been invested in digging those galleries into the rock-face. Here, then, was the place of stories and legends, a series of workings more or less on top of the ruined settlement, not near but actually *inside* Lost Souls' Mesa. Above and around him towered the rocks, now viewed from within. Small wonder, then, when he was hunting Gillespie along Dry River Canyon, the outlaw had always led him into Dead Man's Pass and given him the slip. But how had Billy and the girl come to discover its secrets, and more relevantly, why had they brought him into their circle of trust?

He saw the girl dismount, walk a few steps and pass through the doorway of one of those stone-walled, roofless houses – and disappear. Quickly he slid from the saddle, and removed his right-side Remington from its holster. Keeping his horse between himself and the doorway into which the girl had gone, he walked across the smooth floor of the old, un-peopled central space.

When opposite the broken steps, the girl reappeared in the doorway. The hat was gone and the handkerchief had

17

fallen from her face.

She stepped forward, faltered, half stumbled, and turned her face until the moon shone full upon it. Just for an instant Fitzpatrick hesitated; he hesitated until he found a name for the face of the girl.

"Amy Baxter!" he said. He stared at her in breathless incredulity, the recognition baffling him as he thought of her serving customers in the general store in town.

"Yes," she breathed; "I wanted to hide my face until we got up here. I thought if you recognized me, you might not come. I knew you'd only see me as a silly shop girl telling tall stories. But I had to get you to Billy quickly. I'll explain it all later."

"All right," he said, puzzled by what she said.

"Now come with me. I can't go into that room alone. I'm afraid... he may already be... gone."

There was something in her voice that took away his lingering fear of an ambush. Billy must be badly hurt, or worse, after all. Fitzpatrick holstered his gun, took her hand, and led her through the moonlit doorway. As they entered, both sensed the stillness which meant the place was no longer the refuge of a living man. Nevertheless, she called out softly:

"Billy," she said, "Billy – I got your friend Fitzpatrick here... Billy?"

Very slowly, they edged forward, peered into the corner of the resting place of the stricken man. Amy stepped in front, moved forward toward the dark form, just as some wisps of cloud that were partially veiling the moon were swept away.

Then they saw him, slumped against a wall. His eyes were open and staring, and his contorted face plain to see in the moonlight. Amy turned, ran straight back to Fitzpatrick and he caught her in his arms and held on, lest she run blindly out into the darkness and injure herself.

"He's dead – oh he's dead," she sobbed.

"Too late, then, after all," said Fitzpatrick, softly patting her hair. Even in that light, he could see the tears streaming down her face. He wasn't sure what to do, and so he held on to her as her shoulders heaved in sorrow and pain.

"There, don't cry," he whispered, realising how lacking he was, and how poorly he fitted into the distressing situation. Then, he led her back into the open space away from the house; they stopped, turned toward each other.

"He's gone – the last of us, except me – my brother," she moaned.

"Your brother?" he repeated in surprise.

"Yes," she answered, stepping back. Her eyes were wide with shock, but nevertheless she was able to speak, in a faltering voice. "My real name's Amy Gillespie... I changed my name on account of Billy. I came to live in Dog Creek in the hope of finding him and saving him one day. I knew he was at the mine with my father; but folks said he'd gone bad and turned outlaw. I knew then, that something must have happened to my father, and that Billy was desperate for money. He would never have done the things he did –bad things – if my father were still alive."

"Yeah," said Fitzpatrick doubtfully, "that must have been what changed him."

Amy pulled away from him, and her dark eyes flashed with anger.

"And you!" she said; "They said you were hunting him, like a wild animal, and I hated you for it. I still do. Now he's dead. You ought to be satisfied, you and your kind. He wanted me to bring you to him, to tell you of this miserable hole – to show you how we've been living. He wanted the claim properly recorded in my name. He said it would be worth thousands to a big mining company. God knows it gave precious little to us – the silver's in deep, and the ore hard to purify. Billy said you were the only one who could be depended upon to help me file a claim. It's all that's left for me."

"Well... yes," said Fitzpatrick, "I'll help... if I can."

"I've lived here three months with him, praying, hoping, even begging him to give up his lawless life and go away to California, or Canada, or some other place safe."

"But he wouldn't go," said Stevie Fitzpatrick.

"No," she said; "He wouldn't... change his ways."

"They never do," said Fitzpatrick; "So what happened to him, Amy?"

Her eyes regarded him fiercely.

"Yesterday, a miner he tried to rob on the other side of the mesa shot him. Billy knew he was dying, and I managed to get him back here."

"A miner?" said Fitzpatrick, disturbed.

"He's dead too; Billy held him up, but he went for a gun. Billy killed him, and took a bullet in the stomach."

"I see," said Fitzpatrick frowning; "Are you sure the other man's dead? Did you check?"

"I checked," she said, "and I'm sure."

"Well," said Fitzpatrick, "this is a sorry tale. Another man killed, and for what? Did Billy not think of askin' for help? Most folks would, if they're in a spot, instead of thievin'-"

"I tried to stop him," Amy interrupted, "I truly did. He even promised not to do anything stupid, after we saw that man passing us close by. But Billy got the devil in him, an' after actin' all friendly-like, he pulled his gun on him anyway.

20

It was my fault too – my pony slipped and broke a foot on the trail. Billy thought he'd take the man's horse for me, but I'd already told him I'd walk or get back to town somehow..."

"Uh-huh," said Fitzpatrick, "So Billy pulled a gun, an' the man died defendin' himself. Is that about right?"

"I pleaded with him," said Amy, "but I reckon Billy had the notion all along to get that horse. I was... horrified. At first the man seemed to surrender, then he threw his gun from one hand to another and fired. Billy killed him, but he got shot through as well. He wanted to make it back here; it was where he wanted to die, I guess."

She hung her head, covered her eyes with her hands. Fitzpatrick regarded her for some time, then took out his tobacco and rolled a cigarette, which he offered her. She took it, and accepted a light.

"Well, Amy," said Fitzpatrick, "I'm truly sorry for you. I'm going to do what I can. In the morning we'll bury your brother in the mineshaft; he'll be like a king in his tomb. I'll have to see that dead miner, too. Then I'll get you out of here, back to Dog Creek."

"I always knew it would end like this," she said, sitting down on a slab of stone; "but Billy had something in his spirit – the same spirit that made my father almost insane. Once they got an idea in their heads, they stuck to it, come what may. Pa bribed an old man to learn the secret of how to get into this place. Then, he and Billy came here together, and for what? A few hundred dollars – the silver left in the old mine is the hardest to get at. And my father was killed in a cave-in when the old props failed, and lies buried somewhere in the galleries beneath us."

"But I still don't understand," said Fitzpatrick, building

another smoke, "How did you and Billy meet up? I mean, you were in town, and he was living out here."

"I got a letter from my father where I was living back in St George. He must have posted it the last time he went back to Dog Creek for supplies. I got a ride into Dog Creek on the coach, knowing it was the nearest town to Lost Souls' Mesa, and found a job with lodgings at the general store. That's where I saw you a few times. I had a little money, and saved some more, enough for a decent little horse. One day I packed up my things and rode out by Lost Souls' Mesa – alone."

"That was a dangerous thing to do, Amy," said Fitzpatrick. "This place is two or three day's out of town, and only the Bar Z offers any safe shelter nearby. Even then, those ranch-hands are rough, ready and wild as hell."

"Yes," she said, "I saw those boys in town. I saw how folks kept out of their way."

"Yeah," said Fitzpatrick, "But they ain't nothin' compared to Alvarez and his bunch. They've been terrorizin' this part of Utah for a long time. I'll get them one day; only I can't convince a posse to ride up here. Don't blame them none either."

"My father warned me about Alvarez. He said I had to have a good fast pony, which is what I had, until the accident."

"Unfortunate," said Fitzpatrick, "to lose a horse way out here. Still, ain't no reason to turn to robbery, Amy."

She threw a fierce, momentary glance in the sheriff's direction, but chose to ignore his last remark.

"My father told me where the mine was, and drew me a map. I rode out, and it took two days. When I got to Dead Man's Pass, Billy saw me and brought me in. It was then I learned that my father was dead; it was a terrible time for me.

But at least I was with my brother again. He'd changed though, in every way. He'd grown hard and cruel and didn't care who he hurt; and his face – he looked terrible – poor food, worry and overwork had almost done for him. And the chemicals he used on the ore are poisonous."

"Yeah," said Fitzpatrick, "I've heard that a few times."

"Worse still," he told me how he stole a strongbox off a stage. He said when he shot it open it was mainly mail an' papers – but then he was a wanted man. He needed cash to buy supplies from the trading post near Larsonville, so he robbed some others too."

"A good many others," said Fitzpatrick thoughtfully.

"It broke my heart to hear what he'd done; I planned to make Billy leave the mine. But I had an accident on my horse and its foot got busted. Billy had to shoot it. Weeks passed. I've been stuck in these old walls with Billy ever since. There was no-one else for me, and little by little I was persuading him to get him away. Or at least I thought so. And now it's over, it's too late."

She buried her face in her hands once more. Fitzpatrick sat down beside her and lit his cigarette. He drew in the smoke, staring into shadowy ruins opposite him.

Fitzpatrick left her to cry it out for a long time. Finally she stopped, and slowly turned to look at him. She looked, for all the world, like a lost and lonely child.

"First thing in the mornin'," said Fitzpatrick, "we got to get you somewhere safe."

"For me," she said, "there ain't no such place."

She was hugging herself protectively, and shaking like a leaf.

"I know of one," he said, putting an arm around her; "I

23

have a sister who'll look after you. We'll ask for your old job back while we file your claim. You'll be a rich woman, you'll see. What do you say? Will you go back to Dog Creek?"

He gently drew the girl toward him.

"I don't know," she whispered, "I just don't know."

"Listen," he said, "I guess my promise extends to looking after Billy's sister for a spell. Don't get no ideas I ain't the perfect gent in all this. Yes, that's what we'll do. We'll go see my sister, she's got a house with a spare room. We'll see what she makes of all this. Now, Amy, will you go with me, and trust me?"

There was a long silence, as she leaned her head against his shoulder. Her arms were tucked in front of her and his own were placed very lightly around her.

Then the answer came.

"Yes – I will go," she said.

CHAPTER TWO:
CAMP-FIRE LIGHT

That night they slept out in the open square, a miserable camping place that gave them both unquiet dreams in the snatches of sleep they managed. The next morning, after Billy was buried in a mine-shaft, they filled canteens in the trickle of water coming down one side of the mesa. Their only breakfast was the remnants of corn-bread and biscuits from Fitzpatrick's pack. Then they saddled and prepared the three horses, and got ready to travel. Amy rode the buckskin – which had been the miner's pony – and Billy's big sorrel mare became their pack animal. Fitzpatrick distributed the stolen silver between the three horses, with most of it going on the mare, packing it into the saddle-bags.

"This goes to the relatives of the miner," said Fitzpatrick to the girl, "if I can trace them. Otherwise it goes to the county treasury. The same goes for that pony when it's sold."

"Of course," she said morosely.

"The silver from your own mine we bury and leave here," said Fitzpatrick, "and what happens to it is your own affair."

He made her show him the place where the miner had been murdered. It was only a short ride away. The body was still there, but the buzzards had been at work, and it was not a pretty sight. Fitzpatrick told her to wait a little way off while he examined the crime scene.

The dead man had a few papers, including a letter from his wife, and a couple of photographs on him. It turned out his name was Thomas Mannerheim, a Mormon. He had come all the way from Salt Lake City. One of the photographs was of him holding a little girl in his arms. He showed it to Amy. She recoiled in horror.

"That's why most folks go easy with the guns," he said, with pursed lips; "Every action's got its consequences."

That was the first time she shot him a look of something approaching absolute hatred, and it sent a chill down his spine. But he met that look with a steady gaze, and held it, until she turned away. Then he went back and dragged the body into a shallow gulch, and caved some rocks and sand over it; it was a pitiful grave, but it would have to do.

All day they rode in silence. That night they camped near a waterhole. There was a little grass for the horses, and some bushes with dead branches for a camp-fire. Fitzpatrick set about cooking a good evening meal with beans and a jack-rabbit he'd shot with his rifle. The critter had no head, but once skinned and quartered, there was enough meat on it for two. On flat stones next the fire he baked corn-bread, which turned out hard but edible. He made coffee too, of which they both had several cups while they waited for the stew.

Before they'd drunk it, Fitzpatrick had apologised that he carried no sugar. She had shrugged, reached for the brown leather bag she had slung over her back. Unbuckling its flap, she opened it and reached inside. As he glanced up, Stevie Fitzpatrick noted that the bag seemed to hold a fair few of her personal items, for it looked heavy and full.

She took out a small bag of sugar, and tossed it over to him. With a nod of thanks, he opened it and spooned some of it into their coffee. He was about to throw it back when she told him to keep it, to stash it with the provisions. As he was looking across at her, he caught her glance into that bag. It was a strange, furtive look; he thought little of it at the time, though the memory of it lodged in his mind.

Later, as he sat staring into the flames of the camp-fire, he tried to think of something suitable to say to Amy Gillespie to bring her out of her black depression. That would not be easy, since they'd just that morning buried her brother, and later his victim, out on the desert side of the mesa.

Fitzpatrick rose, went to the other side of the fire, where the pots were simmering away on their stick tripods. He doled out the stew onto tin plates and gave her a spoon. He handed her one of the plates and sat down again.

"I was his sister and I let him down when he needed me," she said softly and absent-mindedly, as if she were alone. "I could've been stronger."

"Don't blame yourself," said Fitzpatrick, "He made his choices long ago."

"He made one bad decision and you hounded him further and further beyond the law," she said gloomily.

"Listen," he replied, "If I'd caught him after that first robbery, maybe I could've talked sense into him. But he'd still have to do his time. That's how it works."

"Oh sure," she said sarcastically, "you'd have done him the kindness of putting him in the pen for ten years, and he'd have come out brutal and hurting and gone straight back to his old ways."

"Well, Amy," he said, surprised by her attitude, "How could a man like your brother ever change? How exactly did you propose to, you know, turn his life around?"

"He said he'd come with me to San Francisco; get a job, make something of himself. We'd both find someone to marry, get fine houses, have families, lead a normal life."

"Was that what he really wanted to do, Amy?" said Fitzpatrick, doubt coloring his of voice.

27

"He said he would," she said defensively, eyes scowling at the fire.

Stevie Fitzpatrick spooned a bit more of his food, deep in thought. Amy had hardly touched hers, though they had been riding since early morning.

"Try to eat just a little," he said quietly. "We got a long way to go tomorrow."

"I ain't hungry," she replied, setting down her plate.

"Even so," he persisted, "you got to eat something."

"Won't you let me be?" she said angrily; "I know you're trying to be all brotherly-like, Fitzpatrick; but can't you tell, I just want to be let alone."

The two of them said nothing for a time. Fitzpatrick, not having learned his lesson, that saying nothing might be the wisest policy, was the first to break the silence.

"Why'd he have to go bad like that, anyway?" he said, "I mean, the man started out so full of promise when he punched cattle on the Bar Z. It was that damned silver mine turned his head, I reckon."

Amy shifted uneasily on her blanket by the fire.

"Come to that," Fitzpatrick continued, "why'd he take that strong box in the first place? I mean, he could've used some of his own silver to pay for supplies... it just don't make sense."

The girl turned on him, now fully wakened from her reverie of grief.

"If you can't say somethin' good," she snapped, "maybe you should keep that big trap shut, Fitzpatrick. Ain't you ever done things you were ashamed of? Ain't you ever put just one foot wrong? Or are you just one of those Mr Perfects who go to church on a Sunday an' spend the rest of the week tellin' everyone else how to live?"

The harshness of her tone took him aback somewhat, and he wondered for the first time if perhaps she was as innocent as he had believed. Her dark mood he had taken for an intensity of grief, and guilt that she'd been unable to persuade her brother to take the straight and narrow trail; but could it be that she had taken a more active role in the killings after all? Surely not! He took out the scrap of paper he had prised from Billy's fingers and, shielding it from her gaze, read it again:

> Stevie remember Amy done nothing
> it was all on me
> you got to help her file
> there's silver in the bags if you want it
> you be square
> Billy

A sudden thought struck him.

"Amy," he said, "Do you have a gun?"

He indicated her brown leather bag with his eyes, and the long time she took to answer told him all he needed to know, even before she spoke.

"Yes," she said at last, "Why not, out here? I got a .32, an' Billy taught me to shoot, if you must know. But not so's I could hold up stage-coaches, if that's what you're thinkin'."

"It wasn't that," Fitzpatrick lied, "it's just that we're in Paiute country, and if anything was to happen to me... well, it's good you learned how to shoot, that's all."

"You're a lousy liar," she scoffed, "just lousy. But it's all right, Mr Perfect. I can see it from your point of view. Maybe, just maybe, Billy Gillespie trained his sister to gun down unsuspectin' miners. Or shoot the sheriff when we're almost back in town. I mean, it's possible, ain't it?"

"It wasn't that," he said, his face coloring red with embarrassment, and more than a little anger.

"Or maybe you think I might get riled-up like my brother did, and draw a bead on you?" she snapped.

"Now you're just being foolish," said Fitzpatrick, even more irritated.

"But if I'm so dangerous," she said, "how come Billy thought I needed your help? And if either one of us wanted you dead, how come he didn't just send me to shoot you down outside the bunkhouse at the Bar Z?"

"All right then!" snapped Fitzpatrick, finally losing his temper, and throwing a lump of wood onto the fire. "On the subject of trust, how come you knew exactly where to find me yesterday night? I don't go to that ranch once a year, an' only then to get some money for old Smithy when the hands have smashed up his saloon on a Saturday night. So how could you have known I was there? Tell me that!"

Sparks rose up from the fire, and the flames flickered higher.

"Is that's what's been bothering you?" she said; "Are you so dense you can't work that one out?"

"Yes," he said, "I am. So tell me, how'd you know?"

"Because we saw you go there mid-morning," she said more quietly; "It was just before we met that miner; we were on our way to the other side of the mesa, both of us on Billy's horse, up on the high trail. You passed below us – weren't nowhere else to go in that direction but the Bar Z. We guessed you'd stay the night, it being so far out of town."

"Ah," he said; "You saw me there. I guess that explains it."

"Yes," she said, "I guess it does. And another thing – when we saw you, I asked Billy to ride down to get some help. I told him that I'd heard that sheriff Stephen Fitzpatrick was a decent man, and maybe he should trust you. Can you believe that? I actually asked him to give himself up to you. An' do you know what he said?"

"Well – I guess I would like to know," said Fitzpatrick.

"He laughed and said 'I have a favor to call in from that hombre Fitzpatrick, but I don't expect it extends to a pardon for murder.'"

"Well," said Fitzpatrick, "he called that about right. I'd have gotten you that horse, and taken him in, too – or tried to."

"So," she said, "he saved your life, and you'd still take his. Is that about right?"

"Not exactly," he said; "If I'd seen him on the way to California with you, an' believed that he really was goin' to change, that favor would've extended to letting him go, Amy, I'm sure of that. But the way things were, he was out to do more stupid stuff, stick guns on innocent men, kill when he had to. That's what men on the dodge get up to, Amy. They start off by helping themselves to another man's goods at gunpoint. Then one of them robberies turns sour, a gun goes off, an' they kill. It always follows the same pattern. Ain't that what happened yesterday, Amy, ain't it?"

She threw the plate of food into the fire, and stamped off into the darkness. Some way off, he thought he could hear her weeping over by the horses. This time, common sense got the better of him and he left her there to cry it out, get some of the sorrow and bitterness out of her soul.

An hour later, just as he was stoking the fire and throwing on some big branches for the night, she returned to her side of the fire. He could see from her movements she was still moody and angry, but, nevertheless, she threw a blanket over herself and, turned away from the firelight, and lay in an attitude of sleep. There she remained until just after dawn.

Snug in his own blanket, Fitzpatrick heard her rise, opened one eye and closed it again. Amy Gillespie snatched up her bag, and went down to the water to wash.

It was there she saw the Indian, an old man of sixty, which is old for a Paiute, sitting on a spotted pony. He'd seen their three horses, and thought he might like them for himself. He was small, skinny and wrinkled of face, but he wasn't lacking in courage. After he'd drawn his knife, and given Amy the kind of look that meant she'd better not try to stop him, he slid down and walked towards the horses. She guessed he was going to cut them loose from their hobbles, put collars on them, and lead them away in a string behind his own mount, then return to his people, triumphant.

As he crouched to cut the rope from the buckskin she had been riding the previous day, a shot rang out and the man slumped forward, a .32 Colt slug lodged in his heart.

Fitzpatrick came running to see what had happened.

"Oh my good heavens!" he exclaimed, "Amy what have you done?"

"I had to," she said, "He was after the horses; he threatened me with his knife too. I had to act quick."

"Yeah," said Fitzpatrick, "I guess you did. But a man of that age will be someone very important in his village. Reck'n we'll have the whole Paiute nation down on our heads pretty soon... pack up your blanket, get that horse and let's get goin' – reck'n we got an hour or two before he's missed. Then they'll come for us."

CHAPTER FOUR:
PANCHO ALVAREZ

By ten o'clock they were almost ten miles further along the trail to Dog Creek, and so far they had seen no tell-tale dust cloud in their rear. However, there was no way of erasing their tracks, so it was possible that Indians might catch up with them later in the day, or even the following one. What they really needed was a storm to blow away those hoof-prints; but the weather was hot, sultry and still. And so, covering some distance in the least possible time was the only thing that might keep them safe.

"I'm tired," she said at noon, when they reached a muddy waterhole; "We can see way back if anyone's coming. Can't we stop for some of that coffee?"

"All right," he said, "but the stop is more for the horse's benefit than yours. I guess it won't hurt to make coffee to pass the time."

"You certainly have a way with words," she said, swinging down. "I'll get some dead sticks – they don't give off smoke."

That's smart," he said, loosening the cinches, then leading the horses over to the pool. There was no shade from the glaring sun, so the break from riding was only a partial relief. They drank their hot, bitter coffee in the usual heavy silence, and chewed on some left-over corn bread he'd baked the night before. Then Fitzpatrick kicked some sand into the fire and announced:

"Time to get going; if we make good miles we'll be at the half-way point by sun-down. Then we'll have a real good rest. Keep your eyes skinned for another rabbit – we need some meat."

"We need a grassy spot to feed these horses too," she said, "They've been working for days on a few tough bunch grasses – they won't stick that many days."

"Agreed," said Fitzpatrick; "I'll give them the rest of the cornbread and the last of the oats now. We'll keep an eye open for that grass."

As he was tightening the girths, Amy touched him on the arm.

"Look," she said, pointing towards the horizon. "I can see dust and some men on horseback a mile or more back."

"You got better eyes than me," he said, squinting in the direction of the dust. "Come on, let's get going. If they're kicking up dust they must be goin' some – we better do the same."

They were soon off at a fast lope, so that they too, were putting some of the fine, semi-desert dust into the air. The horses maintained the pace for a time, but after an hour and a half they were struggling to get their wind, and Fitzpatrick decided to rest them once more.

He scanned the horizon again. The dust was closer, and now he could see the men on horseback. He scowled, and shook his head with concern for what must soon follow.

"They're not only gaining," he said, "but they've divided in two. That means they'll send their fastest horses round to the east of the salt flats, while the others come straight for us."

"We could go to the Bar Z for help," she suggested.

"Too late for that," said Fitzpatrick; "They got between us and the ranch already. We got to carry on to town. The trouble is, they'll have fast, desert-bred horses that'll give us a run for our money."

"Can't we outpace them over the flats?" she said. "We can

dump everything we don't need and make a dash for home. And I can change horses and take Billy's big mare. She's got more miles in her than this buckskin. He's almost spent."

"You're right!" said Fitzpatrick; "We'll bury the silver by that big rock, and wipe the tracks with some branches. Then we'll ride on to the base of that low hill yonder, and ditch the rest of our gear. That way they might not cotton on where the silver's been left. In any case, it's no use dying for it."

"Are Indians so bothered about silver?" she asked, as she helped him throw the silver into a hollow and cover it over, "I mean, it's not as if they can spend it."

"No," he said, "they ain't so keen on it, but they ain't just Indians on our trail."

"What do you mean?" she said, watching him cut creosote bushes with his knife and sweep the ground behind them. They got back in their saddles and set off for the hill a half mile in front of them.

"I saw the white dots of sombreros back there," he said as they rode at a fast lope, "and that means only one thing."

"Alvarez?" she asked.

"Him, an' his charming band of men," said Fitzpatrick; "He'd show me no mercy either, not after Billy and I shot several of his friends."

"Billy told me all about that," said Amy, "after we saw his gang some time ago. We had to hide. He said they'd take everything – and that I wasn't safe."

"You can say that again," said Fitzpatrick. "If it's Alvarez, he has a mixed bunch of Indians, whites and Mexicans running with him. The only thing they have in common is that none of them are welcome amongst their own people. It certainly solves the mystery of that old man you killed."

"What do you mean?" she asked.

"I mean he wasn't dressed in Paiute clothes; he had a shirt and pants stolen off a white man somewhere. And his hair was all wrong for a Paiute, too. If he was one of Alvarez' bunch, he must have separated from the main group for a spell, or maybe he was scouting ahead of them. Now, I'm sure Alvarez doesn't care two hoots for his dead Indian friend, but two riders with a pack-horse in silver mining country would interest him mightily. He'll reck'n on findin' some silver, and there's the prize of these three fine horses to spur them on. Then there's you."

"They can't know I'm a woman," she said, "not yet, surely?"

"Oh they know," said Fitzpatrick, "they have ways of tellin' even that."

They saved themselves the further effort of speaking while they cantered for the hill, then dismounted and set to work ridding themselves of everything that might hold them back. Cooking pots, beans, salt, coffee, blankets, spare clothes – all these they left thrown in an untidy heap, in the hope that Alvarez and his men would stop and waste time going through it for valuables.

The items they kept were significant: other than two saddles, they took only the water canteens, guns, ammunition, and two knives.

The buckskin was freed of its saddle, and Fitzpatrick fastened a leading rope to its bridle.

All this was accomplished in a couple of minutes; then Fitzpatrick mounted his gray, and Amy swung up to the leggy sorrel mare and patted its neck.

"I'll be damned if I'll leave them this horse," said

36

Fitzpatrick, looking at the buckskin; "If they want it, they got to catch it. Let's ride."

He kicked his horse forward, tugging at the lead to urge the buckskin on, until it gradually picked up speed into an easy gallop. Meanwhile, Amy put her bandanna over her mouth to keep out the trail dust and set out after him. Once she looked over her shoulder, and didn't like what she saw. Half a dozen riders, their various colored horses plainly visible now, were coming on at speed. The question was, where were the others? Would they be waiting for them on the other side of the flats?

The horses held up well for four or five miles, when the arid land gave way to salt pan. It was an expanse of flat, pale-colored powder without plants or even a cactus. It was only a few miles across, but the heat-haze coming off it in the hot afternoon was telling. Half-way across, they could see the dust cloud was quite close now, no more than a quarter-mile back. The horses were almost ready to collapse, but Fitzpatrick was gambling that the pursuers were equally tired, and that he and Amy could get them across and into some cover.

As they loped off across the flat landscape, they rode side by side now, to avoid the stinging dust kicked up by the flying hooves. When they had all but crossed, it was the buckskin that first sent out the distress signals: a lolling tongue, profuse sweat and an unsteady gait. The leading rope grew taut the as pony slowed. Fitzpatrick swore, for he had set his mind on keeping the animal.

"Let it go!" shouted Amy; "He'll follow on behind the best he can. 'Least he ain't no use to *them* any more..."

Fitzpatrick let go the lead, and the pony was left behind them, gasping and panting for air. As Fitzpatrick glanced back, he spied the men behind. There were six of them, three in sombreros, but that was all he could make out.

"We'll push for those bright red rocks over there," he said pointing, "and I just happen to know there's water nearby."

Amy glanced back, and saw the six men, could make out dark beards, brown faces and grimy hats. One man in front already had a gun in his hand. Fitzpatrick saw the worry on her face and called across:

"Don't fret none, Amy, we're almost there. I've been dyin' to reach them rocks before they do. I know that spot. I'll show 'em what happens when you catch a lion by the tail!"

A quarter hour later they cleared the pan and were into sandy wasteland. That was when the first shot came whizzing between them. The range was still too far to be effective, especially from the saddle. Fitzpatrick called across:

"That's it! Follow me, we're almost there. Those mangy dogs are about to get a little surprise."

He rode straight for the red rock formation, which turned out to be more of a cliff as they neared it. In between two slabs of low mesa was a passage about thirty yards across, and they rode through. No sooner than they'd cleared the neck of the canyon, Fitzpatrick was off his horse and had his Winchester in his hand. He took two boxes of shells out of his saddle bag and angrily stuffed them into his pockets. Amy noted that he had an insane grin on his face, as if he were going to enjoy what came next.

He strode purposefully back to the entrance and lodged himself behind a rock, working the lever of his rifle.

"Go water them horses in the well, fifty yards back, fifty to the right," he yelled. "Fill the canteens an' bring me mine. I ain't goin' nowhere for a spell."

She opened her mouth to speak, but at that moment the rifle thundered, sending weird echoes through the rocky hillsides as if a whole army was at work. She hesitated, waited while Fitzpatrick loosed a few more shots, shouting as he did so:

"Come on in, Alvarez! We bin waitin' for you all this time. I'll teach you to come chasin' after me, you lousy coward!"

There was a brief exchange of shots, then silence. She waited, but Fitzpatrick and the outlaws held their fire. Keeping behind rock formations that kept her out of the line of fire, she took the horses' reins and walked fifty paces back, and fifty to the right. There before her was a little pool of water. The basin in the rock looked as if it had been carved and plumbed there for the pleasure of thirsty travelers. She let the horses drink a spell, but pulled them back before they could take too much and do themselves harm. Then she submerged the two canteens, and hurried back to the neck, where Fitzpatrick was now exchanging fire again with the men on the outside.

"I got your water," she said, hugging the sides of the mesa as she edged forward; "You need a hand?"

"Naw," he said, "there's two of 'em down already. The rest of them cowards are all huddled in a gulch waitin' for dark. Only when it gets dark, we'll be out of here. You give them horses a good drink?"

"As much as I dared," she said; "They're in the shade, like us, an' it feels like heaven. I'll let them take a little more water when they're cool."

"Amy, you're a gem," he said, taking the flask of cold, clear water; "You'll make some rich rancher a damn good wife."

"You read my mind," she said. "I always dreamed of a real

big piece of land, with horses and dogs."

"Ain't that everybody's dream?" he said. He had a good pull at the canteen and closed his eyes with pleasure.

"Yeah," she added gloomily, "I was waitin' for one of them rich bachelors with ten thousand acres to make it to town. Then I'd drop my handkerchief on the boardwalk right in front of their eyes." She smiled a little at her own little joke. "Then I found that fool brother of mine, and ended up in some half-empty silver mine in the back of beyond."

"You can sell that mine an' buy a spread with the money," said Fitzpatrick. "That'd be more your style. You ain't the handkerchief droppin' sort."

"How would you know, sheriff?" she said; "You don't know what I might be capable of."

"Well, that's true," said Fitzpatrick, squinting down his sights; "If there's one thing I've learned doin' this job, it's that *some* women are capable of doing things most men would never dream of."

If only he had been looking in her direction at that moment, he would have seen a look of shock pass over her face. She stared uneasily at the man hunched over the rifle. Perhaps, she thought, Stevie Fitzpatrick might not be quite so naive and credulous as she had supposed...

CHAPTER FIVE:
THE PROPOSAL

Over the top of his gun-sights, Fitzpatrick could see a sombrero lying on the rim of the sunken gulch in front of him. It had been put there to draw his attention, that much was clear; and it was the last point from which Pancho Alvarez had fired at him. Therefore, he knew, it was the one place the man would *not* be. Just as expected, Alvarez popped up thirty yards away, and loosed two quick shots at him. The bullets ricocheted noisily off the rocks, but Fitzpatrick only smiled. The hits were yards away.

"Nice try, Alvarez," he laughed. "Now try stickin' your head up the other side. I'll be ready."

"Hey!" shouted Alvarez, "I'll tell you what. You just throw out your guns, and I'll let you both go back to your little town. All I want is the silver and a few of your dollars, and we'll be on our way."

"Oh really?" mocked Fitzpatrick; "In that case, here they are, come and get them. We surrender, Senor Alvarez, sorry to have bothered you."

There was a silence, and ten minutes of inactivity; then the four surviving outlaws tried a different tactic. They all came up from the dry bed at once and loosed some shots at the place they thought Fitzpatrick was lodged. For the sheriff, it was all basic shooting gallery stuff. He glanced up and noted the faces, an Indian, a bearded white man, and two Mexicans, one of them Alvarez himself. He let them shoot unopposed and descend again, and thought they would try it again. What else was open to them? If they rushed him, he would probably get them all. If they stayed put, they would probably die of thirst.

And so, when the stuck their heads and shoulders up again from a different place, he was ready. He had even predicted one of the spots, a little indentation in the rim of the gulch. When the dark face appeared, he squeezed off a shot and hit – dead center; then shifted five yards right and knocked the bearded fellow back as well. The two survivors ducked, and stayed down. Alvarez had lost four men, and were no nearer to getting Fitzpatrick – or the girl.

"Who's next?" jeered Fitzpatrick; "Who wants a lovely drink of water – we got plenty!"

He unscrewed the top of his canteen and emptied it out, making a splashing sound as it hit the ground.

Alvarez came up again and tried a snap-shot, no doubt fuming with rage, and Fitzpatrick fired. That shot should have ended the fight – but Fitzpatrick had tugged his trigger a mite too hard and pulled off target. The head disappeared, Fitzpatrick swore, knowing he had missed; and with that, it was over for the afternoon. With the shadows lengthening, the two remaining outlaws decided to wait it out.

"Guess we'll just stay put then," shouted Fitzpatrick, drawing out his pocket watch and noting the time. He loosed off a last couple of rounds and left his post.

Amy was sitting on a rock near the horses, thirty yards inside the canyon and over to the right, where bullets fired through the entrance couldn't reach.

"Tighten that cinch," he ordered, sticking his rifle in its boot, "We're leaving right this instant."

"But how?" she said, tightening the girth-strap of the mare, "Ain't we boxed in a canyon?"

"Nope," he said, getting into his saddle, "Whatever gave

you that idea? It's open the other end, only it's ten miles down. Ten miles closer to home, too. We'll just walk our horses through the sand till we get out of earshot of those jokers in the gulch."

"But why didn't Alvarez send men to circle round and get behind us?" she asked, as she swung onto the mare.

"Oh he did," he said; "Alvarez stoppered up the bottleneck with six of his pals, and when the others arrived he waved his arms and sent off them the long way round. I saw them go. They must've been hot, thirsty and tuckered out, but they went. I counted five of them."

They walked on through the sandiest part of the canyon, chatting as they went.

"Why didn't you shoot?" she asked, "I mean, couldn't you have stopped them?"

"Not really," he said, "They were too far out; could've hit the horses, I guess, but I'm not one for cripplin' horseflesh – seems kind of mean an' cowardly."

"Were they the ones that tried to cut us off on the salt pan?" she asked.

"Correct," he said, "They came up just after we got in the canyon, the horses all but spent. If they hadn't seen Alvarez' signal, I'd have got them – or some of them. Anyhow, they'll be working their way around even as we speak. It's fifteen miles at least to circle the mountain, and nine or ten back up the canyon; that takes time. They'll find water, but on tired horses, they'll never make it tonight. They'll have to rest up, which is where we'll get the better of them... I hope."

"But we'll be riding straight toward them," she said, "and in the dark too – the light will be gone in half an hour."

"Correct," he smiled, "but we got two things in our favor."

"Fresher horses, and surprise," she said.

"Right again," he said.

"So what's the plan?" she asked.

"Sneakin' past their camp won't be easy," said Fitzpatrick. "They'll be in the narrowest part of the canyon where they think they can stop us if we try to get past. But the way I see it, we have to be one step ahead of them. That means we have to surprise them – in their own camp."

"But how will we find them?" she said, "Surely they won't light a fire if they think there's a chance of us trying to get through in the dark?"

"No," he said, "not unless they're really stupid."

"So how exactly are we going to 'surprise' them, she said, "if we don't know where they are?"

"We'll muffle our horses hoofs with cloth, then ride up slowly, looking for the glow of their cigarettes."

"*Cigarettes?*" she smiled, "Are you serious? We have to look out for glowing cigarettes in miles and miles of canyon?"

"No other way," he said; "If we stay, they'll come for us, if we hide, they can find us. There's no path over the mountainside, at least not with a horse – and I ain't walkin' home."

"So," she said, "how far do you think those men will be in front of us? One mile? Five? Or at the end?"

"The canyon narrows three miles from the other end," he said; "It's only fifty yards across at that point. That's where they'll be. I'm certain."

"You sure are one for planning things out," she said; "I took you for a straight-laced, simple kind of law-man, but you're crafty as hell."

"Thanks," he said; "I'll take that as a complement."

"I sure wouldn't like to play you at poker," she said.

"I don't play poker," he said; "I'm too damned unlucky."

"It ain't about luck, she said; "It's all skill and bluff."

"Whatever," he said, "I'm lousy at it. I'm fair to middlin' at checkers, though."

"Forget checkers," she said; "With a face like yours, you should play poker. You sure know how to keep your cards hidden."

"So do you," he said, turning to look at her, "don't you?"

"Meaning?" she said, keeping her gaze straight ahead.

"Meaning," he said, "that you haven't been quite honest with me, up to now."

"How so?" she said, now calmly meeting his icy stare; "If you're so smart, you tell me, Sheriff Stephen Fitzpatrick."

"All right," he said, "as we're coming to the most dangerous part of our little adventure, an' maybe one or both of us will come off the worse for it, I'll tell you."

"I'm listenin'," she said.

"All right then," he began; "First, Billy didn't kill that miner, did he?"

"Of course he did," she protested, "he shot him twice, I saw it with my own eyes."

Her eyes flicked away once to the side of the sheriff as she uttered these words. It was a tiny thing, but Fitzpatrick saw it.

"You're good," he smiled, "I have to admit you're good."

His smile was faint, cold, and without humor.

"What do you mean?" she said, a tear in her eye now.

"Billy didn't kill that man," persisted Fitzpatrick, fixing her with his steely eyes."

"I tell you he did!" she said, "Billy had to kill him to save his own life-"

45

"No, Amy," said Fitzpatrick, "It was you."

"Are you crazy?" she said; "It was Billy, I swear!"

"Stop it," he hissed, "you said yourself I was no fool. I saw the two holes in that man – Thomas Mannerheim, that was his name – and one was a big .44 slug in his arm, the other was a small wound over his heart... a .32 bullet for sure."

"I never!" she said, almost weeping now, "I never!"

"A shot through the heart," said Fitzpatrick, "your trademark shot. And I bet the Indian and Mannerheim weren't the only ones either. Once you kill one or two, the next ones come easier, so they say."

Fighting back tears and outrage, she slowly reached down and opened the buckle of her leather bag, which happened to be swinging at her side. She pulled out the little .32 pocket revolver and pointed it at Fitzpatrick's head. He glanced sideways, and there was contempt in his eyes.

"I wondered when that was coming," he said.

Her hand, with not so much as a tremor, lowered the .32 until it pointed at his chest, straight at his heart.

"Trademark shot again?" he said; "Well then, hear me out before you pull that trigger. I've a couple of things to say before you kill your best friend."

"You, sheriff, ain't my best friend," she said through clenched teeth.

"Are you sure about that?" he said; "After all, I'm riskin' my neck to get you to town. I'd lower that gun, if I were you – if you want to live, that is."

"You're a snake," she said, "there ain't a straight bone in your body, not one."

She maintained her aim; Fitzpatrick tried a different tack:

"So shoot me," he said; "God knows I deserve it. I've

46

probably killed more men than Billy."

"Men *like* Billy," she said,

"Some, some," he confessed.

The gun wavered, just a little. She narrowed her eyes at the sheriff, her finger tightened on the trigger.

Fitzpatrick looked across at her annoyed.

"You better quit that," he said looking down at the gun, "if you think I'll run you in after all this is over, you're wrong."

The gun remained in its threatening position.

"You'd run in your own grandmother if she stole a stick of candy," said Amy.

"Listen," he said, "I got something to say."

"Oh please!" she said, looking into his narrowed eyes, "Spare me the lame attempt to get round the dumb woman."

Nevertheless, he persisted:

"Amy, the truth is, I'm gonna ask you to marry me when all this is over. If we survive, that is."

She scoffed in disgust, but the gun came down as she spoke:

"I wouldn't marry you, Fitzpatrick," she said, her eyes full of wildcat fury, "if you were the last man on earth."

"Well, that's plain," he said, frowning.

"I should shoot you," she said; "God knows, you need shootin'."

"I ain't my fault I'm ugly," he said.

"Your mug ain't so ugly," she said, "but you're as sneaky as a damn fox."

"I just might be," he said.

"You took the cartridges out of my gun while I was asleep," she said, "That's why you're so damn cocky with a gun pointing at your heart."

47

He turned and caught her gaze, his composure for once, deserting him, as he heard her next words:

"I saw you do it," she said, "and I loaded it up again."

Sure enough, when he looked closely, he could see some of the small lead slugs in the pistol's cylinder. He felt a cold sweat on his forehead and under his hat.

"Not so cocky now," she said.

He looked straight ahead and tried to look unfazed, but it was hard.

She slipped the gun back in its bag and suppressed the urge to smile.

"Sometimes," she said, "a man can try to be too damn clever, too damn sneaky, trying to manipulate a woman's feelings."

"I'll remember," said Fitzpatrick.

"You do that," she said.

"Anyhow," he said, "I meant what I said."

She cast him a quick glance. His face had resumed its deadpan look once again.

"Would that be the *proposin'* part, or the *not runnin' me in* part?" she asked.

"Both," he said.

They traveled on for a mile or two in silence, as the shadows lengthened, and the floor of the canyon darkened.

"It's nearly dark," she said presently, "We'd better muffle these hoofs while we can still see. I suggest you sacrifice those chaps of yours – we'll cut eight pieces an' we'll tie them on with some thin strips of leather."

"Good idea," he said, "We're getting close to that narrow spot."

Half an hour later, they had the horses' feet wrapped in

squares of leather and secured with long strips of hide. They tried a few steps over some rock and gravel, and the bindings held; the sound was minimal.

"Works like magic," he said. "Which reminds me – we have to listen out for Alvarez and his pal coming up from behind us."

"We'll hear them in the dark before they find us," she said, "at least I hope so."

"Yeah," he said, "me too. Now I'll tell you the plan for when we find those five coyotes down the canyon..."

They continued down towards the narrowing of the canyon, sliding down from their horses as they neared the place. The smell of tobacco smoke wafted to them on the faintest of breezes, and they stopped. As they peered into the darkness, there, a few yards ahead, they saw a bright red glow, as a man drew strongly on his cigarette.

"There," whispered Fitzpatrick, laying a hand on her shoulder, "What did I tell you?"

CHAPTER SIX:
SHOTS IN THE DARKNESS

After they had back-tracked fifty yards, they secured the horses to a bush and the plan swung into action. Fitzpatrick's reconnoiter revealed that there were indeed five men, three on the west side of the canyon, two on the eastern one. He heard a few words of Spanish spoken by the group of three, and noted their exact position as a match flared to light another of those tell-tale cigarettes. Now it would be a game of patience and stealth.

The first man to leave the group on the west side was a short, stout fellow with a dark sombrero pushed back on his head. He took his rifle with him, treading warily, looking out into the darkness. He was planning to relieve himself a few yards away, and presently stopped next to a big boulder. He felt a sharp blow on the back of his head an instant before he blacked out. Fitzpatrick dragged him under a bush, gave the sombrero and jacket to Amy. She took her position by the boulder and waited.

"*Estás bien, Fernando?*" one of the seated men called out softly.

When there was no reply, the man rose and walked tentatively into the darkness. When he saw the familiar sombrero and coat of his fellow outlaw, who seemed to be looking the other way, he breathed a sigh of relief, and called out softly:

"*Eh, amigo, te has perdido?*"

When his companion did not move, or even reply, he grew suspicious, and cautiously took a step forward. Another blow from the butt of a pistol rendered him unconscious.

Amy, wearing the first man's hat and jacket, turned round and nodded to Fitzpatrick. Together, they had now to act fast, before the third man raised the alarm. With the broad-rimmed hat pushed down over her eyes, she walked boldly up to the him, while Fitzpatrick tried to get behind him.

"*Ah, eres tú!*" he said, as Amy approached; but a couple of seconds later the man saw her face, and snatched up his rifle. Fitzpatrick, already behind him, swung his reversed pistol at the outlaw's head. The wooden butt connected with such force that Fitzpatrick thought he's broken one of his best weapons; but a quick examination showed it to be still intact.

"Reck'n you killed him," said Amy, staring at the man on the ground.

"Aw, he'll be all right," said Fitzpatrick; "You know what to do next?"

"Sure," she shrugged, drawing her .32 and disappearing into the darkness. Her task was to locate the bandit's horses, and wait for his signal. She was already past the narrow part of the canyon, which left two alternatives open. If Fitzpatrick could kill or capture the remaining three men, the two of them ride away on their own mounts. But if things went wrong, and Fitzpatrick did not make the correct signal, she was to take one of the outlaw's horses, stampede or shoot the others, and try to get back to town on her own.

Meanwhile, Fitzpatrick took some dried grasses and bits of paper out of his pocket, along with some twigs he'd soaked in the last of his gun-oil, and placed them on the ground. Then he took the match from his pocket and struck it on a rock. He lit the paper and watched it ignite the dried grass and sticks. He placed a few bits of creosote branch on top, and darted into the shadows.

51

Within seconds, the other two men came running towards the fire, calling out in muted tones for the fire to be put out. They had assumed their companions had disobeyed orders and lit it themselves, but when they saw no other men nearby, the penny dropped and they stopped – just for a second. Their hands reached down for their guns.

Two shots in two seconds from Fitzpatrick evened the fight down to one against one; but then his luck ran out. The last man standing had drawn his gun and disappeared, unscathed, into the darkness.

Now it was fifty-fifty as to who saw who first – and so remained alive. Fitzpatrick had ducked behind some rocks, a gun in his hand, eyes trying to discern shape from shadow; and it was not easy when every bush, boulder and pieces of vegetation might be mistaken for a human form. Fitzpatrick knew his best bet was to stay put and wait for the man to creep into his view. It was also possible his opponent would run down to the outlaw's horses – where waited Amy with her .32.

He decided to try something, which might yield a result, and would let Amy know his position, and that only a single man remained.

"Hey, Amigo!" shouted Fitzpatrick, "You're the last man left, you yellow dog! Here I am, now come and get me!"

He waited, but heard or saw nothing. After a full minute, there was still no sign of the last man. Fitzpatrick thought now he must take a chance, and go to Amy. They could take two horses, saddled or not, and head down the canyon and run for home. There was always the chance – a huge chance in fact – that the outlaw was still watching for him, and might drop him when he broke cover, but it had to be done. He could not leave the girl down by the horses alone for too long, for soon Alvarez and his surviving companion from the top end of the valley would come riding down, looking for their quarry. And if those two bandits were already nearby, they would have been alerted by the shots fired.

As he crept nearer to where he believed Amy was waiting, a single shot pierced the darkness, and he froze. It wasn't a particularly loud shot, in fact it seemed like that of a small caliber piece – most probably her .32. But did it mean that Amy had got the last man? He thought it very likely, as he moved from bush to bush towards where he had heard the shot. A few yards on, he saw the outlaws' horses tied in a line. But there was no sign of Amy – or the last man. Then he heard her voice.

"It's all right, Fitzpatrick," she said, "I've got him. He's dead."

He stopped in his tracks as if turned to ice! For the signal that either of them was to give if all was well was a low, double whistle – anything else, they had agreed, meant something was amiss. Could she have killed the last man, and then forgotten their agreed code? He thought it very doubtful. But where was she, and what could have happened? As he was pondering these things, he heard her voice again.

"Over here," she said, and whistled, *once!*

He crept through the bushes, not in a straight line, but circling way out to the right so as to approach her from the side. As he peered into the darkness, in a patch of moonlight he could just make out two figures. One, with his back to him, was a tall, hatless man wearing a light-colored shirt. It was the latter which had made his outline visible. He seemed to be holding a gun on the second figure. Fitzpatrick stared into the darkness, straining his eyes to see – and then realized that the farther figure was Amy, *with her hands in the air.*

Fitzpatrick reined in his emotions on seeing the girl held captive, and determined what to do next. He couldn't shoot the man with the gun, for Amy was almost directly in line with him. It was possible the .36 slug would hit her after passing through the man. He needed to move a little to one side to take the shot. Without taking his eyes his target, he moved his feet slowly, being careful not to stand on a piece of dead twig that might give away his position.

Then, having edged sideways, and about to pull his trigger, another gun flashed and roared from somewhere in the darkness.

Fitzpatrick felt as if somebody had fetched him a mighty blow to his ribs with a sledgehammer. He went down, gasping for breath. As he lay there, Alvarez stepped out of the shadows, grinning with satisfaction. He pumped two more bullets into the sheriff's writhing body – and Fitzpatrick moved no more.

Amy let out a sob of fear and anguish. By the first flash of Alvarez' gun, Amy had seen Fitzpatrick hit, then heard him fall heavily. The second and third shots told her that she was had been left alone – in a nightmare.

Her knees almost gave way, and she felt a wave of nausea well in her stomach, for she believed she had lured Fitzpatrick to his death. She had tried to warn him by her tone of voice, and not delivering the correct double whistle, but evidently it had not worked. He had walked into a trap. But what could she otherwise have done? Alvarez, seizing her and putting a knife against her throat in the darkness, had whispered exactly what she must do; and she had no doubt that he would have killed her in a second if she had refused him and thus rendered herself useless for his intended deception.

Sick with fear and shock, she tried to stop herself from falling, as her arms dropped to her side and she swayed unsteadily.

A grip of iron seized her arm, and it bruised her. She cried out in pain, as she was pushed heavily against a wall of rock. From there she could focus on her three captors for the first time. In the dim moonlight it seemed that evil spirits were at work in the canyon, for the men were three of the most grotesque beings she had ever seen.

One of them, an Indian, immobilized her with a knife held under her chin while the others kindled a fire. As the flames took hold, the effect was even more terrifying. The Indian, dressed in clothes stolen from a variety of his victims, had cold, emotionless eyes like a dead man. A red headband held down his greasy hair, and he cradled in his arms a rifle with feathers hanging off it. The second man was a veritable freak of nature. He was a tall white man with a grizzled beard that only partially hid his scars and lesions, the products not of battles but advanced syphilis. One eye was completely white and blind. His teeth were missing, but that didn't stop him from grinning gleefully from ear to ear. The smell emanating from him was akin to rotting meat.

Then there was their leader, Alvarez. He stood in dusty clothes and a discoloured gray sombrero that had once been white. His overgrown moustache and beard hid a part of his leering, cruel features, but not the eyes. They seemed to dart from object to object, like a raptor looking for prey. His boots had long, sharp spurs attached. More than once, he scratched his ugly, wizened face with the foresight of a loaded pistol.

Amy noticed that, though he was the leader (at least of this remnant of his band) he was unable to look her in the eye, always staring at a point to one side of her face as he spoke.

"Now then, *mi querida*," he sneered, "how many of my men did *you* kill?"

She made up her mind to end her life by forcing him to shoot her. She would grab his gun, or make a run for the horses. But while she waited for the right moment, she knew she must answer.

"Only one," she said; "and I'm sorry. The sheriff made me do it; he did all the other fighting."

"Oh I see," he said, nodding in mockery, "The sheriff made you do it, did he, my pretty one? Then why did you have *two* pistols on you? And my friend Blanco here was killed with a shot straight to the heart. I think are a woman who knows how to handle a gun, no?"

"I never fired one before today," she lied, looking at his .44 and willing it to go off.

"Well, my pretty one," he said, his gaze still not meeting her eye, "perhaps if you let me know where you hid the silver, I shall let you go."

"All right," she said, "I'll tell you. But you've got to put me on a horse, and promise not to follow."

"Sure," he said, turning to his men, "we can do that, my friends, can't we? After all, we only want the money."

"Oh sure," smiled the Freak, "We'll let you go all right. That's a promise!"

"All right," she said, "Then I'll tell you."

"Good," Alvarez said, "Very good; and what is your name, my pretty one?"

"It's Mary," she said, not wanting those filthy men to know

56

or utter her real name.

Alvarez smiled, enjoying the fear he instilled in her. He thought of his dead companions, and how he would make her pay.

"Well, then, Mary," he said, squinting past her shoulder, "Where did you put the silver. Tell me and I'll let you go."

There was a long silence. Amy closed her eyes, trying to overcome her strong desire to stay alive, overriding it with the thought that all this could end, with only a small amount of pain, and that then she could sleep in peace forever.

She opened her eyes, sprang forward and grabbed at Alvarez' gun – but to her great regret, it didn't go off.

Instead, he snatched it sideways, then swung it expertly back so that its barrel struck her hard across the forehead. She fell, dazed, to her knees. The other two men grunted in satisfaction at this more acceptable turn of events.

"That is for Federico," he snarled, in an altogether different tone of voice, "who your dead friend killed this afternoon. He was my brother."

"I'm sorry," she said – and Alvarez exploded!

First he struck her a straight punch to her face, then caught her as she fell and slapped her a half dozen times on either cheek, before throwing her to the ground.

She cried out in pain, and hated herself for showing weakness, crawling like an animal on all fours. She tried to stand up.

Alvarez kicked her to the ground, and put one foot on her.

"I will tell you what will happen," he said, "and if you once try to defy me I will give you more pain than you can ever imagine. First, you will tell us where you hid the silver. Second, you will consider yourself my woman for a few days, then I shall give you to the others. You will do everything I say. Even if I tell you to smile – you will do it. Now, take off those clothes. You dress too much like a man for my taste. I want to have a look at the goods that has cost us all so dear."

He took his foot off her back, and prodded her with a pointed boot. When she didn't move, he drew his long knife and knelt down beside her. He let out a long sigh.

"Then I guess I shall have to cut those clothes right off you."

He caught hold of her hair and pulled her head back, till it seemed he might break her neck. She gasped with pain, but he only pulled the more, bending down and whispering in her ear:

"Well, now, my pretty one, you're beginning to look much more interesting from down here!"

He began to cut off her shirt with his knife, putting the blade into the cuff of a sleeve, and opening it up to reveal her bare arm and shoulder. As he did so, there were more grunts of satisfaction from the Indian and the Freak – for there was nothing they liked more than to see a woman get badly hurt and horribly humiliated... other than actually killing one, that is.

Alvarez, still cutting at her shirt, opened his mouth to speak more obscenities. Then he froze. He looked into the dark space under the horses. Something had caught his eye. There, sticking out of the darkness was an arm; and at the end of the arm, a hand holding a gun.

The last thing Alvarez ever saw, as he knelt there on the ground, was the muzzle-flash of that Remington .36 Navy. The slug entered the middle of his face, and went straight through, lodging in the Indian's knee three steps behind him. The

Indian fell, clutching his leg, but another discharge of the gun sent him rolling into the shadows. The Freak, at the first shot, had jumped up in the air like a startled jack-rabbit, and bolted for the safety of the darkness. But he tripped over the trailing rope of the horses' tether-line and fell flat on his face.

He never got up. Amy had snatched one of Alvarez' guns from its holster, turned to the Freak as he tried to rise, and emptied all six bullets into his body.

The odd thing was, he was still alive, for a few seconds, even after the sixth hit. For once Amy had missed her trademark shot; but within a few seconds the man had bled out, and his eyes ceased to flicker. He died with a smile on his lips, as if bemused by the unexpected manner of his passing.

As Amy recovered herself a little, she remembered with a start that Fitzpatrick, with three slugs in him, had somehow managed to crawl under the horses to bring about her deliverance.

She pushed the horses back, knelt over the bloody form of Fitzpatrick, and lifted his head into her lap.

"Sorry," he said, "I let the wolves get you, Amy."

"They're dead wolves now," she whispered.

"Me too, maybe," he breathed; "How many times they get me, Amy?"

"Three," she said, a tear leaving her eye.

"That's bad," he said. "Reck'n I'm just about done for."

"Hush – and let me take a look," she said, looking at the blood welling through his jacket and shirt.

When she unbuttoned his clothes, the full extent of his injuries was revealed. His third gun – in its shoulder-holster – had taken a hit on the very edge of a walnut grip. A few fragments of lead had got past, and lodged in his ribcage. This had been enough to knock him off his feet, but it was a shock from which he would recover. As for the other two bullets, one had hit a rib and skidded through skin and muscle, causing a great loss of blood, and was the most dangerous of his wounds. The third bullet, fired as he rolled on the ground, had only put a groove into his tough old hide, and a few stitches would deal with it.

"You're a lucky dog," she said, "looks like he missed your vitals."

"A lucky dog?" he winced; "Sure don't feel like it."

"That gun'll need fixin' though," she said, removing it from its holster and showing him.

"Saved me a couple of times before, that one" he grimaced, "but never like that."

"You're breathing all right," she said; "that's a good sign."

"Ain't got no taste of blood in my mouth neither," he said.

"That's even better," she said, "but you're still losin' too much blood from your chest; I got to see to them wounds."

"You know how?" he asked.

"Not really," she said; "I seen it done once."

"You got to boil some cloth," he said; "Them fellers will have a pan somewhere – if not, do it in a canteen. You got to press it on them holes real tight. There's sulphur powders in my saddle bags. When the bleeding stops, you pour the powder on the wounds. Can you do that for me, Amy?"

"I guess," she said.

"There are caves in the rock face near here," he said, "and water. You can put me in one and go for help. We're less than a day from town."

"No," she said, thinking of how she had left Billy alone, "Reck'n I'll stay. You might be all right in a day or two."

"Yeah," he said, closing his eyes, "I might…"

"Well then," she said, "We'll rest up a while, then travel back to town. The horses will be rested. There's even a bit of grass for them here."

"Sure," he said, "We'll rest the horses, then go back together. It'll be a breeze."

CHAPTER SEVEN:
A WOMAN OF MEANS

After his return to One Dog Creek, it was two months before Stevie Fitzpatrick was able to resume all his duties at the county sheriff's office. His assistant, deputy Bud Morton, nearly seventy years old, was an experienced hand at running things while his young boss was away. In the past this had been while Fitzpatrick was heading a posse, or investigating crimes out of town. So, having to take over while the sheriff was recovering from serious gunshot injuries was something Morton took in his stride. Luckily for him, no challenges to his authority had occurred in his boss's absence.

On Fitzpatrick's first full day back in his office, late in the afternoon, Morton sat in his usual wooden armchair, chewing a match as was his custom. Fitzpatrick sat on his desk rolling a cigarette, deep in thought.

"Well, Bud," drawled Fitzpatrick, "what do we know about Amy Gillespie? What's she been up to these last few days?"

"That's the seventh time you've asked me," said Morton. "Why don't you go ask her yourself, I'm thinkin', especially as she called in twice to ask after you."

"Yeah," said Fitzpatrick, "About that – I'm not sure what to do. I mean, she killed a man back there, then nursed me back from the brink, an' escorted me back to town when I could barely ride."

"So you said," said Morton, rocking back in his chair, his eyes hooded contentedly as he chewed his match; "but nobody except me, you, an' her knows about that miner. Seems to me she deserves some consideration for what she done for you."

"But hell, Bud," said Fitzpatrick, "I just can't do it. She

killed a man, an' I'm obliged to act."

"You left it a bit late," said Morton, "The girl's sold her claim at Lost Souls, an' the word is she's leaving town tomorrow."

This piece of news caused something of a shock-wave to pass through Fitzpatrick – though the only outward sign of it was a two second delay in him striking his match to light his cigarette.

"That so?" was all he said.

"But I've had an idea," said Bud Morton, "to finally clear all this up."

"Go on," said Fitzpatrick, lighting his cigarette.

"You may not like it," said Morton.

"You reckon?" said Fitzpatrick, inhaling deeply.

"I reckon," said Morton, throwing his own mutilated match into the bin.

"Well," said Fitzpatrick, "Let's hear it anyway."

"All right," said Morton, "Then listen. How about if we get the girl to come in for an interview? We'll ask Judge Stevens to attend. You can ask her all about that first killing, then explain to the judge how she assisted you in the apprehension of the Alvarez gang. Let *him* decide how to proceed."

"What if he says she should go to trial?" said Fitzpatrick. "What if he says she should hang?"

"That's the risk," said Morton; "but that way it's all above board and legal."

Fitzpatrick drew on the last part of his cigarette, tossed it on the floor, stuck out a foot to crush it out.

"I don't think I could do that to her," said Fitzpatrick. "Not after her helping me out like that."

"Saving your bacon, you mean," said Morton with a wink.

"Yeah," said Morton uncomfortably, "you could put it that way."

"So," said Morton, "you want to ease that dead-straight Fitzpatrick conscience of yours without getting the girl who saved you hanged. Is that about it?"

Fitzpatrick winced.

"Just about," he said.

"Fitzpatrick," said Morton, "You're a damn fool."

"Yeah," said Fitzpatrick, "I know. But the whole thing's eatin' away at me."

"In other words," said Morton, helping himself to another match, "you feel grateful she saved your life and helped you wipe out Alvarez and his bunch, but at the same time you feel bad about letting a *possible* murder go unpunished."

"Not a *possible* murder," said Fitzpatrick; "It was a real one; that girl and her brother killed an innocent man; and it's very likely *she* was the one that did it."

"Oh well," said Morton, glancing out the window, "guess we'll soon find out."

"What do you mean?" said Morton.

At that moment there was a loud knock on the door, and Judge Stevens marched in.

"Howdy, gents," he said, removing an enormous cigar from his pocket, "Everything ready?"

Fitzpatrick stared as if he'd seen a ghost.

"Almost," said Morton.

"Hang fire a second," said Fitzpatrick, "What's goin' on here?"

"Don't monkey with me!" snapped Stevens tetchily, "I'm here for the hearing you fellows asked me to preside over."

Fitzpatrick turned to Morton for an explanation. There

64

was a loud rap on the door and Amy Gillespie walked in. She was dressed in a sober brown dress, stockings, and flat shoes like a spinster schoolteacher. It took another six seconds for the penny to drop for Fitzpatrick.

Then he glared angrily at Bud Morton.

"Things move mighty quickly around here sometimes," said the sheriff.

"Yeah," said Bud Morton, "but it was Amy here who suggested the meeting in the first place."

"Well," said the judge, "whoever called it, I'm here now, so let's get to it. I understand this girl wants to make some kind of a confession."

"Amy!" said Fitzpatrick, "you don't have to do it."

"Yes, sheriff," she said coldly, "I do. I'm going to get this out in the open, once and for all."

In a few minutes, with all parties seated around the sheriff's office, Amy began her testimony.

"It all started when I rode out to Lost Souls' Mesa," she said, picking up Fitzpatrick's tobacco pouch from the table. "My brother Billy found me, and fetched me into the site of the old mines. He said he needed my help, that he wanted to go straight an' he'd only be able to do it with me by his side. We were always real close, Billy an' me. I'm a year older than him. I kind of mothered him at home after my mama died."

"Yes, yes," cut in the judge, "that's all very nice, but cut to the chase and tell us about what happened over by Lost Souls' Mesa. I gather from Morton here, there was some kind of a gun-fight, in which you were involved – tell us about that."

"Well," said Amy, continuing to roll herself a smoke, "we were on the trail near to our claim, that's the Lost Souls' Mine that I sold the other day, when we met a prospector at the head of Dead Man's Pass."

"Go on," said the judge, lighting his cigar, which soon filled the room with clouds of smoke.

"That man," said Amy, pausing to seal her cigarette with a dainty lick of her tongue, "was all smiles at first, and walked along, talkin' friendly-as-you-like. Then he said he wanted to follow us back down the pass, thinking to learn the secret of how to get to our mine. I told him we knew nothing about silver mines, but he just laughed – Billy was covered in dust and muck from our claim, which had given us away. I begged the man to get goin' while he still could, but he said it was a free country. Because me an' Billy had only one horse between us, we couldn't shake him off. It was plain then, he wanted to muscle in and stake his own claim next to us."

"Which he was perfectly entitled to do," puffed the judge.

"Yeah," said Amy, "Despite him bein' already weighed down with silver from his own claim that he wasn't sharin' with us. Anyhow, he was bold, an' got pushy, said he wouldn't go back, or take no for an answer. That didn't go down well with Billy. He drew a gun and told the fellow to rustle. But the man only laughed, he thought Billy was bluffing, and he said so."

She paused, and placed the cigarette between her lips. Morton struck his match on the desk, and she drew in the smoke, a long, luxurious inhalation that took several seconds. Then she blew smoke across the desk in Fitzpatrick's direction, covering him in a blue-white cloud, before she continued:

"It was then that Billy said he was going to take the fellow's horse and goods, so that me an' him could get to Larsonville for some supplies."

66

"Larsonville?" queried the judge, "why would you want to go to that den of thieves when One Dog Creek's about ten miles closer?"

"Billy was a wanted man," said Amy, "an' he wasn't ready to turn himself in, not yet. Larsonville's not so choosey about who comes and goes. We could've gotten our stuff without a hitch."

"I see," said Stevens, "Please go on."

"We needed supplies – we were out of most things, including coffee and flour, but there was a big problem. My horse broke a bone and Billy had to shoot it, the day before we met that man. So, when we saw that prospector, Billy took me on one side, and tried to persuade me that we had to take that man's horse and goods if we wanted to make Larsonville. He said that I needed the buckskin more than the stranger, and he promised me the man would come to no harm – and, fool that I was, I believed him."

"So," said the judge, "Billy had already decided to take the man's horse and his goods at that stage, is that it?"

"Yes, sir," said Amy, holding her head down for the first time.

"And didn't you try to stop your brother robbing that miner," said Stevens, "I mean, couldn't you have dissuaded him from committing a robbery at that point?"

There was a pause, as all eyes scrutinised Amy's face. Finally she looked up, and went on:

"No," she said, "there was no stopping him at that point. I begged him to let the man go, but he took no notice."

"Then what happened?" asked the judge, "You'd better tell us everything. Spare no detail, Miss Gillespie."

"Billy suddenly fired a shot," said Amy, "right past the

67

fellow's ear, an' then we all knew Billy was not going to stop till he'd got the horse, the man's gun, his money, everything."

"Tell us what Billy said to the man," said Fitzpatrick; "Did he threaten to kill him."

Amy looked up, stiffened, and gave the sheriff such a horrible look of cold contempt that the others thought she might attack him; but then she seemed to compose herself again, and said:

"Sure he threatened to kill him, sheriff. He said he'd knock him off that damned horse if he didn't get down that instant. When the man got down, he told him to hand over his gun. We could see it stickin' out of his pocket. The man sort of sneered at Billy, and slowly took it out. He removed it real careful, with two fingers, but there was something in the way he did it that showed he was going to try something."

"Which is not surprising," said the judge, stubbing out his cigar on the underside of his shoe, "considering that he was about to lose everything he owned. But please, do go on, Miss Gillespie."

"So the man took his gun out with one hand," said Amy, "then threw the gun to his other hand. It was a trick – only it went wrong. Badly wrong."

She paused, drew on her cigarette and held in the smoke.

"How wrong?" said Fitzpatrick.

Again she showed him that look of contempt, her eyes flashing angrily as if, at that moment, she were capable of just about anything.

"Let me finish," she hissed, breathing out the smoke. "The man threw his gun into his other hand, and I knew Billy was going to kill him. So I leapt for Billy's gun to try to stop him shooting... only I was too late. Both guns went off, and the

68

man fell back, with a big hole in his arm. He fell on the ground, and sat there staring up at us, a look of shock on his face. Then Billy aimed his pistol at the man – on the ground – and pulled his trigger. Only his gun didn't go off. It was a mis-fire; and when he tried it again, the pistol wouldn't shoot. It had jammed – and I was glad, because I thought the man was safe."

Here she paused, her face torn with emotion, her hands shaking. She tossed the butt of her cigarette on the floor, and wrung her hands together in distress.

Fitzpatrick had rolled another cigarette, which he offered her. She snatched it out of his hand, and Morton lit it.

"If I might just say," said Fitzpatrick, "when I recovered Billy's gun, it was still jammed. It had a cap stuck in between the cylinder and the frame. It's a common enough thing. It's happened to me, before now."

"Very interesting," mused the judge, scratching his chin.

He gave Amy a bit of time to compose herself again, before he whispered:

"Go on," Miss Gillespie. "Please – in your own time."

"I thought... I thought the man was safe," she said, "but I hadn't reckoned on Billy. I knew he had a temper, and that he was hard, but I had no idea how hard he was – not till then. He threw his gun on the ground, then grabbed me by my jacket, and took my .32 from my inside pocket."

Fitzpatrick stared at her, and she glared back, with fury in her eyes.

"You never told me that," he said.

"You never gave me a chance," she said, shaking.

She took such a draw on her thin cigarette that over a half of it turned to ash before she removed it from her lips. Then she exhaled noisily, before continuing:

"I fought him for that gun," she said; "I got a grip on it, but he socked me on the jaw, and I let it go. I fell in the dirt, and then I heard the gun go off. I didn't need to look up to know what he'd done. I just cried, and told him he'd promised me he wasn't going to kill the man. Only... a promise like that meant nothing to him."

She finished her cigarette, smoking the thing till the last tiny bit was burning her finger-tips; even then she puffed on it again, and dropped the last remnant of burned paper on the floor.

"I gather," said the judge, as he watched her, "that Billy had been shot in the first exchange?"

"He told me he'd got what he deserved," said Amy; "He was my brother, and I loved him, but God forgive me, he was right. Billy had grown so hard over the years, I didn't really understand it till then. I'm only sorry I ever went to him. I had to see my brother with a slug in his belly, and I had to see that other man lying there dead. I had to see and do a lot of terrible things. Things that made my heart sick. That's why I could never go back to that mine. My father and my brother are buried in those shafts. I've paid the undertaker in advance, a lot of money, to bring their bodies back to town, when they're found. But in a way, it would be better for me if they stayed where they are. It was the silver that turned their heads, made both of them crazy, in different ways, turned them into hard-hearted strangers. So maybe it would be better if they stayed where they were."

She shuddered at the thought of her brother and father, what had happened to the men of her family that she had loved so dearly, for all their faults.

Presently, with the three men still looking on her, she said, quite softly-

"That's all I got to say; I'm going to leave town tomorrow; if any of you gentlemen got anything more to say to me, I'll be in the Gold Bar Saloon in the corner, alone. I need a few drinks, an' I ain't ashamed to say it. But more than anything else, I need an apology, and I need it said to my face."

With that, she stood up, turned and walked slowly out of the county sheriff's office. After she closed the door, Bud Morton let out a long, low whistle of surprise.

Fitzpatrick had a hangdog look of shame on his face; he couldn't look the other two men in the eye.

"Well I'll be damned," said the judge, "if that ain't the sorriest tale I ever did hear! That poor kid – she's been carrying that burden around all this time – and you, Fitzpatrick, never thought to let her tell her side of the story. Heck, Bud here said you were afraid she would hang for murder! You ought to be darned ashamed of yourself."

"Yeah," said Bud Morton, with a twinkle in his eye; "You ought to be really ashamed – what with you bein' a sheriff an' all. What were you thinkin', Stevie? I tell you what – that's one hell of a woman that is. Get yourself down to the Gold Bar an' cut yourself a big, huge slice of humble pie, my friend."

"Yeah," said Fitzpatrick, slowly getting to his feet, "I guess I'll wander down and see how she's doin'. Don't like to see a woman in a place like that, all alone..."

He found her in the saloon, just where she'd said she'd be, with a tumbler of whiskey in one hand and a cigarette in the other. On the table were the bottle and an empty glass. Fitzpatrick took a seat, poured himself a measure, and downed it in a single gulp. Their eyes met: hers piercing and bold, his sheepish and guilty-looking. He opened his mouth to speak, but she put a finger across his lips to stall him.

"Don't," was all she said; "You know why."

He looked across at her, and for the first time noticed that she had with her that brown leather bag, in which she always kept her pistol. Then he remembered with a start that she had always carried that little .32 inside the bag, never in a pocket, and that it had a buckle to keep it closed. There was no way Billie could have wrenched it from her in a struggle and taken the gun to kill the prospector as she had told the judge!

Then, she leaned across the table and kissed him, hard, with the hottest, fiercest, whiskey-fuelled kiss he would ever receive in his entire life.

THE END

BOOK TWO:

HENRY SUTHERLAND'S CIVIL WAR

'The enemy never sees the backs of my Texans!'
-General Robert E Lee

HENRY SUTHERLAND'S CIVIL WAR

CHAPTER ONE:
THE VOLUNTEER

In March of 1864, Henry Sutherland was in the last year of his military cadetship in the East Texas Military Academy, which was situated just outside the little town of Homer. He was only sixteen years old, but like thousands of other young men he dreamed of serving his country, which happened to be the Confederate one. He had already tried to join up two years earlier as a private soldier, or even a drummer boy, but was refused on account of his age and looks; for though he was fourteen at the time, he was small of stature and baby-faced to the extent that he looked a good deal younger. Though many regions of the Confederacy were not especially fussy about recruiting boy-soldiers into its army, at Huntsville Barracks, Texas, Henry Sutherland was summarily rejected for immediate active service. Instead he was directed to the East Texas Military Academy, a residential training institute set up in a big country house in April 1861 to educate young men for service as officers in the new Confederate Army.

Being an orphan, he was unrestrained by parents in the matter of risking his life by joining a very dangerous war, but two years in the Academy would at least delay the inevitable hazards to life and limb. As for his guardians at the County Orphanage in Huntsville, they were more than happy for him to go. Indeed, after Henry put the idea in their heads, the orphanage's governors sent all the other boys above the age of twelve to become cadets too, in order to save the county a portion of its modest welfare costs.

Although the East Texas Military Academy's original principal volunteered for real military service in November 1862, along with two of its best tutors, the Cadets did not disband, but remained under the command of an elderly gentleman called Colonel Wentworth. Under his direction the boys, in their smart gray and red uniforms and caps, were taught drill, musketry, gunnery, and camp skills. At gunnery in particular, old Colonel Wentworth imparted his considerable expertise, the boys all being able to load, lay and fire the Alamo era cannon in their grounds, and reputedly knock a blue-jay out of a cottonwood at five hundred paces, which is more than can be said for many of their adult Confederate Army gunner counterparts. Not for them the point-and-hope techniques of ill-trained soldiers of the day; the Colonel taught them the importance of range-finding, consistent, measured powder-charges and disciplined rapid re-loading with all types of projectile. When he spoke, boys listened; when he ordered, they obeyed. Henry, in particular, revered old Colonel Wentworth, and he wrote copious notes on everything he learned from him.

Henry and the other lads, as the war dragged on, made themselves useful in running messages for the officers of the troops quartered nearby, or by guarding railroads, bridges, and suchlike from Union saboteurs – of whom there were absolutely none for the entire course of the war in that part of Texas. Fifty-one Academy boys had graduated to the Confederate Army by 20th March 1864, which is when life suddenly changed for Henry Sutherland.

The stunning news was that Texas was soon to be invaded

by the Union Army! Or so the newspapers claimed. What was factually correct is that 'The Red River Expeditionary Force', under Major General Nathaniel P Banks, which consisted of some fifteen thousand men, with the potential of being reinforced into a much larger army still, was just across the state line in Louisiana. What is more, this Union force was on a winning streak, with several minor victories under its belt already. It was well equipped, well led, and well supplied with munitions, and stopping it in its tracks would not be easy.

Homer, Texas was to be the rallying point from which a Confederate Army would sally forth and give those Yankee imposters a damned good thrashing. General Richard Taylor was the man given the task of opposing Banks' advance along the border. General Taylor realized immediately that the greater part of his army would be made up of Texan units. So, at Homer, he set up a temporary headquarters in the Town Hall, and began organizing his regiments and putting a workable plan together.

Like all of his fellow cadets, Henry was ordered to report to General Taylor's staff to be assigned 'special duties'. So, snatching up his cap and pack, dressed in his neat cadet's uniform, Henry went off to see whether he might be of service. Several hundred men of the Confederate Army of East Texas, as it had been named, he found congregating in the streets of Homer, and its leaders on the steps of the Mayor's office in Main Square.

Henry was much impressed by the ordinary soldiers, those sturdy men in gray, singing, gossiping, and smoking, as they seated themselves on their packs or the hard ground. He had heard so much of these wonderful men, stories that had trickled through from The War, that vague, mysterious place that had sucked in and spat out a great many fathers and brothers from the region already. He remembered too, that of the fifty-one graduates of his Academy, more than half were already dead, wounded or captured. Nevertheless, he hoped to be yet another useful addition to a hopeless war and do his bit for Texas.

As for those gray-clad soldiers milling around the town, with their everlasting jokes and songs, their ever-ready hand-clasps and equally ready fists, their rifles short of ammunition and holes in their tunics, their anger at the inferior equipment and intermittent food, and their dogged determination to fight on when all the signs said they could never win - were there ever, thought Henry, more noble beings than they?

And there in the Square young Henry met a familiar face, old Sergeant Fredericks of Hubbard's 22nd Texas Infantry. This fellow, who was liable to get his words a little mixed when he was excited, used to shout, "Cursed be all Yankees!" and "God Bless Thomas Jefferson!" outside the Star Hotel bar, after a few drinks with his pals; but now, back home with his regiment, his eyes were strangely sullen and mournful. But to Henry, here was a fabled hero in the flesh, safely returned from the terrible battles of Shiloh, Chancellorsville and Gettysburg.

"What's up, Sergeant Fredericks?" said Henry

"Howdy, son," said Fredericks; "And where're you goin', young Henry, in yer smart 'ol uniform!"

"I want to join a regiment," said Henry, "What shall I do?"

"Go home son," said Fredericks, "War's already lost. We're just bidin' our time till the Yankee devils come ridin' into Texas. *'Woe to the inhabiters of the earth and of the sea! For the devil is come down unto you, having great wrath, because he knoweth that he hath but a short time.'*"

78

"Sergeant Fredericks!" said Henry, crestfallen, "Don't speak like that! We'll pull through, ol' Texas'll pull through, you'll see."

"Oh, sure it will son," said the Sergeant, "Sure it will. *'And God shall wipe away all tears from their eyes; and there shall be no more death, neither sorrow, nor crying, neither shall there be any more pain: for the former things are passed away.'* "

"Don't mind him," said a private barely older than Henry; "He caught a Yankee rifle butt on the side of his skull two months ago, and now he's even stranger than before – if that's possible."

Leaving the group of soldiers, Henry pressed forward to where some officers were talking with the Mayor, in the hope of learning something of the Army's probable movements. His curiosity was not to be unsatisfied, for, in response to a familiar bugle, he shortly found himself parading with several fellow Cadets, who had also gathered there to play their part in the coming struggle. They were informed by their aged Colonel that the Army of East Texas – and many more volunteers who were on their way – were to camp just outside the town that night, and that the Cadets were to go with them to be of what service they could. The entire army was to march across the border into Louisiana and offer battle to the Yankee army of the Red River Expeditionary Force very shortly.

The cadets were divided into batches, but Henry was not one of those in the first lot to march off with the Confederate soldiers, and so he waited. Regiment after regiment marched by, and the group of eager cadets diminished until only three were left with the Colonel.

Almost last came two companies of those wonderful

beings whom the Cadet Commander had never tired of lauding, namely Griffin's 21st Infantry, locally recruited fellows to a man, all bearded, wild-eyed men with angular cheeks, dishevelled uniforms and sprigs of willow in their caps to represent the rout of enemy raiders in a skirmish at Willow Creek, Missouri. As they marched, a big man in front, evidently a Scotsman, played abominable music on an instrument he carried under his arm. That was the first time Henry had ever seen or heard the bagpipes. He was suitably impressed, and pressed forward that he might be chosen to go with that famous formation.

Alas, Henry was disappointed, when the other two cadets were allocated to the 21st, and he was left alone with the old Colonel. It was already getting dark, and almost all the soldiers had now moved off to camp for the night. He was tired, hungry and his spirits were beginning to sag, when his commander spoke up.

"Now then, Henry," said Colonel Wentworth, "You may be wondering why I've saved you till last."

"Sir?" said Henry, puzzled.

"Look," said the Colonel, "That is your unit."

There was a faint rumbling of wheels and clatter of hooves on the stony road in the distance. Presently, a column of artillery could be seen approaching. There were cannon, most of them sturdy 12 pounder bronze Napoleons, with limbers and caissons attached, and behind these, about forty supply wagons. After these rolled four big iron howitzers, monsters forged by the Confederacy in their own new foundry outside Houston. It took four good horses to pull each gun and its carriage, and six or seven men to fire them under ideal circumstances. Some of the faithful crew sat stoically on the limbers and the leading draft-horses, while the rest followed up on their own mounts.

"Oh sir," said Henry, busting with excitement, "Am I to go with the artillery?"

"Not exactly," intoned the old soldier; "That would be far too dangerous."

"Too dangerous, sir?" said Henry, crestfallen. "But that only leaves-"

"The supply wagons," said the Colonel. "That driver in the front is in need of an assistant. The request came direct from Captain Hollis, Quartermaster in charge of Requisites and Supplies. Congratulations, Sutherland, you're in the army now."

Henry's disappointment at not becoming a gunner was soon forgotten, however, when he saw those two great horses pulling the first cartload of shells. Here was something worth waiting for! If he had admired the tough old horses before the guns and limbers, he absolutely worshipped those elegant giants towing the billowing supply wagons. The pair hauling the lead wagon were about seventeen hands at least, rippling with muscle and dapple-gray from nose to base of tail.

"Beauties, ain't they?" drawled a gnarled old Texan driver with one wooden leg, one eye, and one arm. Henry noted he also had an ear missing, and that all these abnormalities occurred on his right side.

"Hey, boy," said the driver, regarding Henry with his single, hawk-like eye, "Your father never tell ya it were rude to stare? Stop gawping an' climb aboard, you're holdin' up the entire Confederate Army."

"Sorry," said Henry, slinging his pack up onto the driver's box. "It's just that, you know-"

"Shiloh in 61," said the old timer; "Yankee shell almost killed me. Lost an arm, a leg and a few other things too. Yep, woke up in hospital an' the surgeons told me 'Son, you've lost one of everything, an' I do mean everything.' "

"That's tough," said Henry.

"Speak up, boy," said the man, "Got no ear-drum that side. The names Jim Bolt, by the way. Folks call me Calamity Jim. Can't think why."

"Pleased to meet you," said Henry, offering his hand but withdrawing it when he noted Jim Bolt had no spare hand to give in return.

"Yeah, likewise," said Jim. "This, by the way, is Bates' 13th Infantry Battalion, and them guns you saw in front are Batteries D and H, run by Major Jeffries, the best damn gunnery officer on planet Earth. They got 12 pounders, bronze beauties they are, and the Yankees hate their hearts."

"I just bet they do," said Henry, "and what about those iron guns in the rear? They look like howitzers to me, an' big ones too."

"Well now," said Calamity Jim, "I see you know your guns young feller. That's Battery Q, that is, under Lieutenant Ritchie. We call them the suicide squad. They were six guns, an' now they're four. The others blew up when they got too hot, back at Gannon Hill. Iron guns ain't a patch on the bronze 'uns, but they're cheap an' Jefferson Davis loves cheap. Them's guns from Houston, an' everyone know that Houston makes damn good hats an' coats, but terrible artillery. That's why they only got four left, an' the next battle they'll be down to three or two, no doubt, if they has to rapid fire. If ever you become president, young feller, don't go ordering no iron guns."

"I'll remember," said Henry; "But what about us, Jim, what unit are we in? I saw a W on the side of the wagon."

"You've a pair of eyes, you have," said Jim; "We're part of the 13th too, but we got forty wagons, an' our job is to supply the whole darn Army of East Texas, an' carry the baggage so to speak. This is Supply Company W, Wagon 1, which is why we got the best horses. Those two used to win prizes at county fairs for a farmer called Nobbs. He damn-near shot himself when we took 'em for the army."

He laughed a little at the memory.

"Where we going, Jim?" asked Henry, innocently.

"If I told ya, I'd have to shoot ya," said Jim seriously.

Then he broke into a lop-sided, semi-toothless smile: "Louisiana, son. We're going to war. We're Union-fodder."

"Will there be a battle?" asked Henry.

"For sure," said Jim; "Every time we travel we end up in a battle, We do it for a livin'. See them holes on the sides o' the wagon?"

Henry craned his neck around and saw there were half a dozen big splinters missing from the planks behind him, and a number of smaller bullet holes.

"Yankee shells," said Jim; "We get special attention wherever we go. Wagons one to six carry mainly shells. Artillery wins wars. But artillery is just lumps of useless bronze an' iron without these-here shells. Remember that."

"Where in Louisiana we goin', Jim?" said Henry, "I mean, is it far?"

"Never mind that," said Jim, "it's miles an' miles an' miles. Five days, mebbe. All we need to think about is cookin' time. That's when we stop at sundown, and I gets down to cook. An' I'm the damn best cook this side o' the Mississippi."

"That's good," said Henry, "very good. I ain't eaten all day."

"Well we won't eat for another hour," said Jim, "but when we do, you'll make a neat little fire and it'll be downwind. Can you guess why, young Henry?"

"Sparks, I guess," said Henry, "And tons and tons of shells."

"That's right," smiled Jim, scratching the hollow under his eye-patch, "You're a right smart lad, an' you' an' I'll get along jus' famously so long's you remember one thing, you savvy?"

"I savvy," said Henry. "What thing?"

"Ye can't mention stuff that happened 'fore Shiloh in 62," he said, turning to see Henry's reaction, "I had a wife, a farm and pots of money 'fore that damn shell did for me. My Martha upped an' left me for a no-good sneaky preacher, an' now I'm just an ol' cripple who sits here all day belly-achin'. It's all I'm good for. Nobody wants ya no more when half is blowed away."

Calamity Jim, lead driver of the supply column, and Henry Sutherland, Cadet First Class, lost no opportunity of chatting about the war, food, cannon, horses, the officers in charge, the rightness of the Confederate cause, the stupidity of Yankees, anything and everything – so long as it did not drag up events that happened before April 1862...

That night, the column pulled to a stop on a big open plain. Cattle were grazing nearby, and several foraging parties were sent out to turn some unsuspecting steers into beef. Back in camp, there was plenty to do. Men were busily engaged seeing that the horses got oats or hay-fodder. Others made fires and got out the cooking gear and coffee pots. Pipes were lit, a flask or two of whiskey passed round, and all was content and relaxed.

Before they crossed into Louisiana, all evenings passed like this. The drivers simply stopped their carts on the side of whatever road or trail they were on. Even so, sentries were posted to watch the column, and mounted patrols plodded past in the night in case of raids or saboteurs. Later, Jim explained, they would make an armed camp every evening, and be prepared for cavalry attacks at any time, for both sides took great delight in disrupting and destroying each other's supply trains, for obvious reasons.

There was, however, one incident that concentrated the minds of those in the Army of East Texas, even as they were about to leave 'The Lone Star State'. A young sentry, made nervous by stories of Yankee saboteurs and night attacks, was left to guard the rear-most wagons of the column one evening. The password for the night had been 'Bluebird.' But another young private, on his way back from a latrine, when challenged for the correct word, thought it would be very funny to say 'Bluebellies' instead. So he did; and the rifleman duly shot him dead – the first casualty of the campaign.

CHAPTER TWO:
CAMP INVINCIBLE!

The drivers were an easily recognizable bunch in the Army of East Texas, since, being civilians, they dressed in whatever clothes they liked, and walked around unarmed and immune to most aspects of army discipline. They were very popular, since they carried all the food and ammunition. That would explain all the friendly offers of cigars, card games and nips of whiskey. In return, a few extra items of food might make their way back to friends amongst the soldiers, and heavy items from the infantrymen's packs were sometimes accommodated on the wagons.

Amongst the other drivers, whom Henry was frequently asked to assist about camp in the evenings, was a man called Will Tanner. He and Henry soon became particularly friendly, and, when both were off duty, Henry and Will had long chats about a number of things, but the progress of the war, and the coming battle were favorite topics of conversation. Like most soldiers and drivers, Tanner was not optimistic about their chances.

"Back east, them Bluebellies got all the money, they got all the men, and they got all the fancy guns," said Tanner one evening; "We ain't never gonna beat them on their own sod; but in Texas we can lick 'em every time."

Jim Bolt, who was sullenly smoking his pipe, chipped in:

"Don't make no sense to go chasin' after them Yankees; seems to me we should hold fast in Texas an' look after our own."

"So why's we goin' to Louisiana to fight?" said Henry.

"Guess we gonna try to stop 'em there," said Tanner;

"General Banks has fifteen thousand Bluebellies marching up the Red River towards Shreveport. But he may take a left and go for Texas instead; he got the men to do it. So we got to show 'em it's a bad idea to mess with we Texans. Otherwise, they'll be gettin' funny ideas about marching on Longview, then on to Houston. Just hope they don't join up with another o' them big Union outfits. I heard some of 'em's got twenty thousand men with new repeatin' rifles."

"But can't we Texans fight better'n them, Will?" asked Henry naively.

"Yep, we sure can," said Will Tanner, "but they keep right on comin'. There are four times more men in the Union ranks than the armies of the South, an' they got six cannon to every one of ours. But there is one thing we sure do better'n them."

"That's good, Will," said Henry; "What is it?"

"Die," said Tanner. "Almost every fightin' man here's either been wounded or he's a replacement. We left our friends an' comrades buried everywhere from Antietam to Gettysburg. An' where's it got us Texans, young Henry? All the way back to Homer to regroup, get more young blood like you, then hurl ourselves at the Yankee colossus like a bucket o' water chucked on a prairie fire."

"Well," said Henry, "they'll never take ol' Texas. Mebbe they'll give up."

Jim and Bill spontaneously burst into laughter.

"They might," said Jim, "They just might!"

"The Yanks got all the money and food, but we got all the damn mosquitoes," said Tanner, slapping an insect on his leg.

"I doubt that," said Henry; "As for food, we do all right. What we eatin' Jim. Sure tastes good."

"Same's yesterday," said Jim, "Rustled steak, onions an'

beans with plenty o' pepper. It's pepper makes a darn good meal on the hoof."

"Speakin' of hoofs," said Henry, "Why we been packed in tight as peas in a pod with the horses these past two nights? Horses an' mules can't get enough grass jammed in like this."

"Ah," said Jim, "Ain't you heard? We're in Louisiana now. The General says we have to cosy-up like this every night."

"That's right," said Will Tanner, "Every sun-down the senior officers place the men and supplies in a series of squares to deter a surprise attack. General Taylor calls it 'Camp Invincible.' Let's hope he's right."

"Yeah," said Jim. "An' the tighter the box, the more they fear an attack, to my mind. There's a crossroads 'bout a mile ahead. Reck'n the infantry will block it off tomorrow an' wait for the Bluebellies to try an' take it back. We're in the way o' them Yankees an' where they want to go. They'll attack tomorrow, noon at the latest. That's the word."

"Rumors, more like," said Will; "Still, I wouldn't be surprised to see some Yanks turn up real soon. That crossroads is smack in their way if they hope to take Shreveport."

Henry had stopped eating, and looked around at the other men. They looked mighty solemn he thought, though they continued to spoon down the beef stew; but a sense of great excitement had overcome Henry, as he contemplated the thrill of being in, or near, a real battle.

That night, he went forward with Will to watch the gunners of H Battery cleaning their 12 pounders, and lost no opportunity of learning the names of their ordnance and how they worked. Lieutenant Prosser of H Battery proudly told him:

"We got six 12 pounder brass Napoleons, they're smooth bore, and kill at a mile an' a half. They ain't the most modern gun in the word, but they're versatile, an' they're deadly. They fire solid shot, shell, and canister, and we shoot fast an' accurate enough to make them Yankees quake in their boots. Last time we fired 'em, we knocked a Bluebelly Colonel off his horse at eight hundred yards. We've been offered captured breech loaders, an' Parrott Rifles, an' other styles of guns, an' we said no. We love these guns like some folks love their kids. Guns like these'll win a war."

Later, they paid a visit to company Q, and were soon examining their 24 pounder monsters . These were howitzers, shorter-barreled guns of sixty-four inches tube length that took two pounds of powder and hurled shells of about eighteen pounds weight, despite their name that suggested heavier projectiles.

"If you'd only got a little more strength in yer wrists," said a sergeant called Tom Kinnock, you'd be welcome to stay an' be a loader, an' learn to fire the ol' things yourself. We're a few men short this campaign. Damn Yankee cavalry gave us a short back an' sides last time out – that's after two guns blew up in our faces when the lieutenant told us to increase the charge."

"What did you do to increase the charge?" said Henry.

"Well," said Tom Kinnock, "since you ask, we increased the powder an' popped in two shot."

"That was a mistake," said Henry; "If you double-shot a cannon, the extra pressure automatically increases the range without adding extra powder."

"Oh really," said Kinnock, bemused, "and how would a young whippersnapper like you know such a thing?"

"Because our Colonel at the Academy told us so," said Henry, "an' I tried it on the range. Worked like magic. *'Little powder, Much lead, Shoots far, Kills dead.'*"

"Well," said Kinnock, "I wish you'd tell the lieutenant that before he blows the lot of us to kingdom come. Say, we could use a smart brain like yours in Q Battery – how's about joining us?"

Will had to shepherd Henry away from the lure of the howitzers. There was little doubt they would adopt Henry if he asked to join, but Will was eager to keep the youngster with the teamsters, where he was also badly needed. For his part, Henry longed to be able to stay with the batteries. He even asked Jim and Will if they might let him go.

The response was unanimous.

"No, son, we need you here," said Calamity Jim. "You'd not last long up with the guns, 'less you can run faster'n a Yankee horse."

"Or a Yankee bullet," said Will; "Tom Kinnock an' twelve others were the only ones to survive at Gannon Hill when they got cut off four months ago. They lost thirty men in sixty seconds, an' only a counter from the 11th Mounted Infantry stopped the guns being stolen away."

"Besides," said Jim, thumbing some tobacco into his pipe, "Didn't I tell you we got our own work to do? These-here shells don't just supply our own three batteries you know, they go to every gun in the brigade, not to mention the bullets an' powder for the rifles we carry."

"Are there only shells for the artillery, Jim?" asked Henry. "Don't you have chain or grape-shot as well?"

"I say shells, sonny," said Jim, "but there's solid shot an' canister too. Grape we don't use loose these days, and chain-shot died out with Napoleon an' Wellington. But canister with iron balls inside we got a-plenty, and shells by the box-load. Shells are what wins the battles in a modern army. They go straight, an' they go far, as you'll soon see, and they does terrible things to men an' beasts. But when them shells run out, that's when things turn bad. Why, I seen the guns simply starvin' for ammunition. I've seen the gunners hanging round the guns cryin', 'cos they've run out o' shells, and there was the poor beggars in the lines gettin' smashed to bits by the Yankee fire. Oh, it's horrible, son," said Jim, "simply horrible. We're the supply train, but they depend on us, so we got to make sure we don't let the shells dry up."

And he pulled fiercely at his pipe, with a strange look in his eyes that somehow prevented Henry asking any more questions just then.

That night after super, when the horses and mules were corralled in the narrow spaces between the wagons, and the artillery positioned to repel a surprise attack, pickets were posted around the camp, and riders sent out to patrol. Two companies of infantry, instead of pitching their tents, had been allocated to sleep under the wagons with the drivers, which did not go down well with either group, especially when the rain began pouring down at about an hour before midnight.

Henry, Jim and Will had made their beds on the flat space above the ammunition boxes in Wagon Number One. Jim was soon snoring, but Will and Henry, as was their habit, were talking for a while before they slumbered. Will used to drive a big wagon for the cavalry in peacetime, and discussed the merits of different kinds of carts, the deeds of various regiments of soldiers before and during the war, and a hundred and one other things; but Henry liked best to get Will to talk about his past adventures. If Jim was awake, events that took place before '62 were off-limits, but that night, as the rain rattled down against the sturdy canvas over their heads, Jim was snoring loudly and the topic became the first part of the war.

"Were you at Shiloh, Will?" said Henry.

"Sure," Will grunted, "I was there."

"What did you carry that time?"

"I had boxes of powder and ball for the men," said Will, "an' my job was to run my cart up an' down behind the line when the balls an' powder got low. On the way back they put wounded in the back, but there was so many, I'd only be able to take a few. After the battle, the whole wagon was bright red with blood an' it took me a day to scrub it clean with soap."

Henry's curiosity to know what it was like in a battle was strong, and he pressed Will for more details.

"When a man gets shot," he wanted to know, "does it, you know, hurt real bad?"

"When a man gets shot," said Will, "most times he ain't killed right out. Oh sure, a few are lucky that way, but most leap up in the air then fall to the ground, and crawl around yellin' like crazy. If they's shot in the gut they often die in a minute or two, stickin' their fingers in the dirt an' callin' for their mama, but some get gathered up an' hang on for a day or two an' go all green an' rotten under their bandages. Limb-shot fellers, they mostly get the saw; four men hold 'em down an' they bite on a mini-ball to soak up the screams. Sometimes they champ that lump o' lead clean in two. After Shiloh, there was a barn where a surgeon plied his trade, an' just outside was a heap of arms an' legs almost as high's the barn itself.

They laid them amputees in lines across the fields till as far's you looked was nothin' but men in the open beggin' for water, or another drop o' whiskey. But the only one to get the last o' the whiskey was the surgeon himself; that feller worked for two days solid, drunk as a lord, singing hymns to take his mind off his work which was, as you might imagine, well-nigh impossible. That was a very hard way to earn a livin'. Nobody knows more of what war's really about than an army surgeon, young Henry."

Thereafter, Henry's imagination was fully satisfied and he asked no more on that particular subject. Which was just as well, considering what happened the next day.

CHAPTER TWO:
DAWN ATTACK...

A few minutes before dawn, several huge explosions awoke the camp. Dozens of sentries and riders on patrol had failed to detect the enemy arriving in the night. A battery of eight Union 6 pounders was positioned on a hill three-quarters of a mile way, directed by a 'wig-wag' signaller sitting in a tree. This man sent messages to the artillery commander by moving his lantern and flags in various positions of the wig-wag code. Thus, he was able to home the guns onto the wagons and soldiers in the camp – for a short while.

The enemy gunners were hoping to take the three Confederate Batteries by surprise, but despite good intelligence that had told them where these guns had been positioned, they discovered the guns had been moved off in the night. General Taylor had decided to include them in his blocking force sent to the crossroads, after hearing that the Red River Expedition might occupy that crucial position before his own forces could deploy. So, luckily for Batteries G, H and Q, they were long gone by the time the Union field artillery made their play. But their luck was the supply wagons' misfortune – for now there were no guns to counter those of the attacking force.

In the dawn light the opening Union salvo was not accurate, most of the shells falling way short. By the time the signaller had corrected their aim, and the battery began dropping shells nearer to the wagons, a large body of Confederate cavalry had formed up. As some sharp-shooters blasted the signaller out of his tree, the cavalry spurred their horses into a charge. But, as they reached the spot where the

Union guns had been a few minutes before, General Banks, predictably, had arranged another little surprise. Banks, being something of a chess player, had worked out his opening strategy in advance. The 6 pounders had already been rushed off the field; and just as the cadet-gray riders lost momentum at the now deserted hill, they themselves were charged by an equal number of Union cavalry.

Close-range cavalry battles had evolved into a new form of mounted combat by this late stage of the war. Few men now put their faith in sabers at the onset of a skirmish, but might take one up when their side-arms were emptied. Revolvers were the thing: a pair gave the rider twelve shots, twelve chances to kill. Ten feet or less was the sort of range that got results. Shooting a stationary target from the saddle was hard enough; but hitting a fast-moving target *from* a fast-moving target took even more skill – or luck. Factor into this the fear of being hit by bullet or shellfire, falling under the hooves of charging animals or careering headlong into another horse and rider, and the challenges faced by cavalrymen might be envisaged. Small wonder, then, that actions generally descended into disorder, chaos and carnage.

On the little hillside, both sides pushed for an advantage. Major Simmons and his Confederate cavalry, though taken by surprise and lacking momentum, nevertheless drew pistols and carbines and turned around to face the counter-charge. As Blue met Gray, there was a prolonged, ragged volley of gunfire, and simultaneously, a gigantic rolling cloud of black-powder smoke covered the battlefield. Men, horses, guidons, flags and weapons went down into the freshly created mud. There were collisions, shootings, bugle-calls, battle-cries, screams of injured horses and shouts of dying men. Within ten minutes the melee would have been complete, except that both sides, having hacked and shot their way from one end of the battlefield to the other, rallied, turned and did it all again.

Meanwhile, the Confederate infantry were forming ranks to face the Union lines that were already advancing on the crossroads. They had a bit of uneven ground and woodland on either flank to deter the horse-soldiers, but in any case the two cavalry were already hell-bent on annihilating each other on and around that little hill. The pesky battery of Union 6 pounders that had initiated all the action in the first place had, by this time re-deployed safely, and set up their guns on the opposite flank, guarded by some companies of infantry.

Back in the camp, Henry had observed first-hand the effect of shellfire. Though the enemy guns had miraculously failed to hit a single wagon, they had dropped half a dozen rounds into the gaps between them. Henry had been most amazed to see a pair of mules not fifty feet away do a somersault and fall to earth kicking and lifeless. A man who had been trying to calm these animals had seemed to disappear. When Henry ran over to see what had happened to the driver, he was stopped in his tracks not by the sight of the dead animals, which was horrible enough, but by the corpse of the man, now lodged half-way up a thorny tree. Bloodied and broken, the body hung limply as a rag-doll, the fellow's face with lolling tongue somehow fixed in an expression as if stopped midway through a cough.

Henry stood and stared; only a pat on the back from Will brought him out of this nightmare.

"C'mon, son," he said, "Ol' Mike-there's cashed in his chips, ain't nothin' we can do for him now. We got to get them horses hitched."

By the time they got back to wagons One and Two, a messenger had given a piece of paper to Jim, who read it and handed it to Will Tanner.

FIELD ORDER
Wagons two and three follow rider to Pineridge Wood
go rear of batteries H and G.
12 pounder   ammunition as follows:
100 rounds each / 70% shell / 30% canister
dry wad & fr primers x 200
plus 10,000 rounds .58 mini, cartridge or bullet/powder,
percussion caps 10,000
Maj. H T Jeffries

"Them again," said Will; "Always gettin' into scrapes an' askin' for more ammunition before they've even emptied their own limbers. One day, I'm goin' to run down to the Major an' tell him not to panic at the first little pops on the other side of the darn battlefield."

"Even so," said Calamity Jim, "orders is orders."

He shouted to the drivers of Wagon Three, a short way off: "Hey, there Dick Riley! Jack Berry! Hitch 'em up an' follow Will, you hear me?"

"Wish I could go," said Henry.

"Tain't the place for the likes o' you," said Will, knocking out the ash of his pipe. "You stay in the camp, and help Jim send the right stores out to where they're needed."

"Well, I could go and come back in a while," suggested Henry.

"You can't walk that far back in time," said Will; "Besides, the Major'd want to know all about it."

"I'll ride over on a mule," persisted Henry. "I should be

able to find you, an' help you unload."

"Don't do it, sonny," said Will, "You'll get shot by a sentry, or lost, blown up, or run down in a charge. New hands like yourself is extra vulnerable – seen it before. We'll unload the gear ourselves, an' be back in no time. Shot an' bullets will be rainin' down that end by now, or my names not Will Tanner. Leave it to us."

"I'm a cadet," said Henry rather foolishly, "I ought to go."

Will's sarcastic grin rather annoyed him.

"Sorry, General," said Will with a mock salute, "but your place is here in case you're needed. Ain't that right Jim?"

"You'll get shot at soon enough," said Jim, "if that's the sort o' caper you like to dance. Then you'll see things a different way, to be sure."

Henry watched the two wagons depart to drop off their shells. Another note came through, for ammunition to the opposite flank. Jim saw the boy's great interest in the matter and tried to nip Henry's enthusiasm in the bud.

"You ain't a-goin'," he said firmly. "Stay here an' stop tryin' to get yourself killed. We got another delivery to get ready."

After loading the next wagon, Henry secreted himself in the shadow of a tree. The wagon was having its cargo verified, by Jim and Captain Hollis. Henry's ears strained to catch an inkling of its destination. When everything was ready for departure the drivers were mustered for a few final instructions from Jim. Henry slipped around the back to inspect it. He found to his delight that there was plenty of room to hide himself inside, for the stack of boxes did not entirely fill up the wagon. Henry clambered in and crouched down behind some cases of shells, and presently heard the men coming back. With beating heart be heard one of them tie down the big cover, while the other roused the mules. In a few moments there was a grinding of the big metal tires on the road, then a rumble as they set off across the grass through open country. It was one of the smaller, lighter wagons, and was therefore pulled by only two mules.

Beside them rode a trooper, and occasionally a messenger or a swiftly-moving body of horsemen would thunder by. Now and again Henry heard the tramp of marching soldiers. It was very dark and stuffy in his hiding place and he was beginning to feel sore from the continual bumping. He almost wished be had not come, and for the first time began to wonder what would happen when he was found. Supposing the wagon was attacked when isolated and he fell into the hands of the Yankees? Or supposing they were hit and the cart blew up with him inside? He remembered with a start the fate of Mike, who'd ended up in the big thorn tree.

He told himself that though he was doing wrong to be there at all, yet he must see the thing through. If he was questioned by an officer, he must attest he had been sent with the wagon and was merely acting on orders given him back at the camp.

A great explosion and the sudden stopping of the wagon told him that something was amiss. Then there was an even more deafening roar which seemed to shake the ground. Outside, riders hurried by, more orders and questions were shouted. Then the wagon moved on a few yards and stopped again. Then a strange thing happened. Something hit the ground and exploded so close to the wagon so that it almost turned over sideways, then righted itself again. The tarpaulin over his head was torn away in an instant, and Henry Sutherland fell sprawling among the boxes, some of which landed on top of him. For a few seconds he was blinded. As his senses returned, he thought it odd that, despite all that was happening to him, the world had turned completely silent. Presently he was able to push away the boxes on top of him and stand up. Gradually his hearing returned, but there was a continuous buzzing in his ears. He looked about him and realized what must have happened. The driver lay dead, slumped to the bottom of his box. His companion had been blown clean off his seat, for he lay on the ground face down, and by the contorted way he had landed, it was plain he too, had been killed. Henry licked his lips, took in the rest of the scene around him.

One mule had taken a great mass of shrapnel in its side and had died at once. The other, shielded by its companion, was unhurt, though mightily distressed. The corporal who had been riding beside the wagon, evidently unhurt, was attempting to get the dead animal out of its harness with the aid of four or five other men. How they had managed to react so quickly to the near-direct hit of the shell was a mystery; certainly it spoke volumes about the urgency of the shipment of ammunition.

"Glory be!" said one of the men looking up, "Hey, Corp, there's one left alive up there. Must be a miracle!"

"Hey, boy," said the Corporal, "can you drive?"

"I guess," said Henry.

"Good," said the corporal, "We got half the infantry stuck in a farm up ahead with ammunition almost gone. There's artillery too, almost out of shells. "

"Lead the way, then," said Henry, climbing into the box, "But look – we only got one mule, an' this stuffs mighty heavy."

"We'll try it with one," said the corporal, "An' if it can't pull it, we'll all go round an' push. We got more'n a mile to go – if the Yanks ain't broken through already, that is."

The near-side mule dragged away, Henry took up the reins and whip, and stirred the remaining animal into motion. The mule was reluctant at first, but a touch of the long whip on its tail worked wonders and it leaned into its collar gamely and began to heave the outfit along.

"She's a good 'un," commented the corporal, lending assistance from the saddle by tugging on a canvas-hoop on one side. The men ran along behind, catching up and pushing whenever they hit rough ground.

"How long you been a driver, son," said the corporal.

"Oh, for a while," lied Henry.

"Well, son," said the corporal, "you're doin' a grand job.

Just as he said these words, a mini-ball hit him in the chest with a resounding thud, and he toppled from his saddle.

"Keep goin', kid," shouted the men behind, "We'll see to him. You go on, straight over that ridge, the buildings are on the right."

The single mule just managed, with some brutal persuasion, to haul the cart to the summit, and then stopped. Henry gasped at the scene before him. Not a quarter mile away was the ruined farm. Several ragged lines of dark blue soldiers were advancing over the far horizon towards it. The attackers' rifles had bayonets fixed, and here and there were standard bearers showing the positions of various companies and regiments. Defending the farm were cadet-gray soldiers on the roof of the house, in the corral, along a hedge and all the way along a fence to where it joined some woodland on the right flank. Down below, on the left flank, were four cannon in front of a large barn. Henry recognized them as Q Battery by the shape of the guns, and the distinctive color of some of the horses hidden behind a hedge, four of which were so light gray as to be almost white.

Between the barn and the wagon, it appeared a bridge had been broken by enemy fire, and some engineers, or men with tools at any rate, were repairing it under heavy fire, both from rifle and cannon. Henry ducked as a shell came whistling over and exploded fifty yards behind him.

Evidently, this part of the Union line was well-endowed with artillery, manned by some decent gunnery officers too, judging by the number and direction of the explosions. A few moments later there was a roar and a crash louder than any that had gone before, and the wagon shook and almost turned over again. Henry was rocked in his seat, and felt a sharp sensation in his left leg. He looked down, and there was blood on his thigh. His first concern, however, was the mule; but though it was far from happy, having been showered with gravel, it nevertheless stood on its feet, waiting for orders.

"You all right, son?" said a voice beside him on the ground. It was one of the soldiers following him.

"I got a bit o' metal in my leg," said Henry, "but I can manage. I'll see the surgeon later. Give me a push – looks like they fixed the bridge."

As they were completing the last bit of the journey, the enemy gunners found his range. Shell after shell landed close to the wagon, but Henry consoled himself with the thought that, if one scored a direct hit, he would know little about it.

"Look behind – there's two more wagons coming up," said one of the men who were pushing.

Henry turned his head, and sure enough, two more

wagons were cresting the ridge. Then, there was a gigantic and prolonged explosion that made the individual shell-bursts seem like pops from champagne bottle corks in comparison. His own wagon, along with every other thing in the vicinity, rocked from side to side.

"One's gone up already," said a voice behind him, stating the obvious.

Henry craned his neck to see, but all that remained of it was a pall of smoke. As for the driver – he had vanished.

"Good-bye and good luck," said Henry, hoping and praying that it hadn't been Will or Calamity Jim.

As the mini-balls whizzed and zipped past his head, or thudded into the wooden sides of his wagon, Henry urged his mule over the newly-repaired bridge and into the relative safety of the area behind the barn. The remaining wagon soon drew up beside him, its painted identification mark W2 very familiar to Henry.

"Well I'll be darned!" Will Tanner said, as he stepped down from Wagon Two. "What in the name of tarnation are you doin' here, you young fool?"

"Never mind that," said Henry, "Who was driving that wagon back there, Will? Don't tell me it was-"

"No," said Will, "Not Calamity Jim, but Jack Berry and his pal Dick Riley... God rest their souls, poor beggars."

Willing hands began to unload boxes of shells from Wagon Two, and rifle ammunition from Henry's wagon.

"An' how in heaven's name you didn't go sky high," said Will, "I'll never know. I mean – look – there's about a hundred holes in your wagon. An' that mule – she's been plastered from head to foot with dirt. You too, for that matter."

"Well," said Henry, looking at Will, who was also covered

in muck, "if that ain't the pot callin' the kettle black, I don't know what is."

Will told him that he had dropped off the 12 pounder ammunition for Major Jeffries, then been ordered with another cart to find the regiments holding the farm along with Q Battery. Henry explained briefly how he'd stolen a ride, and then taken over the driving on that same dangerous journey of death and destruction.

"Well, you're a plucky 'un," said Will, when Henry had finished, "but you an' me is goin' to get into no end of a row when you're found. Question is, what to do with you now? Chances are, we'll both be blowed to kingdom come in the course o' the next quarter of a hour."

"Well," said Henry, "before we do, I think we're goin' to see somethin' special. Them Yankees are mighty close."

He peeked round the corner of the barn, where the four big iron howitzers of Q Battery were being loaded and laid prior to action. Henry noted they were being used as close infantry support to help hold that part of the line. Then, just as the lieutenant in charge raised his arm to give the order to open fire, a terrific explosion sent all five members of Number Three crew sprawling into the dirt. It wasn't one of their own cannon exploding this time, but an enemy shell that had found its mark.

When the smoke and dust settled, an orderly was attending the sole man of that crew left alive.

Unfazed by this, Lieutenant Ritchie kept his nerve; he ran to Number Three, checked the aim, and picked up the cord.

"Number one gun - FIRE!" yelled the officer. Without waiting to see fall of shot, he yelled again: "Number Two Gun – FIRE!" and so on down the line, firing Number Three Gun, which was still 'on-target', himself.

About three hundred yards distant, and about thirty yards apart, the four big shells exploded in the ranks of dark-blue soldiers, creating vast gaps in the ranks. It was a superb piece of gunnery. Union soldiers further away from the detonations were checked, or staggered, but then – on they came.

The lieutenant ordered two men from other guns to man Number Three, an experienced gunner and a rammer. Then he looked around, as if calculating his next move. Short of personnel, an idea suddenly came to him.

"Hey!" shouted the lieutenant to Will and Henry, "you two there, lend a hand on Number Three Gun! I'll lay myself. Look lively, and do as you're told!"

Truly, it was a fearful situation that now fully revealed itself to the drivers as they emerged from behind the barn. Mini-balls and bullets were whizzing through the air, while exploding shells up and down their lines were the biggest threat of all. At Number Three Gun Henry crouched in imitation of the experienced men. There were supposed to be six men for each gun, but now they had to manage with four or five men crews. A corporal, hardly older than Henry, showed Henry and Will the ropes. Battery Q was unusual in that it used the slang names, rather than numbers, to identify the members of the crew: runner, sponger, spike, gunner, chief.

Will was made a 'runner', told to bring over the charges from the limber. Henry was assigned the job of 'spike' who attended the vent. Henry recognized the terms from the Academy, and knew the routine, including his own role which was to wait until the piece was fired, then put his thumb over the vent as the next charge went in. This prevented a spark getting in, and cut off the oxygen to the powder below. When the charge was rammed tight, he thrust a spike down the vent to pierce the burlap cloth around the powder, before standing back. Another man pressed the primer in the vent. The gunner aimed by elevating the gun on a screw, and moving it left and right via the hand-spike attached to the trail. The chief then pulled the primer's cord, or ordered it pulled, to fire the gun.

All these actions could be done in ten to fifteen seconds by an experienced and well-rehearsed crew; with Battery Q, short-handed as it was, and with novices slowing things down, the process took a little longer.

"Reload – shell! Down fifty – right fifty – all guns! Fire when ready!" shouted the lieutenant. He was giving the correction in yardage to direct the fire himself, rather than leaving the targeting to the individual chiefs. The layers expertly moved the screws and adjusted their trails to shoot the howitzers fifty yards closer and fifty to the right, into another part of the massed ranks of attackers. One by one the second volley exploded among the lines of blue, with equally spectacular results, this time at only a hundred and fifty yards. Meanwhile, the Richmond rifles of the Army of East Texas rattled and thundered from one end of the line to the other; but the surviving Union attackers, their bayonets angled forward purposefully, continued to advance.

On both sides, men – many men, in fact – were throwing their arms in the air and falling over, or rolling on the ground digging at the earth with their fingers, calling for their mothers, even as Will had described to Henry. But, as the battle reached its climax, the living were far too engrossed in their work to pay much attention to the dead and dying.

In truth, a good third of the both the Confederate and Union strength had become casualties around the farm and fields by this time. Several of the gunners were struck by ball or shrapnel – and still the others stood or knelt faithfully by the guns, defying death with every second that passed. More men were drafted into the gun-crews, mostly to fetch the charges; meanwhile the experienced artillerymen took over the tasks of fallen comrades, as they had been trained to do, in order to keep the howitzers firing.

Another volley roared into the Union lines, with deadly results – and still the attackers came on. Then came a second big explosion within the battery, hard by Number Four Gun. The lieutenant, who had stepped across to help lay the gun, clutched at his stomach, and fell to his knees. Sergeant Tom Kinnock was also down. Men ran to their assistance, just as three senior officers and a couple of troopers arrived on horseback. They reined in their horses and dismounted right behind the battery, with little regard for their own safety. A trooper led their horses to shelter behind the buildings.

"Good God!" shouted Brigadier General Parsons, ignoring the wounded lieutenant, and pointing at the attackers, "Look at that! They're awful close. Reload, men, reload! Get back to your guns!"

Henry looked up at the ever-nearing ranks of dark blue. Suddenly, he left his gun and dashed back behind the barn.

"Henry!" shouted Will, "Come back, that's a court martial offense, that is!"

But to no avail, for young Henry Sutherland had deserted his post!

CHAPTER THREE:
THE SECOND LIEUTENANT...

The officers scowled, made a mental note to have that young coward shot – if, indeed, any of them survived long enough to see it through. Their main concern, however, was that Battery Q had faltered in its rhythm, for both the lieutenant and its principal sergeant had already become casualties.

Brigadier General Parsons had shouted for the men to reload. But, as he was not an artillery man, untrained in the finer points of gunnery, he had failed to impart two vital pieces of instruction, namely *what* to reload and *where* to shoot.

Again he ventured:

"Reload those cannon, I say, damn you!"

By now the surviving gunners were back by their howitzers, hesitating, even arguing as to what charge to load next. Most had one eye on the advancing Yankees, who were now almost up to the perimeter of the farm, and one eye on their guns, elevated way too high to make any inroads on the enemy. Now the dark-blue men were coming at them at a run, their bayonets glinting in the sun.

A shrill but surprisingly loud voice from behind the guns brought everyone to their senses.

"RELOAD – DOUBLE CANISTER!" shouted Henry Sutherland, as his gunnery training came flooding back to him. Gun crews turned round to stare at the kid in his grimy cadet uniform.

"Ain't got no canister!" said a gunner, "we only got shell in the limbers – an' precious few o' that left too..."

"HERE, BOYS, QUICK!" yelled Henry. He was dragging an

ammunition box, with its lid removed, by its rope handle. Inside were the cylindrical shapes of 24 pounder canisters. The ammunition came with powder and sabots attached, and was ready for ramming, for canister has no fuse to set; and, as it said on the wooden box, each was one packed with *one hundred and fifty* iron balls!

Will and two other runners had the presence of mind to get some more of the correct boxes out of Wagon 2. Meanwhile, other members of the crews loaded the first charges. These consisted of a canister tin attached by tape to a wooden disc, the sabot, with this in turn taped to the pouch of powder. Thus, the guns were loaded with something akin to a cartridge without an outer casing. Henry, to provide the extra canisters, separated four of the tins of iron balls from spare charges by hand, using his pocket knife. It was an easy enough job to cut the twine and tape separating the two parts. The second canisters, free of their powder bags, were then rammed home on top of the original charges. 'Double canister', as every artilleryman of the period knew, was the last expedient before positions were overrun by infantry or horse, since the second container created a lot of extra pressure, which might cause the gun to blow up. Every man in Battery Q was aware that the reputation of the 'inferior' iron howitzers forged in Confederate foundries. Nevertheless, desperate situations sometimes necessitate desperate remedies. Were they not, in any case, nick-named 'The Suicide Squad'?

"ALL GUNS – DOWN ONE HUNDED, FLAT!" yelled Henry, causing the muzzles to be aimed in a flat trajectory, no higher than chest height; but he had one small act of genius yet to administer. "NUMBER ONE GUN – TRAVERSE – LEFT, FORTY-FIVE DEGREES. NUMBER FOUR GUN – TRAVERSE –

RIGHT, FORTY-FIVE DEGREES."

By this expedient, guns One and Four were left pointing their cone-shaped field of fires way over to the left and right respectively to sweep *along* the ranks rather than shoot straight at them. With Two and Three covering the central area before the farm, a huge frontage was then targeted by the four 24 pounder howitzers. As Henry knew, the same tactic had been used on the British at the Battle of New Orleans in 1812, to devastating effect.

There was a pause, as Henry waited for the attackers to come just a little closer. The cheering Yankee soldiers that had defied all defending rifles were now converging on the farmyard itself. The foremost men could have been hit with a well-thrown stone – but still young Henry Sutherland held his fire.

The Brigadier General and his two staff captains, who had been very calm until then, un-holstered their pistols, drew beads on the enemy and, as one, commenced a brisk fusillade.

"ALL GUNS – FIRE!" yelled the battery commander.

All hell broke loose – for the Union Army attackers, that is. The effect of *one thousand two hundred* marble-sized lumps of death skimming through the air from ankle to head height, not to mention the fragments of the tin cans that held them, was devastating. Dozens and dozens of men were knocked off their feet, in four great arcs of destruction. Long sections of those dark blue ranks were decimated. Some men were lifted off their feet, others spun round in the air. The front-most troops were killed to a man. Officers, leading their men, lay dead or wounded. Gaps opened up in the lines behind them – and the attack faltered. For a few brief seconds, the Texan infantry stopped firing, as men looked on in awe.

Even the Brigadier General was shocked to his core.

"Great God!" he shouted; "Look at that!"

Then he realized that the riflemen had paused in their shooting.

"Commence fire!" he urged, "And you there, by the guns, give 'em more canister, boys!"

This was soon accomplished, the guns reverting to single canister charges, raid-fired. The Union attack, centered on that farm, broke up, the murderous gunfire making the difference between the two sides.

Within half an hour, Confederate reinforcements arrived, though they were hardly needed. Only the Union artillery took the shine off things a little, for they continued to pound away from a distance, until the Confederate cavalry hunted then down and gave them a very bad time indeed. Finally, the Confederate lines were ordered to stand down, but maintain their field positions for now.

"Who are you, son?" said Brigadier General Parsons, walking up to the boy commander, "and what uniform is that you're wearing under all that muck? More importantly, who taught you to handle guns like that?"

"I'm Officer Cadet Sutherland," said Henry, saluting, "an' this-here's a Military Academy of East Texas uniform. As for who taught me, that would be Colonel Wentworth, who made his name fighting the Mexicans in '48."

"Well I never," said Parsons, "I know that old bird – he fought against Mexicans all right – and the British too! He's been around since the time of Adam. Well, Sutherland – the way you handled those guns was outstanding."

"Thank you sir," said Henry.

"You will remain here as battery commander," said the

Brigadier General, as his horse was returned to him. "You are a second lieutenant as of now. I know a natural leader when I see one. We may need your services tomorrow. Lieutenant Garvie, you're about his size – give young Sutherland your hat and tunic."

A young lieutenant reluctantly relinquished his gray jacket and kepi, his lips compressed with suppressed annoyance.

The gun crews and soldiers watched all this with amusement. As the Brigadier General and his staff rode away to inspect other parts of the line, water was passed round, and men were allowed to smoke.

"Any orders... Sir?" said Will Tanner, grinning, as he puffed at his pipe.

"Yes," said Henry, sitting on an ammunition box, examining the wound in his thigh, "Somebody find us some food – I haven't eaten all day. And get me a dressing to put on my leg; it's really beginning to hurt."

"There's a surgeon back in that farmhouse," said a corporal, "I'll go fetch him... lieutenant."

He saluted, smartly, and left.

"There's a field kitchen back there in the woods," said another man; "At least, there was this morning."

"Well, go," said Henry, "and bring us back some grub. You others, see to all these wounded. And post some pickets to watch out for a counter attack."

"Well," said Will, sitting down next to him, "That was one hell of a day – looks like all that training wasn't wasted, eh, *lieutenant?*"

"Perhaps," said Henry, wearily, rubbing his leg; "Or maybe just a bit of beginner's luck."

"Guess we'll find out," said Will Tanner, "if them Yankees

come at us again."

But that was the last they saw of the Yankees that day. The two newest members of Battery Q camped with the other weary combatants in the woods nearby, but not until the guns were thoroughly cleaned, the limbers replenished with ammunition, and all equipment checked ready for the following day. Then there were the draft and riding animals to see to, before food from the field kitchen could be consumed. All in all, it was a long and exhausting day

Reveille was an hour before dawn. Another pre-daylight placement of the guns and infantry put the Army of East Texas in positions ready for battle on the next day, the 9th of April. 1864. If the experienced Union forces of the Red River Expedition were to have any chance of taking Shreveport they were going to have to dislodge General Taylor's stubborn Texan and Louisianan army; and for that to happen, they would need to face those resolute Confederate batteries all over again.

CHAPTER FOUR:
THE TEST

"OPEN FIRE!" yelled Lieutenant Sutherland to his four howitzer crews, as a troop of Union cavalry crossed his front from right to left. It was an hour after dawn, and Q Battery, in their new position, was about to fire the opening salvoes on day two of what was later to be called 'the Battle of Mansfield'.

They had briefly rehearsed their laying and re-loading routines before the enemy showed up, to give new hands some practise in their various roles. Henry had made sure each howitzer had a very experienced and capable man in the capacity of layer, for obvious reasons. In addition, he told crews to check that each of the little burlap bags of powder held exactly the correct charge to propel their shells and canister. He stressed the importance of carrying out his instructions to the letter; and, lastly, he made sure the ammunition limbers were positioned far enough behind the guns so that a direct hit to one of these would not result in the loss of an entire crew – or the whole battery.

Now they would see if his innovations paid off. The four shiny iron monsters erupted with flame at their muzzles and recoiled back on their big wheels. Henry peered through the smoke to observe the effect of his gunnery, as the shells whistled forward towards the enemy...

The four shells slammed into the ground only thirty to fifty yards short of their targets, three-quarters of a mile away.

"Reload, shell, concussion fuses!" shouted Henry, "Layers – up fifty, traverse left, one hundred and fifty..."

The fifty yards increase in distance would drop the shells on the road in front, and the one-fifty yards correction to the left was to adjust for the number of yards the Union troopers would cover at a canter before the next salvo arrived. True, he could have left the aiming entirely to the chief-of-guns, but he wasn't sure they'd allow sufficient yardage for the rapid movement of men on horse. Henry Sutherland's text-book method of targeting had paid off the day before; so now Battery Q trusted his judgement and laid their howitzers according to his orders.

Down a long straight road lined with poplars the enemy cavalry traveled, a lane so long and straight that a man could see about a thousand yards of it. They had thought themselves out of range – but they thought wrong. Henry Sutherland had disobeyed orders and put his guns forward of the position the Brigadier General had allocated him. This was both good and bad. Good, because those troops of cavalry, and any other Union soldiers using the highway to cross the battlefield were now in range; bad because if the cavalry charged, or even a determined infantry assault came at them, they had neither cover nor infantry support to help protect the guns. Nor would they have time to get the guns hitched up to the horses either, for Henry had ordered the drafts and rides several hundred yards back into some woodland to keep them safe – perhaps too safe.

At the first salvo, those troopers had merely speeded up from a trot to a canter. Anxious eyes had been cast on those falling shells. But shells usually take a while to home in on a distant target – don't they?

"FIRE!" yelled Lieutenant Sutherland, and the answer came in four dreadful explosions right among the loping horsemen. Three shells landed directly on, or within feet of the road, the other passing higher and taking the top out of a tall poplar tree. Some landowner or other had taken the trouble to plant those Lombardy poplars from Europe to make that road look a little more like England, or France perhaps. He would never have dreamed those distinctive trees might one day be used as markers for 24 pounder howitzer shells.

The four explosions killed only a half-dozen men and their horses, but sent one half of the company (of a hundred and twenty) reeling back up the road the way they had come, in complete disarray. The infantry reserves, coming up behind, who had been marching to their right flank, were forced to leap out of the way of the returning troopers, into the safety of the margins of the road. Meanwhile, the other half of the company galloped onward in panic. Some of the horses had taken the bit between their teeth and bolted. War-horses are trained to be 'bomb-proof' and accustomed to loud noises – but, like men, they have their breaking point.

Back behind the guns, Lieutenant Sutherland told his layers to keep their howitzers trained on that same position, reckoning, correctly as it turned out, that some fool or other would order men along that same avenue of trees before long.

There was a bit of wait before it happened, however. That lull in the action lasted for two hours. There were sounds of rifle and cannon fire both to left and right, and the faint din of small-arms to their front, far away – involving cavalry, Henry suspected. The gun crews of Q Battery, their howitzers loaded with concussion-fused shrapnel shells, sat smoking their pipes, or talking in relaxed tones a few feet from their cannon in the weak April sun.

There were more sounds of firing, not so far off this time – and then the enemy shell-fire started to drop. A full five hundred yards away at first, then a little closer. A despatch rider came galloping up on his pony, and skidded to a halt. He saluted Henry smartly, before giving him a note, which read:

FIELD ORDER
Stay put. Infantry coming.
Main enemy advance to your front.
Brig. Gen. M M Parsons.

Henry called Will and his corporals over.

"Look," he said; "We're in for a hot time, it seems; but this first line, 'infantry coming'. Does he mean *ours* or *theirs*?"

"Not sure, lieutenant," said a corporal; "I think it means ours is coming to consolidate us."

"No," said another, "it's perfectly clear, it's a Bluebelly infantry attack on us from the front, for sure."

"Well," said Henry, "It says 'stay put', so I guess we'll find out fairly soon."

The shells began to land a little closer.

"We'll dig some shallow pits," said Henry, remembering something in a training manual, "in case that artillery homes in on us."

"Lieutenant, something just flashed over there in the sunlight," said a corporal, squinting through his telescope; "I think they've got a spotter on that main road..."

"We'll use one gun to try to winkle him out," said Henry. "Show me which tree he's nearest to."

One of the poplars was pointed out; and a gun adjusted to land a shell on or near its base. It was not easy to hit the mark, but after four tries, the last one hit the exact spot. The glint of sunlight on field glasses or a telescope could then be seen a hundred yards right of the original spot, indicating that either the man had moved, or another fellow was now in the role of spotter. Meanwhile the enemy shells kept coming closer. To add to their woes, a large body of Union infantry was forming up just behind the same stretch of road. There was nothing for it, but to engage them with their howitzers.

Round after round was dropped on that big formation, but instead of retreating or taking cover, the Union men stood and took the punishment.

"I don't like this," said corporal Thomas, "we'll need more shells at this rate. The limbers are getting empty."

"You're right!" said Henry, "some battery commander I am, letting the ammunition get down to this level. Send two riders over to the supply column immediately.

He wrote out two identical chits, and gave one to each rider in case one or the other failed to reach the supply camp:

Battery Q Shreveport Rd
½ mile North-East of crossroads
Request 24 pounder shells 100
shell 75%/ canister 25%
    LT. H Sutherland

The two riders, who were instructed to show the wagon drivers the quickest route back, then galloped off, and Henry was handed a big spotter's telescope. He examined some smoke to his extreme right front. On this western horizon lay a smouldering heap as the ruins of a big country house burnt itself to ashes, testimony of the skill of the enemy's own batteries. Henry knew that the house was supposed to be held by two companies of their own mounted rifles. He could just make out long ranks of gray soldiers, static in front of the blazing house. He could see big Yankee shells bursting; some fell a few yards short of them, some a few yards too far. But where were the enemy guns? Henry waited for signals from his other spotters. There was no point firing blind.

He swung his scope in a wide arc, watched the Bluebellies in front for a time, observing that men were now crouching or even lying down, a sure sign they were not moving off for the time being. A twinge of fear came to him, and he turned to survey the area behind him, which consisted of a large expanse of rolling grassland with occasional patches of conifer woodland. It was the prospect of enemy cavalry that made him most nervous.

A movement caught his eye beside one of those wooded areas. He saw something fluttering in the breeze – then sighed with relief when it revealed itself as the Lone Star Flag. A handful of gray-clad men surrounded it. Then he saw of the rest of them: hundreds and hundreds of their own soldiers appearing as if by magic out of the trees. A rider came bolting up to the battery with a message. Henry read it, his brow furrowed, then read it again.

"Well, Lieutenant?" said Corporal Thomas, "are we being relieved, or what?"

"Not exactly," said Lieutenant Sutherland; "This is a message from General Taylor himself. His orders are to hold this spot until further notice. He's sending three regiments of infantry and more artillery to hold up the Yankees in front of us. We're told that if necessary, 'we must fight to the last man'. Now what sort of an order is that? It says he plans to roll up the enemy flanks from the east."

Suddenly, a star-shell burst with a blinding glare overhead and everybody in the battery instinctively ducked their heads.

119

"Lieutenant," said Corporal Thomas, "We'd best get on and those hollows for the guns and men. It'll shield us from some of the shrapnel and bullets if things get bad. We'll be here a while – something tells me we're about to get it in the neck."

"Good idea, Corporal," said Henry, "see to it, will you? I'm going to ride over and speak to the commander of those regiments behind us."

Henry picked one of the horses that were kept saddled for despatch riders near the guns, and rode across country to meet a big-bearded Colonel on a gray horse.

"Good morning, Colonel," said Henry, saluting; "I am the commander of Q Battery holding the position in front."

"Those damn guns are in the middle of nowhere with no infantry cover," said the Colonel gruffly; "Lieutenant, where are your horses?"

"Why, there, sir," said Henry pointing to a belt of woodland.

"That, lieutenant," said the Colonel, "is where you are supposed to be."

"Yes, sir," said Henry, a little red in the face, "I moved up a quarter mile to shell the enemy on the Shreveport road. I thought it might ease the pressure on some of the others, and deter a frontal attack."

"Well," said the Colonel, "you have disobeyed orders and made a mistake. In about twenty minutes the entire center of a Union army is going to attempt to break through this front. Our job is to stop them."

"With four guns and three regiments?" gasped Henry.

"That's what I said," said the Colonel; "I'm Colonel Douglas, by the way, of the 14th Texan. Those are Colonels

120

Kidd and Wymark, of the 11th and 3rd."

The others nodded.

"With all respect, Colonel," said Henry, "I believe my position is the best one to hold up the Bluebellies."

"Indeed," said Douglas, "and why is that?"

"Well, sir," said Henry, "there are two long stretches of woodland to my left and right. You could position a good many of your men in there and enfilade the enemy without risk of cavalry, or having your flanks nipped."

"A reasonable plan," said Kidd, "but who will hold the center-ground?"

"I will," said Henry Sutherland. "We have shells with concussion fuses, and canister rounds to break them up."

Henry was surprised to hear the three colonels roaring with laughter.

"Are my suggestions so ridiculous?" said Henry, shamefaced.

"Not at all, lieutenant," said Colonel Douglas, "we are simply amused by your bravado, and the wisdom emanating from what appears to be a very old head on very young shoulders."

"That's one way of putting it, George," said Colonel Kidd; "So what do you say, gentlemen? Shall we adopt this young man's plan and *enfilade the enemy from either flank*?"

"As good a plan as any," said Douglas. "With a little modification. I shall hold the center with the 11th. Those guns need some rifles to support them. Philip, you take that left wood with your regiment, and William might like the right."

"And how old are you, lieutenant?" said Colonel Wymark, himself an old fellow of about seventy with sad gray eyes and a white goatee beard. They had stopped walking and paused for a moment

"Well... sixteen, I guess," said Henry.

"And how long have you been a battery commander?" asked Kidd, a big red-cheeked man of middle-age with a long walrus-like moustache.

"Since yesterday, Colonel," said Henry.

"I thought as much," said Colonel Wymark, "That uniform is all wrong. You have an infantry lieutenant's jacket and hat. Why is that, young fellow?"

Henry briefly explained how he acquired them, and how he had come to be promoted to second lieutenant by Brigadier General Parsons. This caused more amusement among the three colonels.

"Well gentlemen," said Douglas to the others, "we have fifteen hundred men to hold this ground against ten thousand, and four guns in the hands of a cadet. We should have a very interesting day."

He turned to Henry; "Especially," he said, "If that Brigadier General of yours isn't on the ball today – he's the one supposed to roll up the enemy by the flanks while we sit tight in front like ducks in a shooting gallery."

Again the three colonels laughed heartily, before Douglas ushered Henry back to his men.

CHAPTER FIVE:
RAPID FIRE!

By the time Henry Sutherland had regained his position among his guns, and explained the plan to his non-commissioned officers, the pits were beginning to take shape.

"That's it, men," said Henry, "shovel that earth up in front for added protection.

Another star-shell exploded overhead, its lethal cargo of lead balls raining down on the infantry, who were taking up their positions. A couple of men were hit, and went down.

"I know where they're shooting from," declared Will Tanner, "I just saw a muzzle-flash."

He pointed out the position way over to their left, where there was a small copse of trees and scrub, the distance being rather less than the road directly in front. Henry, judging it as being a thousand yards, laid one howitzer to send a ranging shot. A puff of smoke appeared a mere twenty yards short of his target. One of the hidden guns then shot a fused shell in return. It landed a hundred yards behind Q Battery, hit the earth and smouldered for a second before exploding, a sure sign that it had been armed with a time fuse rather than the more modern concussion ones of the 24 pounder howitzers.

What ensued may best be described as an artillery duel; single shot against single, until a big explosion in the distant copse signaled that the Q Battery gun had hit a limber or pile of ammunition. The crews let out a hearty cheer on seeing the distant smoke rise. But then, ten minutes later, another star-shell announced that there was still at least one Union gun in good working order. More of Q Battery's precious stock of shells was expended as each side tried to knock out the other.

Henry reasoned that destroying enemy artillery was a sensible use of his resources. He noted with satisfaction too, that although he had hit enemy positions, his own battery still had all guns intact and crews unscathed, despite some near misses. His guns were in shallow pits, and when not required to serve the guns, the crews were piling banks of earth in a protective horse-shoe shape to their front and sides.

Then, as Henry was contemplating whether to hang fire for a while to conserve ammunition, a sharp-eyed gunner suddenly turned to his commander.

"Look!" he said, "They're coming! By the trees! It's them! The whole darn Union army's coming this way!"

All eyes scrutinized that avenue of poplars, through which line after line of dark-blue soldiers were emerging. Even at that great distance they could hear the rattle of drums urging them on.

Henry felt a hand touch him on the shoulder. It was Colonel Douglas.

"Can you drop some shells on those men?" he asked.

"Why, yes, of course, said Henry.

"Then might I suggest you stop your men digging for a moment and get to it, lieutenant," said Douglas sharply.

As Q battery was preparing for its first combined salvo on the enemy, a thundering of hooves and rumble of wheels caused them to turn round. A very welcome sight met their eyes: a cavalcade of mounted artillerymen, and the six 12 pounder Napoleons of H Battery had arrived to reinforce them. They immediately began to deploy four hundred yards to Henry's right. Douglas's men were already forming a dense line of riflemen that spanned the open ground from just beyond H Battery, across to a point fifty yards to the other, left side of Q Battery. With Kidd's and Wymark's regiments already holding the belts of woodlands on either side, the defensive position was now quite formidable.

"Thank God," said Colonel Douglas, "Now at least we shall have a battle."

Henry continued to target the enemy's battery, or part of a battery, with Number One howitzer, and thought he had weakened their strength further when the fire on his position became even less frequent. Simultaneously, his other three guns dropped shells into the advancing Union lines.

Major Jeffries, commander of H Battery, soon had his own guns belting out air-burst and ground exploding charges to upset the enemy advance, which had halted about three hundred yards away. Both sides were rattling off rifle fire, which was only partially effective. Men were falling on either sides, but the small-arms fire would only be decisive if the range was closed, or – and this was Douglas's greatest fear – General Banks and his staff on the Union side realized that his opponents were weak in comparison to his own, and simply charged.

Henry, after sending Will tanner to check, discovered the shell situation was worse than he thought.

"Only a dozen shells left, plus forty canister rounds," said Will. "Shall I send another messenger for more?"

"No," said Henry, "I'm sure one will have gotten through. Something must have happened to the train. We'll wait, and let H Battery do most of the shooting.

At that moment Major Jeffries himself rode up.

"Look here," he said to Henry angrily, "You've slackened your fire in the middle of a battle, with the enemy in easy range. I know that Brigadier General Parsons gave you some kind of field-promotion, but either you buck up, young fellow, or I'm sending one of my men to take over."

"It's the shells, Major Jeffries," said Henry, "We're terribly low. We've been engaging the enemy all morning, and knocked out some of their batteries, and destroyed cavalry. But we're down to a dozen shells plus canister – I sent out two messengers for more, two hours ago; and I've heard nothing."

"My God," said Major Jeffries, "this is worse than I thought. We were relying on you to up the rate from this end – we were engaged ourselves on the western flank for two hours this morning, and our shells are almost spent too. Our riders requested more some hours ago as well. There's been a cock-up."

"We have plenty of canister rounds," said Henry.

"We'll damn-well need them, at this rate," said Jeffries, "in fact they're coming at us now. I suggest you load some of them right away!"

"We already have," said Henry, "We're just waiting for them to get within two hundred yards."

"They're almost two hundred yards now," said Jeffries tetchily.

Henry ran to each gun and checked the elevations, then stepped back, before giving the order to fire.

The storm of lead did its usual deadly work, cutting gaps in the Union ranks, though not quite as spectacularly as those close-up, decisive rounds of the previous day.

But even Major Jeffries had to admit it was fine gunnery.

"Well judged," he said grudgingly, "I can see you know your ranges. That's the most difficult thing to teach a second lieutenant. Mine keep shooting over the top of those damn Yankees."

Sergeant Macdonald, of H Battery, who had ridden across behind the firing line, then approached Colonel Douglas.

"What is it?" asked the latter anxiously, "I left you to oversee your section."

"I wouldn't have come across, sir," said the sergeant, except we need your orders."

Colonel Douglas, standing nearby, sensed something was amiss and joined the little conference.

"Is there a problem, gentlemen?" he asked.

At that moment another star-shell exploded way over the right and they all ducked, except Colonel Douglas who completely ignored it.

"It's the ammunition column, sir," said Sergeant MacDonald; "It's been caught by enemy cavalry, and many of the pack mules and wagons have been destroyed. General Taylor wants to know how we stand."

"How do we stand, Sergeant?"

Enough to last us ten minutes, sir, at present rate of firing," replied the other. "Shell, in other words, all spent. We're using canister, but at two hundred yards we'd do better with shrapnel shells."

"That's bad," said the Major. "I'll speak to the men myself."

He rode back to deliver orders in person his crews. Then his anxious sergeant handed him a note from another messenger. The Major read it, and closed his eyes in exasperation.

"Well, MacDonald," he said," Captain Hollis at Supplies says we are not likely to get any shells at all. The few boxes that have escaped are being sent on as rapidly as possible, but as we're almost the last they will reach, there won't be much left for us. Not sure if there's any at all for Q Battery at all.

They're the only 24 pounders we have, and their stuff's the hardest to come by."

"What are we to do, sir?" said the sergeant.

"Carry on a desultory fire; we'll use up the last canister. I fully expect them to rush us the second they realize our ammunition is spent. If we have to, we'll blow up the guns and save ourselves as best we can. By that time the Yankees will probably be on us. I'm told they've got a huge concentration of cavalry on the loose, too. That's all we need! I just hope they don't come at us from our rear. See that the men have their rifles and side-arms handy, would you?"

"Very good, sir," said MacDonald.

The sergeant saluted and withdrew to carry out his orders. Mechanically he passed word along to the gunners to double the length of the intervals between each shot, and told the men to get their rifles and pistols ready for the hand-to-hand fighting that was surely coming. Now and again he looked anxiously down the trail leading to their rear in the hope that the welcome sight of an ammunition wagon might gladden his eyes. But the hope was vain. Slower and slower, the guns sent for their fast lessening stock of ammunition, nearer and nearer drew the sound of the Yankee firing. The Union front ranks halted, and formed a dense line a hundred yards away, and raked the defenders with volley after volley. The Confederate defenders repaid them in kind, but, being fewer in number, were getting the worst of the exchange. Only the pits and earth walls saved the men from Q Battery from the same murderous fire.

Still no wagons. A faint cheer in the distance, and a sudden increase in fire, told Henry that H Battery had received 'a few to go on with,' from a couple of pack-mules, but still none reached the howitzers. Major Jeffries, though several of his gunners had been killed or wounded, sent an experienced lieutenant to 'observe' Lieutenant Sutherland, which made the young commander uneasy in his decisions.

Both batteries had paused firing as the ammunition all but ran out. Each had each conserved a few canister to try to stop the inevitable bayonet charge, but these would not be enough to stop all the Union infantry massed before them. To make matters worse, the Confederate infantry were also very low on ammunition. It was time to consider their options.

The observing lieutenant had with him the instructions for putting the guns out of action if they had to be abandoned, but they would not do it till the last second.

Then the Bluebellies advanced, bayonets levelled, a note of triumph in their loud cheering as they came on.

"All guns... FIRE!" yelled Henry.

Again the canister wrought carnage; but not enough to stop the advance. Now, only a single charge was left for each gun. Henry looked across at H Battery; and saw the same hesitation as Major Jeffries pondered whether to blow up his own guns, or fire off the very last round at the enemy.

For the first time in action, Lieutenant Henry Sutherland froze. He knew the two courses of action open to him: either, to shoot the last charge of canister, and risk the guns being captured intact; or, to put earth or rocks in the barrels and use the final round to destroy them.

That was some dilemma for a battery commander! The loss of guns in working order to the enemy brought shame on a regiment, and could be a permanent black mark on a commanding officer's record. On the other hand, a final salvo might just prove decisive in a closely-fought battle...

"Load the last canister!" shouted Henry Sutherland, "I'll not blow up my guns. We'll fight to the last with our pistols – and pray for a miracle!"

Back at H battery, however, Major Jeffries had already given the order to load his last canisters. The gunners swore softly between their teeth as they gathered and laid rocks and stones in little heaps beneath their gun-muzzles. One man kicked an empty limber in frustration and received a reprimand. Others stood grim and silent at their useless guns, clutching their rifles and watching, waiting for the infernal ammunition that never came. Now that the guns of H Battery had ceased, the emboldened Union lines in front made a general surge forward. Drums rattled, and the attackers yelled to give themselves courage.

"That's it, sergeant," said Major Jeffries, "It's all over for us. You know what to do."

Macdonald turned, opened his mouth to give the order to fill the barrels with rocks.

Then, a voice called out:

"Major, for heaven's sake, wait! There's a single wagon coming."

All eyes were turned to the track. Sure enough, from behind some nearby trees there rolled a covered wagon, lurching and pitching among the ruts. It had almost reached them without being seen, screened by a grove of conifers. It was pulled by two big dapple-gray horses. All held their breath as an enemy shell whistled over their heads and missed it by a few yards.

Nearer and nearer it came, and the men rushed forward to meet it. At last it came to a standstill in the midst of a cheering group of H Battery gunners. They seemed oblivious to the mini-balls zipping through the air around them.

"What kind o' shells you got, Jim?" shouted a burly corporal.

"Them at the back's your shells," said Calamity Jim, "12 pounders, ten boxes, eight to a box, that's eighty pops. And I got seven boxes of 24 pounders at the front; they're six to box which is... hell, you work it out. I got rifle rounds too, 10,000 in the red boxes. Don't touch the green case in the middle. That's the whiskey."

Ready hands untied the canvas and started to bring out the 12 pounder shells and infantry ammunition, and in a moment the guns were firing again.

"Ten rounds – canister – rapid fire!" shouted Major Jeffries. All artillerymen live for those moments of rapid fire, each gun competing with his neighbor to get the job done in the fastest time with the greatest accuracy.

Meanwhile, Jim Bolt drove on to Q battery, which had loosed off their last volley and were running to meet him. Had he been empty of 24 pounder shells, it is doubtful he would have lived too long after those wild-eyed men men found out! As things panned out, for a short while he became the most popular man in the entire Confederate Army of East Texas.

"What happened, Jim?" said Will Tanner, as he grabbed an ammunition box, "We needed you two hours ago!"

"Damn Yankees fired up all my wagons," snapped Jim; "All of 'em save this 'un. I made a run for it, an' run smack into a bunch of Texan Mounted Infantry – saved my skin, they did. Only got young Henry's note twenty minutes ago. Came straight over quick's them hosses could pull me..."

His voice trailed off, as Will Tanner dragged one of the heavy boxes over to a gun-pit. Half-way there, a bullet knocked him off his feet. Jim gasped, made ready to get down from the wagon, but was relieved as Tanner got up again and pulled the box to the nearest gun.

The massed Yankee infantry continued to advance in solid waves of blue, as desperately, the two batteries and defending infantrymen attempted to hold them back. The ten artillery pieces cut swathes through the ranks of attackers – and still the blue horses came at them. To their great credit, Colonels Kidd and Wymark lent troops from their woodland positions to try to shore up the center; and their men among the trees loosed volley after volley at their assailants; but without the arrival of reinforcements, the simple mathematics of the situation dictated how the unequal struggle should finally end. All along the lines, the thicker waves of dark blue met and merged with the thinner one of gray. Even the men in the woodlands were finally overwhelmed. By bayonet and pistol shot, the Texans fought to stop them. The simple truth was that for once, through no fault of his own, Jim Bolt had arrived a little too late.

How ironic for the men of the batteries, and the three regiments of foot, that the successful flanking maneuver of General Taylor descending from their right should ultimately bring about a crushing victory for the Army of East Texas. Ironic too, that the six guns of H Battery, and the four howitzers of Q Battery remained intact and in place, despite the fears of their commanders that they might be carried off by the enemy. Had there been horses to do it, the army of the Union might well have tried; but then, the Yankees soon had problems of their own to address.

For, even as the few surviving infantry and gunners took to their heels, Taylor's flanking movement was already rolling the Yankees into a disorganised mass. The temporary victors were now, in their turn, forced to flee. Luckily for them, there were no Confederate cavalry on hand to further compound the Union losses. Nor did the Union cavalry show itself at this crucial point in the battle, for both armies' mounted units were busily engaged against each other seven miles away, in a huge but ultimately indecisive action. Thus, it was left for the infantry to settle who should take the important ground by the Shreveport road, and so win the Battle of Mansfield.

It is doubtful if there ever a shorter, and less heart-felt cheer of victory than that of Taylor's men at the end of that day. For they stood among the bodies of fifteen hundred gallant American men; and there was four times that number of wounded to gather and care for, before darkness set in.

As Wellington noted after Waterloo, 'Next to a battle lost, the saddest thing is a battle won.'

CHAPTER SIX:
A HOLLOW VICTORY...

When Jim Bolt emerged from his hiding place under the spare roll of canvas at the back of his wagon, he had a bottle of whiskey in his one good hand. He had angry words for Brigadier General Parsons as the fellow rode by. There was the man who had let three regiments take the full brunt of General Bank's attack, before he himself arrived to take control of the battlefield – with over eight thousand men!

"Hah! Come to claim your victory, have you, you bunch o' snails an' turtles!" shouted Calamity Jim Bolt. "Well, this ain't none o' your your doin'. You're steppin' on the bodies of the men that won this battle, and you know it!"

Luckily for him, Parsons chose to ignore this rebuke from a civilian teamster. In any case, Parsons was only following *his* orders from General Richard Taylor. Jim Bolt threw his bottle on the ground, and got down from his wagon. The first thing he saw was Lieutenant Henry Sutherland lying a few yards away, next to one of his howitzers. He had a pistol with all chambers empty lying next to him, and a big gash across his forehead. Next to him was the body of Will Tanner.

"You seen our commander?" said a dazed-looking artilleryman with blood all over his tunic, picking up the whiskey bottle. He took a big pull from the bottle and handed it back to Jim.

"That kid lieutenant – you know the one?" he asked.

"I know the one," said Jim, fighting back a tear, pointing at the boy. "Let's see if he's alive."

Jim clambered down and hobbled across to examine the 'kid-lieutenant'. He saw, on the way, that Will Tanner lay with his eyes staring lifelessly into the sun. He made the sign of the cross and moved on. The two men found that Henry Sutherland was still breathing, though very shallowly.

"He's alive," said Jim; "Take more'n an enemy rifle butt to kill that one. But he's concussed, and that's just as well, 'cos his best pal's lyin' dead beside him. Come on, give me a hand to get him on a blanket, and somebody fetch the surgeon."

Henry was alive, but only just, and it would be a long time before he was able to resume his duties. But when he was a little recovered, lying in hospital, he managed to explain to Brigadier General Parsons how he had ordered his battery to fire at the enemy until there was no time left to destroy the guns. He was mortified to have to admit this, until he was told that both Q and H battery guns had been saved – but only a handful of the doughty gunners.

"That was some fight," said Brigadier General Parsons; "We lost the better part of three regiments including Colonels Kidd and Douglas killed. Wymark is wounded and will be out of it for a few weeks. We also lost Major Jeffries, Captains Frost and Denman. Sergeant MacDonald, and young Lieutenant French who came over to assist you at Q Battery are alive, but will never fight again. And I'm sorry for your friend Tanner as well. But I wanted you to know, it was never intended that all those men should be sacrificed in that way. We were held up on that flanking movement by a withering Yankee fire for over two hours."

"Yes sir," said Henry, "I thought that was what had happened.

"It's a hell of a profession we are in lieutenant, to see so many good men pass away so young," said Parsons solemnly.

"Yes," said Henry, "it is terrible. But I must go back to fight again. I would never forgive myself if I didn't. I owe it to all those men."

"Well," said Brigadier General Parsons, "That is why I'm here. Some young officers are broken by engagements like that. I wanted to see you for myself."

"I am perfectly fine, sir," said Henry.

"Well," said Parsons, "we must see what can be done for you. There is a place for you yet in the batteries. I have asked for you to be transferred to one of the newly formed ones with some captured Parrot Guns."

Thank you sir, said Henry; "But I'd like to have my own guns back; and hand-pick another four crews. I'll need seven men per gun, and control of our own pack-mules or a light wagon for supply."

"Good Lord," said Parsons, "You never stop do you?"

"I needed to keep my mind busy, sir," said Henry, "so I've been planning it all out in detail."

"I'll see that you get those guns back," said Parsons, "if that's what you want. Anything else I can do?"

"Yes, sir," said Henry, "I need the services of a good army tailor to make me the correct uniform of a second lieutenant of the 13th Texas Infantry."

"That is one of the easier requests I have received of late," said Brigadier General Parsons; "One of my staff officers will see that you get that uniform."

FINALE:
THE CHEER...

When Second Lieutenant Henry Sutherland received the order to go to the Military Academy of East Texas, his heart sank. He thought that perhaps his superiors had ordered him back for basic training, or even that he would be taken on as an instructor to the cadets. His superior officers had a *carriage* pick him up from the military hospital in Nacogdoches, an event he thought rather unusual. Perhaps something good awaited him in Homer after all. He wasn't quite recovered enough to take up a new command as yet, but as he was told to put on his new uniform, he remained hopeful. The order, in the form of a note written by his regimental commander, stated that he would be meeting 'a few old friends'. So, in his newly completed uniform and hat, he set out for the Academy.

He was delighted to find the Academy was now, as well as a training institute, an armed camp, the grounds being covered with tents for as far as the eye could see.

As he alighted in the parade square, he saw that some kind of ceremony was to take place in the open air. Soldiers of various regiments were present in smart, clean uniforms with every piece of leather and brass polished to shine like the sun. There was even a photographer present with his huge camera on its tripod, and boxes of equipment ready to record the event.

After chatting with the survivors of Q Battery, the 13th Texas Infantry Battalion, Henry was ushered to join a line of other officers and men *who were going to be decorated.*

This was all the more remarkable for the fact that the Confederacy didn't generally confer medals; but on rare occasions this rule was broken. This was to be one of them, the medals paid for by the good people of Houston and Fort Worth in gratitude for their deliverance from the threat of the Union army of the Red River Expedition.

As he waited in the line of nervous and self-conscious men, the first person Henry recognized, from having seen his picture in newspapers, was none other than General Samuel Cooper, Inspector General of the Confederacy. He was moving along the row of soldiers to be decorated with some other high-ranking officers. Another group of men looked on solemnly, amongst them being General Taylor himself, and Brigadier General Parsons, along with some smartly dressed civilians in their frock-coats and ties.

The men received their decorations one by one. Then, General Cooper stopped by Henry Sutherland, who was the last in line, and fixed him with an intense look.

"This is the young man, sir," said a staff Captain; and then he recounted Henry's actions on those eventful days of April 8th and 9th, 1864.

He brought his gloved hand to his cap in salute. Then the other officers saluted, too. Henry was just able to murmur his thanks and return the salute when the general said:

"The Confederate States of America is mighty proud of you, Second Lieutenant Sutherland. You certainly played your part in the Battle of Mansfield. As you probably know, our government does not usually issue medals, but these ones we confer today were paid for and minted by the people of Fort Worth, Houston, and greater Texas in recognition of the importance of our victory. You are the youngest recipient, I am told, and you should be real proud."

But though Second Lieutenant Sutherland accepted his

decoration, as to the praise, he would have none of it.

"May I address the men, sir?" said Henry.

"Well, yes," said the General, somewhat taken aback, "I suppose you may."

"This, boys," shouted Henry Sutherland, "is not for me. This is for all the men of Q and H Batteries who gave their lives for Texas and the Confederate States of America, and the right to choose their own government and destiny."

The others in the camp, upon hearing this, let out a resounding cheer, and all joined in. Without waiting for orders, the military band struck up 'Dixie'. Some soldiers and cadets threw their hats in the air, others clapped, but they all cheered – they cheered themselves hoarse.

THE END

BOOK THREE:

BROTHER OF THE WOLF!

'Each man is good in the sight of the Great Spirit.
It is not necessary for eagles to be crows.'
           -Sitting Bull.

'Sometimes I ran after *them* but most times they were
running after *me*.'
           -Kit Carson, speaking about Indians.

BROTHER OF THE WOLF!

CHAPTER ONE:
COLD-BLOODED MURDER

Between Kurt Danvers and death stood a fire of pine, two pieces of canvas and the will to live.

Danvers was engaged with the methodical preparation of his camp, if such it could be called. It consisted principally of an enormous fire, for whose replenishment he had gathered a large quantity of pine cones, broken branches and twigs. Near the fire, and in the doubtful shelter of two huge trees which happened to grow close together, he pegged down the smaller of his waterproof pieces of canvas as a groundsheet. The larger one he deftly fixed above him by means of long cords which he attached to suitable trees and bushes. The remainder of his outfit consisted of a frying-pan which showed obvious signs of long and hard service, a still more work-worn enameled coffee-pot, and a small canvas bag containing his slender stock of provisions.

It was the slenderness of this stock that worried Danvers more than anything else, though he had other worries, too, to give him unquiet dreams at night. He untied the string securing the mouth of the sack and tipped the contents out onto the groundsheet.

"Two pounds o' bacon, if that," he muttered, weighing in his large hand an unsavoury-looking chunk of that delicacy. "Pound an' a half o' biscuit, barely. Coffee? Let's see..."

He opened a tin canister and peered inside.

"Good, almost a pound. That's better. Not so weak on

coffee. A man can get through most things with a bit o' hot coffee in his belly."

The last item in the larder was a gory mess wrapped in a portion of an old shirt, part of a small deer Danvers had snared the previous night, its foot caught in a wire set for rabbits.

His inventory completed, Danvers produced from an inner pocket a flint and steel, and contrived to set his fire going. That accomplished, he scooped several handfuls of snow into his coffee-pot and frying-pan, and set them near the fire to melt. As the resin in the pine spluttered and flared, and the flames took hold of the bigger sticks, the warm, flickering light revealed something of this lonely wanderer who had been till now no more than a somewhat solid shadow moving about among the trees.

Kurt Danvers was a big man. He stood a clear six feet in his socks, and in normal times he turned the scale at fifteen stone. He didn't weigh that now, of course. Semi-starvation rations of biscuit and bacon don't keep a man's belt tight. He was long of arm, large of hand, a man of physical strength well above the average. His features, or as much of them as could be seen through the heavy beard, were almost brutal in their ruggedness. Here, by all appearances, was a man you wouldn't want to meet on a dark and stormy night – or any other time, come to that. His character was written in his face: belligerent as a grizzly bear with a bellyache, anti-social and cruel as a wildcat. Unsuited to spending much time in human company, the loneliness of the woods agreed with him in many ways. Therefore, he lived as a mountain man of the old school, heedless of home-comforts, hard as iron, and resourceful as an Indian.

And yet, unlikable and anti-social as he was, there was something pathetic in the lonely figure squatting near the fire. Around him on every side stretched the vast forest, lifeless as far as sight or sound might tell, but peopled, as he well knew, by an infinite variety of living things. And among all that host of creatures, great or small, fierce or timid, furred or feathered, there was not one but was his enemy. Between him and them stretched ten thousand years of fear and hatred.

Between him and death stood a fire of pine, two pieces of canvas and the will to live.

It had been that same will to live that had brought him thus far from the company of his kind. Four months ago, in a saloon in Trenton, a little town on the Siksika River, he had seen fit to put into execution his own ideas of punishment for an injury received. It was a foolish, unplanned crime in all conscience, and it was to cost him dear.

By trade a trapper, he had come into Trenton to exchange his furs at the general store which doubled as a trading post. He had come to town earlier in the trapping season than was usual for him in order to buy a replacement for his old mule, which had become incurably lame. After selling his furs, but before buying his provisions for another trip into the mountains, he took his hard-earned money and went, as was his custom, to spend a portion of it in the Big Medicine Saloon and the gaming rooms of the Grandee Hotel. On the first evening of his projected spree he had been persuaded into a game of poker by one Lionel de Vere, a professional gambler with a talent for relieving drunken fools of their hard-earned cash.

Within an hour this sportsman had fleeced Danvers of the bulk of his liquid assets, but in a misguided effort to hasten the completion of this interesting task he was so foolish as to deal himself a card from the bottom of the pack instead of from the top. Or rather, he made the mistake of allowing Danvers to witness this little informality.

Danvers decided to administer a suitable correction there and then, and with this end in view be made a praiseworthy attempt to fell the gentleman with the whiskey bottle which rested, when it had the opportunity, by his side. But the other three men in the game overpowered him, and eventually hustled him out of the saloon and down the street towards the boarding-house where he was to sleep.

This was distinctly unfortunate for Danvers, because, had he actually slain the gambler in the saloon in the heat of the moment, it is probable that he would have been awarded a light sentence, if not acquitted altogether. Siksika River juries take a lenient view of killing under such provocation as Danvers had undoubtedly been given.

As it was, Danvers elected to lie in wait for his man and accost him some three hours later, long after blood had had time to cool in the chill air of that northern town. Danvers stepped out from the shadow of a wooden frame house and hit the devious gentleman over the back of the head with a murderous piece of pine weighing the best part of a stone and frozen as hard as iron. He hit him not once but many times, and rifled his pockets, and left him there to freeze in his own blood, for the crime took place in the dead of winter.

Nor did the man's wrongdoing stop there. Within ten minutes Danvers had broken into the general store, and, discovered by the owner in the act of theft, gave the proprietor a tap on the head with his frozen lump of wood. From the store he stole a sack-full of provisions, tinned and otherwise, and from the livery stable nearby, as he reunited himself with his horse and camp-gear, he helped himself to somebody else's mule, a pack-saddle, and some blankets. At this point in time the shopkeeper's wife, who had discovered her husband unconscious on the floor, began screaming and shouting for help from her neighbors. As Danvers saddled his horse, and loaded his gear, he could hear raised voices and cries of alarm that prevented his returning to the boarding house to retrieve his firearms; and so was forced to set off unarmed – a situation far from favorable to a mountain man and fugitive in that neck of the woods.

He rode through the night, and all the next day, encountering not a soul, which was not surprising considering the remoteness of those mountains and the freezing winter weather. He was making for the Canadian border, a few hundred miles away to the north. He hoped to do the journey in a week or two, being well equipped and having in mind a route through the mountains to keep him safe from the county sheriff, bounty hunters or other instruments of the law.

Unfortunately, circumstances were against him from the onset. To begin with, he had no guns and ammunition with which to get wild game for food. Furthermore, he had slightly overloaded his horse with surplus items his mule could not carry. Ordinarily, this would not have mattered too much, but the first night and day's travel through snow, without rest, badly exhausted the beast, to the extent that it probably needed several days' rest to recuperate. The old mare had some stamina, but she was a plodder rather than a racer. Rest, even for a day was out of the question. Danvers assumed, correctly, that he was being closely pursued. Therefore, he continued, spurring his mount on cruelly, till on the third day she stumbled on a patch of ice and fell. Her hind leg broken, and having no gun to administer a coup de grace, there was nothing for it but to leave her to the wolves. Cursing his own folly, he was forced to jettison a quantity of his supplies, taking only as much as he thought the mule could safely carry. By now he was well into the narrow mountain tracks that he hoped would convey him safely northwards. He walked steadfastly onwards leading his mule, and at first made good progress. He expected to lose any pursuers by this time, but he was in for an unpleasant surprise. From the heights of a mountain-side, he was able to see back several miles towards Trenton, and was amazed to see three figures on horseback riding along the very same path he had earlier taken.

Had he not been so far ahead, he would have been seen that the first of these riders was a Blackfoot scout, and the two behind him were troopers of the United States Cavalry! For, unknown to him, the mule he was riding was an army pack animal, and a certain lieutenant of the Seventh Cavalry Regiment who had it on his inventory had no intention of letting Danvers keep it. When the townsfolk had pointed out that a murderer was on the loose, and that the missing army mule had enabled the fellow to take to the snowy hills, Lieutenant Ritter took the decision to dispatch his best scout, his most stalwart corporal and a hardy trooper who knew the mountains to apprehend the thief and murderer.

As Danvers was to discover, although the army mule was a good one, his pack-saddle and bridle were in poor condition. Therefore, he spent some weary hours patching and repairing them, improvising with twine from his stores.

He made good progress nevertheless, and every day saw

him a little farther from the frozen corpse of the gambler he had left behind him in Trenton, and a little nearer to the safety of the border. Unfortunately, the trio on his trail also made good progress, and very nearly caught up with him on the tenth day. It was only by traversing a treacherous ridge atop a mountain that he stole a march on the man-hunters. For, just as he crossed and began his descent again, a terrible storm blew up to cover his tracks and force the army men to hole up in a cave. The tempest blew for almost a day. Meanwhile Danvers, now at lower altitude, remained on his feet and plodded gamely on. Nor did his pursuers easily pick up his trail when they finally crossed that inhospitable ridge. They thought of giving up and going back to Trenton; but the Corporal, a man called Carpenter, told the Indian to take them further on, and cast about in a wide arc to attempt to pick up the fugitive's path in his own time.

Thus Danvers forged ahead, and picked his way through the hills and peaks, in a zone and clime he knew of old. His spirits were still sky-high. Every night, as he squatted by his fire and ate his supper, he told himself that he was winning the race. For a race it surely was, between him and three men who he believed could not know the terrain and all its hazards as well as he...

Had he known that a Blackfoot scout called Komzitapi was acting as tracker he may not have been so confident. This son of a local chief was known up and down the Siksika River as a great hunter and warrior. Following a white man with a laden mule was not exceedingly difficult for him. Only the two soldiers, Corporal Carpenter and Private Peters, of Company C, the Seventh Cavalry Regiment, served to slow him down a little.

CHAPTER TWO:
BROTHER OF THE WOLF

Day after day, Danvers plodded on, weary, hungry, cold, but never despairing. As a trapper, he was able to catch rabbits, ptarmigan and other small game with the dozen wire snares he had with him. Even a pungent martin provided a meal one day when tastier items were not forthcoming. Then there was the time he snared a young deer by the leg, a fluke catch which enabled him to feast, for a time. But he couldn't carry all the meat with him, and soon he was back on a diet of rabbit or game birds, supplemented with small amounts taken from his dwindling supply of beans and corn-flour.

More seriously, his small bag of oats for the mule was empty, and no fodder was to be had in the mountains. When the beast faltered, and stumbled along for a whole day at less than the speed he could achieve by walking, Danvers took the fateful decision to turn her loose. He watched her amble away into the darkness where, no doubt, she was duly privileged, like his horse, to provide a meal for the wolves. Perhaps the animal tried to retrace its path back home, or search for something edible in that frozen landscape, but for whatever reason, it did not try to follow him, and he felt even more vulnerable and alone.

Now he had to carry his survival gear and provisions on his back. He left behind the greater part of his stores, his coffee pot, even his canvas groundsheet. He kept one skillet for cooking his catches, and thawing snow for drinking water. As he walked through the frozen land, for the first time he wondered if he would ever cross that distant border at all; but if he did not make it, his failure would not be for lack of effort.

Murderer and robber though he was, he possessed a dogged courage with which he fought his uneven battle against the unsympathetic wilderness.

He followed the course of the Little Snake River for several miles, and then struck due west to avoid the small town of Deweyville in his path. Thus it was that he had come at last to edge of Lake Brogan, within a few miles of the Canadian frontier. He was, comparatively speaking, within sight of freedom, but fortune had decided to put one final obstacle in his way.

His left heel, which had been troubling him for a week and more, had finally intimated that it was not prepared to carry him farther without a period of rest. Pain from a large sore on a heel had become unbearable, and Danvers realized that he would have to rest up for at least a day before tackling the last lap of his long trek. He had an inkling that he was far ahead of the trio on his trail, but in any case, as he could not walk, he had no choice but to risk laying up for twenty-four hours.

Irritated though he was at this delay, Danvers philosophically cooked and ate his supper. Having done what he could for the heel with an old rag roughly sterilized in water boiled in his pan, he stoked up the fire and settled down comfortably for a sleep.

It was very still in the frozen forest. The only sound that broke the silence was the hiss of the burning pinewood and, now and then, a little clatter as a log fell into the heart of the fire. Gradually the man's head drooped between his knees, his eyes closed, and with a little grunt of surrender he rolled over on to his side and lay still.

A hundred yards away, a wolf slipped from the cover of his

bush. He was old and lame, an outcast of his tribe, displaced by a younger, stronger male. Unable to share in the kills of a pack, his overmastering sensation was extreme hunger. He was suddenly aware of an intense desire to investigate the scent brought to him on the faint breeze a little more closely. The hunger was with him day and night, and it was now made more than usually insistent, not by the sharp, dangerous stink of man, but by the fragrant odor of roasting rabbit.

The wolf stopped and lay down. For half an hour he remained almost motionless, summoning up his courage to find the food. At long last he rose, and with infinite caution, stopping every few yards to sniff and listen suspiciously, he worked his way in a wide sweep towards the little clearing. His stealthy journey occupied a full sixty minutes, though the distance was less than quarter of a mile. To his surprise, when the clearing came into view, the man was lying motionless on his side, apparently fast asleep. Suspicious to the last, the creature paused to make sure that this was not some trap. And as he stood watching, his quick ear caught the faint noise of Danvers breathing.

As a matter of fact, the trapper now was very near to death as he lay there in the snow. For his fire had gone out and he had, for the very first time in his life succumbed to the drowsiness that sweeps over a man when his temperature begins to drop. Without activity or warmth, death comes gradually without great pain to warn the sleeper to arise. So it was with Danvers.

For whatever reason, the wolf snarled, perhaps to ensure the prostrate figure would not strike out as he went for the cooking rabbit.

With a snort of surprise the man woke up, feeling very

cold and dizzy. He raised his head and the first thing he saw was a wolf. The beast was rooted to the spot. Every instinct told the creature to be off as fast as its three good legs would carry him, away from the sight and sound of a human. But sheer amazement robbed the wolf of the power of motion. Likewise the man, unable to stir through a combination of freezing fatigue and curiosity, locked eyes with the animal and stared.

And so the two outlaws gazed at one another across twenty yards of snow. Danvers looked it over from muzzle to tail. He noted the unnatural thinness of the flanks, the scruffiness of the coat, the damaged paw that he held clear of the ground.

"All on your own, like me," he muttered. "Your buddies've finished with you, eh?"

A sudden thought struck him.

"Well now, I believe it must've been you that woke me. Did you now, wolf?"

The big dog-wolf bared his teeth, and once again the savage snarl smote Danvers's ears.

"That snarl o' yours'd wake a corpse," he said; "Perhaps you saved my skin by wakin' me like that. My hands and feet feel like blocks of ice, and I don't feel right. Here, take this..."

Despite his dizziness and cold limbs, with a quick jerk of the wrist Danvers threw the unwanted remnants of his rabbit supper – consisting of the entrails, a few bones and the skin – towards the wolf.

The wolf sprang back, snarling savagely, but the sight and smell of the scraps were too much for him. With his eyes on the man, his teeth bared in fury, he crept forward. A lightning snatch, a gulp, and the entrails were gone. Another snap of the great jaws consumed the bones, and then the wolf was off among the trees to make what he could of the skin. Danvers laughed as he smote the fire, and fed the ashes with dry twigs until it blazed.

"Guess you was some hungry, old timer," he said aloud, "So all-fired starvin' you couldn't even stop to thank me!"

Danvers' injured heel had not completely healed, but on the next day he felt compelled to complete his final dash for the frontier. In some ways he had benefited from the delay, since it gave him an opportunity to build up his strength. He was lucky with his snares, and he'd caught another rabbit overnight. Luckily, he found it before the wolf. True, he'd begun to tire of the sight of charred rabbit, but it was wholesome enough; and now that he had no coffee to warm his belly and raise his spirits, hot rabbit meat was a comfort.

As the hours had dragged along, a strange understanding had grown between man and wolf. It never reached the level of friendship, because neither wolf nor man could bring himself to fully trust the other. But the wolf hung about nevertheless, limping through the trees around the camp waiting for more scraps of rabbit, always careful, always suspicious.

The morning of his departure, Danvers prepared his pack. He'd given the wolf the offal from his breakfast meal, but kept a small part of the roasted rabbit for later. However, he was not destined to travel far. It was an hour after dawn. He had traveled but a thousand yards when a familiar noise brought him to an abrupt halt.

The sound of shod hooves on frozen ground could mean but one thing. Danvers glanced quickly around him. Twenty yards away to his left there was a thick tangle of undergrowth.

Like an arrow Danvers sped across the ice and burrowed deep among the bushes. Even as he hid himself, he thought this would be a forlorn attempt at finding safety since, if the men could follow him thus far, it would only be a matter of time before they finally caught him.

From within the bushes the fugitive cursed as he saw the Blackfoot scout, closely followed by Carpenter and Peters. He knew they must already have come upon the ashes of the camp, and spotted his tracks. They would know their quarry was close, very close. Danvers, however, believed there was still a chance, albeit a slender one, that the three men might miss his trail into the bushes and pass by, since much of the ground there was covered with solid ice – not the easiest of surfaces on which to trace footsteps. Perhaps he might then make a run for it, through the denser cover, and delay his capture – or even reach the border!

The man-hunters were approaching along a narrow avenue between the trees. A few yards or so from Danvers's hiding-place this avenue forked, one fork leading to a promising path used by deer and other animals – the trail he would have taken – and the other straight to the tangle of bushes in which he hid.

Danvers could not resist the temptation to peer through the bushes towards the fork and learn his fate. If they missed his tracks and passed by, he might yet give them a run for their money.

On they came, on foot now, leading their horses; the Indian, as usual, was a little in front. His dark eyes were busily scanning the icy ground. As he reached the fork, the Indian stopped, hesitating over which branch to take. To the left looked like a dead end. To the right the animal track looked promising; but where were the footprints? The Blackfoot squatted, puzzled, and then Danvers discovered his lifeline: the three men set off on the wrong path!

Danvers crouched lower among the bushes. The path the tracker had chosen would take the pursuers within ten paces of him before it took them past him and away. Already he could hear the breathing of the horses, and the conversation of the two soldiers.

"When we get Danvers I'll tell him he's the toughest man in the world!" said Carpenter.

"Yeah, I didn't think any guy living could get this far on his flat feet, Corp," said Peters.

"Sure," said Carpenter, "an' to think we'd lost his trail for almost three days. That's Canada over there. He almost made it."

"We haven't got him yet," said Peters. "How far ahead is he, Komzitapi?"

The Indian merely put his fingers to his lips and pointed to a point just up ahead, and beckoned them on.

It was all that Danvers could do to suppress a cry of joy, as they came along the wrong path.

Suddenly he heard a rustling noise, and saw the wolf. It had followed the men up from the old campsite, keeping to the side of the track. Near the fork it stopped, sniffing the air curiously. It could smell the part of a rabbit Danvers had packed and taken with him.

For some reason Carpenter turned, and with a gasp, spotted the wolf, not fifty yards behind him.

"Stop!" he hissed, and motioned his companions to the cover of a tree; "There's a wolf back there in the bushes..."

He unslung the rifle from his shoulder.

"A wolf?" said Peters, "Don't shoot, Corp, you'll let Danvers know where we are."

"No shoot," warned the Blackfoot; "To kill brother wolf is bad, bad medicine."

"Not to me," said Carpenter, loading his gun.

The Indian, visibly disturbed by Carpenter's actions, tried a different approach:

"Maybe you make our man run faster," he said.

"Then," said Carpenter, "He'll only tire more easily. Now hold still, the pair of you – I want that wolf-skin."

Danvers, who had been hugging himself in delight before the wolf arrived, grew anxious upon hearing this new development.

"Kill that old wolf," he muttered, "coming to me for his breakfast? Why, that would be a sin!"

The wolf crept a little closer. Danvers stretched out his hand and picked up a lump of wood.

Half a dozen yards away Carpenter stood peering round the bole of his tree. His fingers caressed the rifle lovingly. He was an expert shot. A decent wolf-skin would sell well in Trenton. His eye caught the movement of the wolf as it flitted from one tree to another. His cheek nestled against the stock, he closed one eye, and the sight moved smoothly over its target. Komzitapi and Peters could only watch, waiting for the crash of the rifle, their concentration centered on the wolf.

But the shot was never taken.

Thump! Danvers' lump of wood took the constable off his feet, hitting him fair and square on the side of the head. The rifle went off, firing harmlessly into the snow, and Carpenter toppled over, stunned. A trickle of blood ran down his cheek.

Peters, a few feet away, swung round, revolver in hand.

"Get 'em up, now!" he barked. "No tricks, Danvers, or I'll plug you into a pepper-pot!"

Danvers slowly raised his arms. He looked behind him once, and caught the last shadow of a wolfish body disappearing forever from the sight of men. He smiled weakly at Peters, a thin smile of satisfaction, then nodded a greeting to the Indian, who had his rifle at the ready.

"You're lucky I didn't shoot you dead," said Peters; "An' if my friend here is hurt bad, I may still do it, you crazy piece o' dirt."

Without taking his eyes off the prisoner, Peters spoke to the Indian:

"But say, Komzitapi," he said, "where the hell did he spring from? We've been tracking him three weeks and suddenly he comes at us like a wild animal."

The Indian looked at Danvers with a look of deep respect.

"Three weeks he live alone in snow," he said. "No mule, no horse, no gun. Many time disappear. Then he give up his life – when maybe he go free."

"Yeah," said Peters, pursing his lips, "He's a strange 'un all right."

"And what did he do," said Komzitapi, "that you must take him into town and hang him with a rope?"

"You know the story's well as I," said Peters. "He killed a man who took his money, brained another an' stole some food, then helped himself to a mule."

"I don't deny it," chirped up Danvers; "But, pardon me, gents – that ain't army business! I was expectin' to see the sheriff sniffing along my trail..."

"It was an army mule," said Peters.

"Come again?" said Danvers, "A *what?*"

158

"You stole an army mule," said Peters, "which is why the lieutenant sent we three lucky souls to fetch you."

"An *army* mule?" said Danvers, shaking his head in disbelief; "You chased me all this way over one goddamn lousy army mule?"

He gazed around him at the icy trees, the mountainside, the falling snow, then back at Peters and the Indian, still covering him with their guns.

"But that's just crazy," he said, "plumb crazy..."

"Talkin' of crazy," said Peters, "why'd you go hit the Corp like that? I mean, you knew you'd get caught."

There was silence for a long moment while Danvers studied his captors.

"My wolf," said Danvers finally, pointing into the trees, "He tried to kill my wolf."

"*Your* wolf?" said Komzitapi, staring at the fugitive.

"Sure," said Danvers, "He came every day to keep me company. He's old and mean and crippled like me. I couldn't let you shoot ol' brother wolf-there. It jus' weren't right."

The Indian's dark eyes grew rounder as he took this in.

"Only a spirit-wolf comes to help a man," he said.

"Well," said Danvers, "spirit or not, he came up to the fire an' I fed him. Glad to have his company."

Komzitapi seemed deeply moved by this. He regarded the fugitive for a few seconds. Then his face seemed to lighten.

"You go now," he said to Danvers.

The prisoner heard him, but, conscious of Peters' revolver trained on him, remained rooted to the spot, arms raised.

"You go now," repeated Komzitapi; "You run."

Danvers took a step forward.

"Hell no," said Peters, waving his pistol, "Over my dead

body! He damn near killed the Corp, and he's had us runnin' round these hills like hounds after a raccoon. There ain't no way I'm a-lettin' this son go free now, so get that idea right out o' your head, you damn Injun!"

Suddenly the muzzle of the Indian's rifle moved from Danvers to Peters. The trooper saw the native's face muscles tense as he went from an even temper to rage in an instant. The Indian's large, dark eyes were fierce with indignation. His finger tightened on the trigger of his rifle, which was pointing straight in Peters' face.

"I am Komzitapi of the Blackfoot," he said, through bared teeth; "Who are *you* to tell *me* who shall be prisoner, and who shall go free? My father is a chief, these are my mountains, my woods, my land. *You* are a common soldier, and you know nothing. If I say this man is a brother of the wolf, he *will* go free."

Peters eyed the muzzle of the Blackfoot's rifle and winced. Then he slowly lowered his revolver.

"Don't do it, man," said Peters in a quieter, more respectful tone. "Ain't we come all this way to get him? Ain't we strived an' suffered in the cold all these days to bring him in? The Lieutenant's gonna kill all three of us if you let him go."

The Indian merely laughed at this idea, then lifted his chin at Danvers.

"Go," said Komzitapi, "You go now, brother of the wolf, run like the wind..."

Danvers, thinking himself the luckiest man in the whole north-western frontier, hobbled off down the track, grinning from ear to ear.

Carpenter raised himself to a sitting position, rubbed his

temples and looked about him confusedly, just in time to see the prisoner limping off down the animal track.

"*The wolf!*" yelled Danvers as he ran, "*The wolf! Ya can't touch me, boys – I'm brother of the wolf!*"

THE END

BOOK FOUR:

THE HONORARY BLACKFOOT

'Where did all these damn Indians come from?'
-George Armstrong Custer.

'Of all the Indians I ever dealt with, by far the most unpredictable, and most difficult to deal with were the Blackfoot. They didn't just think they were superior to the white man, they *knew* they were.'
-Kit Carson.

THE HONORARY BLACKFOOT

CHAPTER ONE:
A FOOL'S ERRAND

Late one evening, as Corporal Sam Carpenter was sitting at the edge of a table cleaning his carbine, one of the troopers brought him a message from Major Docherty. He was to see the senior officer immediately.

After his failure to bring in the murderer Kurt Danvers, Carpenter was something of a joke about their camp, which happened to be called Fort Siksika. Thus, Carpenter had every reason to expect his senior officer to give him some onerous task, or offer him some further rebuke. But he was in for a pleasant surprise.

"Ah, there you are, Carpenter," said the latter, as Carpenter entered, "sit down, will you? I've got an easy job for you this time. I want you to ride over to the Long Rock Mine at Mount Lawson. They've got a consignment of gold ore to run to Charlesville. Generally they send their refined gold to Clarkson Springs and down by rail to Denver City; but they want to get it to the Big Hope mine at Charlesville where they have the expertise to extract the metal from the impure rock. As I'm sure you know, that type of ore carries a low risk of being targeted by thieves, since it's very heavy, and difficult to purify. You'll not have a very difficult job. Just go up to the mine and ride back with the wagon. The country's very quiet, so there will be no need to take any one with you. The mine owners think a small escort will attract little or no attention. After all, what kind of fools would try to steal a bunch of rocks when there's other consignments of pure gold on the Clarkson route? However, should any persons chose to attempt a robbery of that ore – which weighs three or four tons, I am reliably informed – the presence of even one uniformed soldier would make it a federal offence. In short, the risk would be simply too great."

Carpenter shifted a little uncomfortably on his chair.

"Right, sir," he said, "but may I ask why, of all the officers and men in the company, you chose me? I mean, I'm just one man, and only a corporal. Seems kind of strange."

"Since you ask," said Docherty, "I shall tell you; or rather you shall tell me. Carpenter, what is the occupation of your father?"

"Sir?" said the corporal, "You already know, since you and my father are acquainted... that he's a banker."

"Indeed," said the Major, "an honest profession, run by honest people."

"I guess so, sir," said Carpenter, "but *I* ain't no banker. Why, I didn't even have the brains to complete West Point."

"Nevertheless," said the Major, "you have been well brought up by honest, upright citizens and so I consider you the right man to accompany gold ore to Charlesville."

"Thank you, sir," said Carpenter, "I'll do my best."

"Incidentally, corporal, my records say that you dropped out of West Point after failing to complete the mathematics component required for directing artillery. Is that so?"

"Correct sir," said Carpenter; "They thought I was a dummy, after my battery dropped shells on the parade ground instead of the firing range."

"But surely they gave you a second chance, man?" said the Major; "I mean to say, West point is an establishment for

166

training new officers, after all."

"To be honest, sir," said Carpenter shamefacedly, "as a cadet I just couldn't master modern gunnery. I flunked all the technical stuff, and some of the written work, too. Thought it best if I just lit out before I was... well, asked to leave."

"Sorry to hear it," said the Major; "But then you decided to enlist as a private soldier in the cavalry. Highly commendable. Planning to work your way up through the ranks, Corporal?"

"Heck no, sir; That is, maybe, sir," said Carpenter. "You see, sir, I'm happy slogging along with the boys."

"Lieutenant Ritter tells me you're writing a book in your spare time. May I enquire as to its title, Corporal?"

"W-Well..." stammered Carpenter, as a matter of fact, sir, it's... *Troopers of the Ninth*, sir."

"But we're the *seventh* cavalry," smiled Docherty.

"It's, er, fiction, based on reality, sir," said Carpenter. "I thought it wouldn't be fitting to write about our own regiment without changing a few names and throwing the readers off the scent a little."

"I see," said the Major, "and would there be a major in charge of this fictitious Ninth Regiment, by any chance?"

"Why yes, sir," said Carpenter, "and a fine gent he is too."

"And does he have a name yet, this fictitious fellow?" enquired the major.

"Provisionally, yes," said the corporal somewhat nervously.

"Well, let's hear it then, Corporal."

"I'd rather not, sir."

"Nonsense, man spit it out," grinned the Major; "That's an order."

"In that case, sir, it's Doolally," said Carpenter, "Major Doolally; do I still get the job, sir?"

"Yes, I think so," laughed the Major

"So when shall I start, sir?" said Carpenter.

"Get away early tomorrow morniig. It will take you four days to get there. You'll see Brandon Roberts, the manager, and I expect everything will be ready for you to begin the trip to Charlesville the next day."

"Will they send any of their own men?" said the corporal.

"Roberts generally sends a pair of older miners with the consignment, then there's the driver. All are armed, but as I said, the risk of encountering banditry is practically zero. By the way," he added, as Carpenter turned to leave the office, "be sure to have your papers with you. It's the first time we've sent a man over, and Roberts will want to make sure you're the right one. See Lieutenant Ritter on your way out, he'll fill you in with all the other details. That is all."

Carpenter saluted and withdrew. As he walked back to his rooms, he shouted across to one of the stable-boys in the yard:

"Here, Pablo, you young rascal, just get my harness smartened up, and hustle it along sonny, or I'll have you court-martialled!"

The youngster grinned, for everyone at the barracks seemed to like the friendly young corporal.

Early next morning Carpenter was in the saddle, and as the sun crept above the horizon he took the north trail to Mount Lawson. He whistled to himself as he rode along; for the track led through well-wooded country, where smiling valleys stretched out on either hand. Now and again he passed prospectors looking for gold, for the area had something of a reputation. Several of the hardy workers crowded round him for the latest news. Some asked him his destination and the object of his journey, but he gave evasive replies. In the wilderness he came upon one or two lonely cabins where pioneers had settled down to the task of earning a livelihood amidst the virgin forests and high pastureland, but he skirted round them without stopping to check how the occupants were faring out in Indian country.

About noon next day he came upon the traces of a recent Indian camp, and at sundown he came across a party of native men and women putting up temporary shelters for the night. He was much relieved that they were disposed to be friendly, and in exchange for a bit of flour, corn and bacon he was carrying, Carpenter persuaded them to build him one of their rough shelters, a sort of wikiup consisting of long grasses tied in bunches and secured over a wooden frame. To his surprise, their chief paid him a visit in his temporary home, and over a pipe of tobacco communicated in reasonable English that they were 'Piikani', which he recognized as the native word for 'Blackfoot'. The old chief, who was called Natayo, explained that certain of his band had acted as scouts for the army, and for this reason were attacked and driven out by tribes still fighting the white man. His band had, he said, been traveling for many months, on their way to a peaceful piece of ground in the foothills where game was still plentiful. His parting words were interesting, a kind of prophesy:

"White man, white man," he said, "When darkness comes, while white and red man sleep as brothers in the same camp, thunder shall come, and there will be trouble. I have dreamed it. Then we shall speak again."

Carpenter was puzzled by these words, noting that the sky was clear other than a blood-red haze to the west, a sign of fine weather for the night and morning. Then, as he was preparing his evening meal, he heard the crash of a rifle from

169

among the other shelters. A few minutes later, one of the Indians, a young man, rushed up in evident distress, and beckoned Carpenter to accompany him.

"Chief say you come, you come," he said. "His son very shot!"

Somewhat surprised, Carpenter followed him to a larger wikiup a little apart from the rest. There, under the shelter he found the chief with one of his sons, a brave of about twenty summers, who was twisting and turning in agony. He had what appeared to be a bullet wound in his shoulder. Close beside him lay an old muzzle-loading rifle. At once Carpenter guessed that the young man had been shot by accident, and the Indians thought that he, a white soldier well versed in the ways of firearms, might have some skill at dealing with such injuries. Perhaps members of the band, if they had served as army scouts, had been treated by army surgeons in the past and so had a degree of respect for the white man's medicine. However, he was himself no doctor; he would therefore have to imitate the emergency treatment he had seen carried out on bullet-wounds in the field – with no guarantee of success.

Telling the man to accompany him, he ran back to his fire. He bade the Indian take the pan of boiling water he had prepared for cooking. Then Carpenter grabbed a few items from his saddlebags and the two men hurried back to the injured man. After his knife-blade, a small spoon and some patches of cloth had been sterilized in the boiling water, he carefully examined the wound, taking care only to touch it with the clean 'instruments'.

He saw that a musket-ball was lodged about an inch into the man's flesh. It took two strong men to keep the fellow still, but by a combination of luck and dexterity, Carpenter maneuvered the piece of lead to the surface. Once it was out, he prepared a rough poultice using a patch of cloth dipped in salt. With this pressed over the wound, he bandaged the shoulder carefully, using strips torn from his spare shirt; then he sat back to observe his patient.

For a time the young fellow was restless, and in agony, but presently the bleeding subsided and the pain became easier. Before Carpenter returned wearily to his own wikiup, the chief expressed his gratitude by shaking his hand about twenty times and repeating his thanks in his native tongue.

Once back in his own shelter, having eaten supper, Carpenter turned in early, for he intended to make a long journey on the morrow. When he awoke he found an old woman sitting outside the shelter. As he rose to his feet and looked out, she got up and at once hastened to rekindle his fire. The Blackfoot head man joined him at breakfast. The whole tribe were astir, and Natayo explained that because food was not plentiful in the neighbourhood, he and certain of his braves would be engaged in hunting that day. He asked that Carpenter accompany them, a request that was politely refused. Carpenter gave the head-man some tobacco and left the camp on very good terms.

He had determined to make his next camp on a small hill about twenty miles from Mount Lawson, which would give him only a short ride for the last day's journey. This would give the manager of the mine plenty of time to get things ready for the return journey.

It was evening as he rode up the narrow rising trail. A flash of light that was reflected off something metallic in the willows up ahead served to warn him of impending danger. He unslung his carbine in readiness. Then, without warning, a rifle shot rang out just ahead, and his horse fell headlong to the ground, stone dead. As he fell, Carpenter rolled clear of the saddle; it took only a second for him to recover his wits and crawl back to the horse and take cover behind it. Then he opened fire with his own rifle, firing where the flash had revealed his attacker's presence.

CHAPTER TWO:
THE BLUNDER

For a while no answering shot came; and then suddenly a harsh command rapped out, and from the shadow of the woods three men sprang towards the spot where Carpenter had been lying. All three were firing as they closed in, but to their surprise they found only the slaughtered horse there; for, during the interval, Carpenter had wormed his way backwards to the cover of a small bank, and as they stood there he suddenly opened a brisk fire with his revolver. With a yell of rage the bushwhackers rushed for the trees, while the young corporal, deeming discretion the better part of valour, retreated in the opposite direction.

For some hours Carpenter worked his way carefully through the undergrowth, hoping to come across some prospectors or even a homestead. Finally, at about midnight he saw dimly through the trees the light of a camp fire, and, making no more sound than a panther, he crept towards it.

It took him some time to get near enough to see the three occupants of the camp, and waited before disclosing his presence. If they were honest men, he decided, he would ask for the loan of a horse. The first words he heard, however, put him on his guard, and told him he had probably been traveling in circles.

A young fellow a little older than himself, was speaking.

"It's no good, Connell, he's miles away by now," he said.

The man he addressed, a burly giant of a fellow, turned on him angrily.

"You shut yer yap, Kenyon," he growled. "I'm tellin' you the young fool won't have got far. Besides, even if he's gone miles we've got to find him. We need his papers and his uniform."

"That's all very well, Connell, but it'll be risky getting it. The fellow's smart – look how he gave us the slip already."

"Well," said Connell, "if you're going to let yourself be foxed by the likes of him you'd best leave this outfit. An' if you ain't got heart to go for him again, well – we've got no use for a man with no grit."

"It ain't that, and you know it, Connell," said Kenyon. "I just don't like killing a man for no reason. I'm willing to do my part to get his duds, an' his papers, an' we'll have 'em right enough, just wait you an' see. But we can do it without killin' him, that's all."

"Oh can you now?" said Connell sarcastically, "Well let's see you do it then! We'll light out early and it won't take us long to pick up his trail. If he don't stick his hands in the air, this time *I'll* make sure of him."

He slapped a hand on the butt of his gun to indicate what he meant by this.

"Now just hold on," growled the third man. "Look boss, we've kept our hands clean so far and I'll have no part in a murder now. If we *have* to shoot the young fool, all well and good. It's different if it's a fair fight, but I won't stand by and see him shot in cold blood."

Connell was about to reply when Kenyon spoke again.

"You're right, Blythe. If it comes to a fight, I'll chip in with the rest of you, but murder is another matter – a hangin' matter – and that was never a part of the plan. Not for no bunch of old rocks!"

"Well," said Connell, "you know as well as I that we can get that ore safely away to our place. There's fifteen thousand worth in them rocks and that's a good day's work. When we get it over to our claim, an' get it all panned out, who's to know it ain't ours? We'll go way south before we sell it; nobody knows us there. But believe me, gents, we gotta do whatever it takes to get that gold into our hands in the first place. An' remember, sometimes you can't eat no beef if you don't shoot no cows."

"That's crazy talk," said Blythe, "theft of a bit of ore gets five years in the pen, but crossin' the line into killin' a trooper means a noose for certain."

"Only if we get caught," said Connell, "and we won't."

"But it was never in the plan, Connell," said Kenyon gloomily, "that's all I'm sayin'."

"Well, things have changed," said Connell, "an' it's like this – if he don't put up no fight, he gets to go see his mama again. If he tries to plug me, I'll do what I have to, an' to hell with you two. We need them papers and uniform to pass Kenyon off as him, so there's an end to it. I was six months working in that mine, waiting for those fools to give us a chance like this."

"Yeah, boss," said Blythe, "an' we're grateful."

"Well then," said Connell, "I'll just outline it one more time. We get the man's uniform, and Kenyon here goes up to the mine dressed as a trooper. He'll come back with the wagon. When they get to Long Bottom Gully the driver will be hangin' on that brake and slowin' the wagon a bit. When they're at the bottom of the dip he'll cover 'em, an' we'll walk out quiet-like and take charge."

"It sounds easy enough, the way you put it," growled Kenyon.

"Just stick to the plan," answered the leader sharply, "and it will be."

Carpenter had heard enough of the plot. Now he also knew how the thieves had received their information about the gold wagon. But what was he to do? He had the attackers within his grasp – but they outnumbered him three to one. His mind was soon made up. He would arrest these men without delay while he had them all in one place.

Cautiously he arose from his hiding place, his .44 army issue Colt at the ready.

"Get them hands up!" he cried sharply, "The first one to move is a dead man!"

Quickly three pairs of hands were raised above the men's heads.

"Now, stand up, you cowardly bunch of thieves," he yelled.

The three men obeyed.

"Now, Connell," ordered Carpenter, "step forward, where we can see you; real slow, or one of my men will shoot you dead."

It was a big bluff, but it succeeded. Connell stepped forward. The three miscreants glanced uneasily into the darkness behind the young officer. Carpenter's revolver was covering them as he kicked a small coil of rope towards them.

"Now, Kenyon, tie up your partners and mind that you do it properly; if you try something, or I get suspicious, I fire."

"Don't shoot, Corporal," said Kenyon, as he stooped for the coil of rope.

"Corporal?" said Connell, "Well, talk of the devil – it's the very same kid in his nice blue uniform we spoke about earlier!"

Then, quick as a flash, something thin and sinuous whistled through the air, as the lash of a bullwhip tightened round Carpenter's wrist. The pain was unbearable, and the revolver fell from his hand. Crying out in agony, he tore the cruel whip-end off his wrist. Its owner, Blythe, pulled it back and almost in one movement cast it forward again with a loud snap. Now it had Carpenter round the ankles, and he was thrown heavily to the ground.

"Nice work!" yelled Connell, as he stooped over Carpenter with the cold blue barrel of a Colt in line with the latter's head.

"Yeah," leered Blythe, "I knew he was alone as soon's he stepped into the light. An' if he'd had anybody with him he wouldn't have needed Kenyon to tie you up."

"Good thinkin'," said the chief of the band; "Now, kid," he added, turning to Carpenter, "you see, you ain't quite as smart as you thought. My friend here used to knock the end off a cigarette in a showgirl's mouth to earn dollars back in Tombstone."

Carpenter eyed the gang sullenly, cursing inwardly at his own carelessness. He had seen many clever feats performed by cattle-men with a bullwhip, for its twenty foot lash is a powerful weapon in the hands of a practised man. His reflections were cut short now, as they made him swap clothes with Kenyon. In a short time the change was effected and Carpenter was pushed to the ground under a tree, and the leader turned to him.

"I guess you heard all about our little plan," said Connell.

It was not a question but a statement.

"Sure, I heard," snapped Carpenter defiantly.

"Too bad," said Connell, putting a gun to his prisoner's temple.

"No!" shouted Kenyon, "You ain't gonna shoot him,

177

Connell. You shoot him and I ain't doin' the job."

"Yeah, Connell," said Blythe, "you just leave him be now. Ain't no cause to kill him now we got what we wanted. You crazy or what? Step back, man, I'll see he don't get free."

"Yeah," said Kenyon, "we'll tie him up while the game's on, but we'll tell the wagon crew where he is before we set them loose. By then we'll be well away; and remember, nobody knows where we're headin' up in the hills."

"If anything goes wrong," said Connell in a fury, "you two look out. I told you my view – but I guess I got saddled with two faint-hearts."

He spat on the ground and paced off toward the horses, muttering angrily to himself.

CHAPTER THREE:
THE ANT-HILL

Early in the morning they made a start. They took Carpenter into the woodland away from the trail, and, tying his arms and legs securely, left him lying there, under a giant spruce tree.

"Well, bye-bye," laughed Kenyon. "Be good. We'll tell the others where you are once we're on our way, you can depend upon it!"

Carpenter watched as they rode away, leaving him bound in the full glare of the sun. For some hours he lay there, and as the time wore on his thirst became intolerable. To add to his misery, columns of wandering ants found him, and he was soon covered with the vicious insects. Struggle as he might, he could not break his bonds, and it was only by the most violent jerks that he could dislodge some of his tormentors.

For hours, it seemed, they scrambled over him; and his face, neck and hands came up in a maddening rash as the ants bit him. By four o'clock the sun had shifted, and a cool wind sprang up. But his terrible punishment continued, for he still could not rid himself of the insects. Now and again he sent a loud call for help echoing through the silent woods; but no answer came, and eventually he gave up hope.

An hour before sundown a curious sound came down wind. It was made by a body of Indian riders, laughing and talking as they rode. The unshod ponies made distinctive hoof-beats on the earth, something which Carpenter recognized. He guessed that the voices belonged to a hunting party, for they sounded relaxed and jovial. He thought of shouting out to them – but what if they turned out to be a war party after all? There were plenty of hostile tribes in these foothills and mountains, and he was helpless. As he pondered his best course of action, the sound died away, the echoes becoming fainter as the riders departed. He decided to risk it, and shouted for help. He would trust to luck, and throw himself on the mercy of the unknown riders. Again and again he called, and eagerly listened, but no repetition of the sound came to him, and he believed he had been left alone, to endure more torture by the ants.

He must have dozed, for he suddenly came to himself with a start. A twig had snapped somewhere on his right, and as he strained his eyes in that direction he could just make out an Indian among the bushes. The figure was well-nigh hidden, but the white of his eyeballs and a couple of red stripes on his cheeks gave away his position. For several seconds he stared, and then Carpenter realized that it was a Blackfoot watching him. The man approached, then broke into a broad grin: it was one of the very same band that Carpenter had camped among and fraternized with not two days ago!

Carpenter uttered a few sentences, but at first the Indian only gazed on in wonder. Then the fellow recognized Carpenter's distress, and in an instant the ropes that bound him were cut. Other members of the tribe arrived on horseback, and one of them got down, bent over Carpenter and bade him drink from a canteen – an army issue canteen – and he looked up and saw the face of chief Natayo smiling down at him.

After he had sipped a small amount the canteen was taken back. The Indians were pointing towards a stream, and using sign language to indicate that Carpenter should avail himself of its cooling waters. He needed no more encouragement. His clothes thrown off, he leapt into the water and immersed himself to get rid of the troublesome ants. Meanwhile, Natayo's men had shaken out his garments, so that by the time Carpenter had finished his bath all the ants were scattered.

A man brought him an armful of a salving plant that grew beside the water, and bade the white man rub himself all over with the cooling leaves.

As he sat before their camp-fire, Carpenter thought hard, and presently, after a meal of venison which he found very acceptable, he thought about his next course of action. Alone with the chief, the two men smoked in silence. Carpenter believed at first that he was utterly helpless. Deprived of every weapon, his first thought was to get to the mine and warn Roberts the manager. Had any violence been intended toward the miners he would have risked it; but he realized that he was now too far behind the gang to stop them before they took control of the ore. The Blackfoot chief looked on with amusement as the young man sat with furrowed brow smoking pipe after pipe; but at last a plan came to him and he leaned toward Natayo to share his idea and ask for the assistance of his band.

After a great deal of talking, he made the fellow understand him, and Natayo returned to the others. For a time they held an earnest consultation, and finally one and all agreed to help Carpenter, in return for food, guns and ammunition. As the Blackfoot were, in effect, the allies of the government, and Natayo and his men were risking their lives on government business, he agreed to their request.

About seven o'clock next morning they set out for Long Bottom Gully. The Indians knew the place from Carpenter's description, and also knew a short-cut through the forest and hills to reach it in less than a day. The hunting party were armed with their bows, arrows and a few old muzzle-loading rifles, while all carried knives and either a hatchet or a club. Later in the day they arrived, and took up their stations in a grove of cedar, and Carpenter eagerly scanned the trail that stretched like a green ribbon away to the northward. There was no sign of the wagon that day, nor the thieves, and as the light faded, Carpenter camped with the Blackfoot once more, in a hollow some distance away from the trail so as to avoid Connell and Blythe, should they turn up for the robbery. Carpenter calculated that the consignment would almost certainly pass through Long Bottom the next morning, and made sure the Blackfoot were still ready for the challenge before he turned in for the night by their camp-fire.

Next morning they breakfasted at dawn, then went back to their stations and waited. Carpenter had noted a change in the attitude of the Indians. They seemed surly, and disinclined to listen to him when he went over the plan of disarming the gang. Furthermore, they had already painted their faces with red stripes before he rose that morning. He thought this a little ominous; however, he was in no position to tell them how to adorn themselves, and convinced himself that a little paint might make the robbers give up more easily.

They had waited for more than an hour in their hiding places, when, coming down from the hills a mile away, a cloud of dust could be seen. Soon they could make out the figures of two horsemen riding briskly towards them. As they drew near, the two men, Connell and Blythe, rode off into the undergrowth, one on either each side of the trail at the very bottom of the hill. From his hiding-place Carpenter watched this unfold, then quietly gave Natayo his final instructions.

The chief merely looked at him, blankly, without acknowledging that he had understood. Despite this, all the Blackfoot crept stealthily forward until they surrounded the two men, fulfilling the first part of the plan.

In the meantime, Carpenter himself made his way through the undergrowth to where the trail suddenly dipped into the hollow, and there he took his stand. The only weapon he possessed was a club that Natayo had lent him, a thick, heavy stick of about three feet in length. At its larger end a large round stone was embedded in the wood and lashed with thin rawhide – a primitive but deadly arrangement.

Time seemed to pass slowly; but presently a creaking and rumbling noise echoed down the hill, and Carpenter could see the heavy wagon approaching at no more than a brisk walk. Upon the box sat two bearded miners, each armed with a rifle, and with them, the driver. The latter, a huge red-headed fellow, handled his team of four horses with the skill born of long practice. At the side of the vehicle, occasionally dropping back as the track became too narrow, rode a man in the uniform of a corporal of the seventh cavalry. Carpenter smiled as he thought of the surprise in store for the guardians of the gold when the man to whom they looked for help declared himself in his true colours.

The trail dipped suddenly at the point where the robbery was supposed to take place; the trail there was rough and strewn with stones and rocks. In winter the small stream that murmured softly through the gully became a raging torrent, and the utmost caution was needed to cross it. Even now, the driver slowed his team down to a walk and stood up ready to take action at the first sign of a stumble. As luck would have it for the thieves, the off leader's foot slipped on a loose stone and the driver had all his work cut out to prevent the animal falling. That was the moment that Kenyon in his stolen uniform chose to act. Seeing the two miners gripping the sides of the wagon, he came up beside the three men on his horse, drew his pistol and pointed it at the driver.

"Pull up or I fire!" he said curtly.

Confused by this action, the driver nevertheless obeyed, believing that the trooper was forcing him to stop because of some sudden, unseen danger, not yet understanding that this escort was a wolf in sheep's clothing. As the wagon slewed to a halt, Connell and Blythe appeared in front. The driver and the miners went for their rifles.

"Drop that," snapped Connell, and beside them came the softer tones of young Kenyon:

"It's a hold-up, boys. You'd best let us take the ore – it ain't worth dying for."

The miners looked around aghast, found themselves staring down the barrel of a stolen army-issue Colt.

"You dirty blackguard," growled the driver, "you're a disgrace to your uniform."

"I ain't no soldier," laughed Kenyon, "Not me! I'm a rich man!"

"Oh yeah?" said the driver, "Well let's see you run for the hills with three tons of rocks strapped on yer back."

And he smiled at his own little joke, till a contemptuous look from Connell silenced him.

It was at this point that Carpenter took a hand in the game. Seeing Kenyon dressed in his uniform, a silent rage overtook him. He stepped forward until he was only a few feet away from the imposter, and with an unerring aim, sent the heavy club hurtling through the air. It met Kenyon's ribs with a resounding thud, sending the man stunned from his horse.

"Now, Natayo, now!" yelled Carpenter.

The next part of the plan involved the Blackfoot rushing forward with an overwhelming show of force to make the three robbers drop their weapons and give up.

But, as Carpenter discovered, the best laid plans often go awry when the call to action comes. The Blackfoot did indeed surge forward out of the trees, to the enormous shock of robbers, miners and the driver alike. Connell was the first to react:

'Hostiles! Quick, shoot 'em boys!' he shouted, and the three thieves turned and fired. The mine company men, not understanding the Blackfoot were in fact their liberators, picked up their weapons and they too loosed off a volley with their rifles. Those first casualties among the Indians altered things completely, sending the Blackfoot into a wild rage. They replied with such guns as they had, and sent arrows winging through the air. Though several Indians had fallen, the others continued their rush for the wagon while uttering aloud the harsh notes of their war-cries. Arrows that missed their objective thudded into the wooden sides of the wagon, but one struck and felled the driver. Another hit Blythe in the back, a fatal wound. There were more rifle shots from either side, as the Blackfoot closed in.

Carpenter, though used to fighting skirmishes with outlaws and hostile Indians on horseback, was now shocked to his very core by what he saw. Blackfoot braves in a frenzy leapt on outlaws and guards alike. Though they attempted to fight back, the white men were quickly overpowered and dispatched by heavy blows to the head, or finished off with knives. It was swift, decisive and horrible – for such is the nature of hand to hand combat.

The vision of Connell, his rifle dropped and pistol empty, brought down by angry braves was something that would haunt Carpenter to the end of his days. Shot, pierced by arrows and screaming in defiance, the would-be robber fought desperately with his hunting knife, turning this way and that like a wounded beast. A criminal he may have been, but the man was no coward. Finally, struck and wounded a dozen times, he fell screaming to the blood-stained earth, where he was executed with blows from a tomahawk. In a second a man was astride his body with a scalping knife; nor did any of the robbers and guards' bodies escape the same fate.

At first Carpenter had attempted to direct and influence the attackers, shouting for the Blackfoot to stop, without success. After a time he fell silent, realizing he was powerless to halt any of the horrors passing before his eyes. Weaponless and immobile, he could only stand back from the wagon and watch the scene unfold.

Then, when Connell and the others were all dead and mutilated, three of the braves with scarlet hatchets and war-clubs began to close in on Carpenter himself. The look in their eyes was chilling.

"No, no!" cried Carpenter in protest, raising his arms in self-defense, but his lamentations came in vain, for the men's blood-lust was up, and he – a solitary white man – was now the sole remaining enemy. A club knocked him half-senseless to the ground. The warriors bent over him with their knives, arguing as to who should get the scalp.

A shout from Natayo at the very last moment stopped the men in their tracks. They seemed to come to their senses and backed away from Carpenter. As the survivor raised himself up a little, loud cries of victory rent the air, as scalps, guns and items of bloody clothing were waved aloft in triumph...

CHAPTER FOUR:
INFAMY

"Your report is very detailed and explains why exactly you recruited hostile Blackfoot to do the army's work," said Major Docherty. "However, it is also testimony to a foolish – some would say reckless – course of action that resulted in the death of three innocent men, not to mention three outlaws who should have been brought in to face a trial."

"I'm truly sorry, sir," said Carpenter, who was now dressed in civilian clothes. "The whole trip to guard the shipment turned into a nightmare. That's why I asked to quit the army – for good, this time."

"Well," said Docherty, "Headquarters decided to let you go quietly; it was either that or have you drummed out in disgrace; but that would have brought more attention from the press, and the Seventh Cavalry is already a laughing stock, I'm afraid."

"As I said," said Carpenter, "I'm sorry, sir."

"If I hear you say that one more time," said Docherty, "I'll come round that side of the desk and knock you down. Sorry be hanged! I've been relieved of my post because of you, Carpenter. Still can't think what the devil got into you, trying to use those hostiles to do your work."

"I thought it the best course of action at the time," said Carpenter. "I used my initiative just as they taught us at West Point."

"Yes," murmured Docherty acidly, "I can see why you failed the course."

Carpenter smarted at the insult, but managed to rein in his emotions before speaking.

"Sir," he said, "may I ask what you intend to do about Natayo and his Blackfoot? After all, they did what they did to help me as a soldier of the government."

"They did what they did for the love of battle and hatred of the white man," said Docherty.

"If that is true, sir," said Carpenter, "why then did they not kill me?"

"You tell me, Corporal," said Docherty. "Perhaps they imagined some kind of pact existed between you and them. As to what will happen to them now, that is an army matter, and you are no longer a soldier. I will tell you this, however, *Mister* Carpenter. When the regiment catches up with them, they will be very harshly dealt with indeed. Wouldn't be surprised if you haven't stirred up a whole new Indian war. Now get out, and close the door behind you."

The Major turned his back and seemed to study the big map of the north-western territories on his wall. Carpenter, through force of habit, stood to attention, saluted and marched out. But, for all Major Docherty cared, the man could have danced a jig with a flapjack on his head, and he still wouldn't have turned round. For, in his eyes, ex-corporal Sam Carpenter was a traitor to his race, a traitor to his class, an embarrassment to the army, and worst of all, a total disgrace to his regiment. It was only a pity the fellow hadn't had the honest decency to perish back there at Long Bottom – along with his shame.

The Major turned, sat down, and examined again the newspaper on his desk. He read the front page, smarting each time his eyes passed over his own name. Then, with a sigh, he opened a drawer and took out his pistol, put it to his head and pulled the trigger.

BOOK FIVE:

CHEYENNE COUNTRY

Don't interfere with something that ain't botherin' you none.
        -Western saying

'Our land is everything to us... I will tell you one of the things we remember on our land. We remember that our grandfathers paid for it – with their lives.'
        -John Wooden Legs, Northern Cheyenne.

CHEYENNE COUNTRY

CHAPTER ONE:
MURDER IN THE BANK

Marshal Mat Campbell was shocked by what he saw in and around the bank. There was a dead man, still wearing his red bandanna mask, lying in the street where his deputy Ted Jarret had dropped him. Jarret himself lay on the threshold of the Walker Brothers Bank in a pool of blood, a single shot having felled him about ten seconds after he got the lookout. Just inside the lobby was the body of Elspeth Turner, the preacher's wife. Her empty purse was lying next her hand. Her jewelry had been stripped from her fingers, ears and neck. Next to her lay Ben Locksley the buffalo skin tanner, easily recognizable from his stained hands and smock. Further in, behind the polished oak counter, sprawled the three bank staff. Joe Quaid and Ernie Hillier had been the tellers; and Barny Lyle the manager. All except Ted Jarret had been shot at very close range, and all had been stripped of cash and valuables.

Behind the counter, through an open door, was visible the empty safe, its heavy steel door ajar. Campbell surmised that though the safe could not be wrenched open by any degree of physical might, the manager had been coerced into handing over the key in the vain hope that by doing so his life would be spared.

Witnesses said that four masked men had gone inside, leaving one man guarding the door – the man that Jarret killed – and a sixth man holding the horses a few feet away in an alleyway. That sixth outlaw, hearing Jarret's shot, was seen to tether the horses to a post, walk around the corner and shoot the deputy dead. This shooter, seeing a number of armed townsfolk gathering in the street outside the Lucky Dog Saloon and Harper's General Store, then fired a few warning shots in their direction. These would-be vigilantes instantly dispersed, though fortunately one of them had the presence of mind to mount up and gallop over to Marshal Mat Campbell's ranch a mile out of town.

It was generally agreed that the four robbers in the bank, though the safe had already been opened, must have panicked upon hearing shooting outside. At any rate, the flurry of shots from within came just after the outlaw outside had loosed off his rounds towards the store and saloon. After the two clerks, the manager and two customers were gunned down, the man outside had yelled: 'Rattle your hocks, boys! They got Jeb!' or words to that effect.

What was particularly shocking to all who heard or read the story of the 'Walkers' Bank Massacre' was the way those five people were executed at close range with shots to the head. It was a case of cold-blooded murder.

As Mat Campbell said in his report to the Mayor and his committee: 'Just what kind of men are we dealing with here? These are no ordinary criminals. These men are out and-out-killers who have to be stopped. And rest assured, I will do the stopping.'

His report detailed his efforts so far, and the fact that even the man killed by Jarret had not yet been identified, though sketches of his face in death were circulating far and wide to sheriffs and marshals, not to mention the Texas Rangers. Campbell expressed also his frustration that he had, temporarily at least, been thwarted in his pursuit and tracking of the five by the fact that they'd ridden plumb into Cheyenne country, about fifty miles west of his jurisdiction. There was a precarious treaty in place, and, at least while it held, Campbell and his posse dared venture no farther.

However, as he told his exhausted posse on their return, while handing out glasses of good quality rye in the Lucky Dog Saloon:

"Could be, we never get to hang that bunch at all, boys. I think them Cheyenne will give them outlaws a very rough time indeed, you mark my words. But if it turns out them mangy dogs get through, sooner or later word will come this way, and then we'll go again, an' make 'em wish they'd never been born."

Digby Slade, the Mayor, put it another way: "Trouble's a-coming for certain, Marshal," he said. "Maybe those varmints will get their just desserts at the hands of them Injuns, and maybe not; but either way them outlaws encroachin' on that valley is like sparks landing in an open powder-keg."

A third voice now ventured an opinion on the fate of the five outlaws who had, after a fashion, escaped justice. It came from Jed Clarke, the oldest member of the posse by far, who was smirking through his bushy gray beard and enjoying his drink of fine whiskey.

"Hah!" he laughed, "You're all wrong, all o' yer! No need for them hang-dog looks. When men go chasin' into a spot like that, it's a clear-cut *fryin' pan case*, that's what it is."

"What the heck are you talkin' 'bout, old timer?" said Digby Slade, more than a little annoyed.

"I mean," cackled Clarke, "Them outlaws is already dead, with no hair left on 'em, d'yer hear me? We chased them sons of bitches right into the mouth o' hell, an' they ain't a-comin' out. It's a clear-cut case of *'Out of the fryin' pan, into the fire!'*

CHAPTER TWO:
SURROUNDED...

Four men found themselves in a fix of their own making. In a valley somewhere in Colorado territory their lives hung in the balance. Thirty-three well-armed Cheyenne Indians, their faces marked with white war-paint, were out to kill them. There was no way out. No help coming. No way to appease or turn the Indians from their task. Not after Lester Croft shot dead the chief's youngest son.

Now all the best warriors of one village – a society of elite fighters calling themselves the Black Dog Lodge – were out to avenge the boy's death, and none would rest easy till the intruders' scalps were dangling as trophies on their belts.

The four white men knew, as soon as they swung down from their horses and took to cover in the rocks, that there was a good chance they would never mount again, never get to spend that fifteen thousand dollars they stole in Pueblo. All in all, things were not going well for the gang. The four had once been six. Jeb Harnsey had already met his maker outside the bank. Bob Tallis lay dead back up the trail.

That raid had been a mere five days back, but it seemed a lifetime ago now. Throughout tough days a posse had hounded them far out into the wilderness. Several times their pursuers had almost caught them up, until a fateful decision was made: they would turn into Cheyenne country. A narrow cleft in the hillside led into a precipitous valley, above which puffs of smoke were already rising. Though the posse hesitated to follow, the five riders felt a new unease. As they traversed some rugged, beautiful countryside, they were on the look-out for game to shoot for food; but not an antelope nor rabbit, deer nor even a bird did they encounter. Twice they spotted shadowy Indian riders on sleek ponies far ahead. Then, two hours into this strange new land, an Indian boy on a striking appaloosa horse emerged from a little stand of pines not thirty paces from Lester Croft, who rode a little behind the others. The Indian, unseen by any but Croft at this time, had in one hand a bow, and in the other an arrow taken from his quiver.

Even as Croft opened his mouth to warn the others, the boy loosed off an arrow that missed him by inches. Cursing the Indian and his kind, Croft pulled his rifle from its boot, took aim and shot the boy dead. As the other outlaws turned in their saddles to see why Croft had opened fire, two Cheyenne hunters appeared from same stand of pines. Upon seeing the fallen boy, they charged the five men without hesitation. A volley of shots from the outlaws knocked them cleanly off their horses. Then, as the outlaws were riding over to the braves' bodies to take a closer look, a rifle shot thundered from further up the valley. Bob Tallis fell from his horse, fatally wounded – and the intruders knew that they had a fight on their hands.

As they turned to ride back out the way they'd come, they saw, rather than the marshal's posse, a Cheyenne war-party in the distance. Thus, there was nothing for it now but to continue riding further into hostile territory, and look for a place to make a stand. This involved riding straight past the sharpshooter who'd killed Tallis, but they had little choice in the matter.

The Indian fired a second shot that brushed the arm of Hugo Lozano, a young man wanted for several murders back in his home territory of south Texas. Lozano, who had been riding to the fore of his comrades now halted, and killed the rifle shooter with his own Henry rifle, and so the four were able to carry on up the valley. A few minutes later, two discoveries in quick succession brought matters to a head. The first was a cave in the hillside with a formation of rocks before it, which might be defensible. The second was the sighting of another group of Indians blocking the path ahead. The outlaws reckoned on there being a dozen to fifteen in either group, one band in front of them, one behind, tough Cheyenne men who were renowned for their fighting skills.

Taking a trail through hostile territory to throw the posse off their trail had seemed a risk worth taking. Now it was revealed, as old Jed Clarke had predicted, a clear-cut case of 'out of the frying pan into the fire.' The Cheyenne had them boxed in from both directions. They had little food, and even less water. It was already late afternoon, and soon darkness would add a new element of danger to their plight. All things considered, they were in something of a fix.

However, the situation of the four men, though serious, was not entirely hopeless. Not quite. For they each had a rifle, a pair of pistols, and plenty of ammunition. Their hunting knives, and strength of arm too, might be called upon. But more important than all of these, was that extra something that fighting men possess. All four men were veterans of a bloody civil war that had left them battle-hardened and skilful with weapons. Moreover, all were cold-blooded killers, desperate men who would sell their lives dearly.

But who were they, these gun-lovers who robbed and killed heedless of the laws of the land, taking risks that other men considered suicidal?

Some men are born bad. Others do bad things when

circumstances dictate, as when revenge gets out of hand. Some men deliberately choose evil, and learn to take delight in another man's pain.

Hugo Lozano, aged twenty-one was the first type. From an early age he had killed without giving it a second thought. And if he hadn't taken a life for a time, at the first hint of a fight he trembled with anticipation like an opium addict long overdue for a fix. He was five feet six, dark-haired, dark eyed, dark-hearted, compact as a little bull, and crazy enough to do absolutely anything.

Kyle Brenner, aged thirty, was the second type: he killed two men who'd slain his best friend, then killed a marshal come to arrest him. Though sometimes he wished for his old life back, he loved the thrilling existence he led, and reveled in the danger of gunplay. He didn't know it yet, but he'd grown to need the heady excitement of near-death experiences in duels and fire-fights. He was six feet tall, ugly as sin, already bald beneath his flat-crowned black hat, with eyes like an angry hawk.

Lester Croft, twenty-five, was the third type. He chose outlawry as his profession, and guns as the tools of his trade. At the age of eighteen he began to imitate the deeds and manner of Billy the Kid, just about the worst role model a boy could be drawn to. First he killed an old drunk in the street who'd laughed at him. Then he shot a deputy marshal in the back, just for the hell of it, a crime that made him notorious and a fugitive. With a change of name, he hid among a Confederate unit called Gurley's Partisan Rangers for the final years of the war – which only served to hone his deadly skills and love of a fight. At the end of the war, he graduated to banditry. Folks who had no idea who he was, or why he pointed a gun at them, were taken for every cent they had. Those who resisted he shot down – and smiled as he pulled the trigger. Bank tellers, stagecoach drivers, shop owners, anyone with cash, valuables or a better horse than the one he rode came under his harsh scrutiny.

As for Rory Tate, the old man of the unit at thirty-three, he was the first type. And the second. And the third. Sometimes he killed for one reason, sometimes another. But without the thrill of battle he felt empty and useless, his spirit at rock bottom. Though he had sufficient intelligence and just about enough self control to channel his violence into robberies that furthered his ends, he could no more have given up a life of murder and blend back into civilian life than a cougar could turn vegetarian. He was six feet two, with hair like matted straw beneath his battered hat, and cold, steel-blue eyes that showed no flicker of emotion even when he laughed – which was generally only in mockery. His laugh would reveal bad teeth, worn and spaced like old tombstones. He wore his two gunbelts crossed over his chest, and would as soon shoot a man as look at him. His face was notoriously difficult to read, and his temper so mercurial that even his fellow outlaws were terrified of his moods.

Fortunately for him, he had reputation enough to attract a gang that were dependable on raids, and help him keep even the doughtiest of lawmen at bay. Furthermore, like many of his kind, he had the luck of the devil. Though he'd been shot seven times, all he had to show for it were holes in his sleeves, his buckskin chaps, his hat – and even his face. A .36 slug had gone through one cheek and out the other as he was shouting orders at his men – without so much as breaking a tooth.

Men outside the law were superstitious about such things.

Life, like gambling, seemed to give huge luck to some individuals – at least for a time. Outlaws whose whole life was a game of chance believed you could do worse than stick real close to a man like Rory Tate. Likely as not, some of that luck would rub off...

"Lozano! Brenner! Croft! Don't shoot till I say!" said Tate through gritted teeth. "Let 'em get cocky so's we get a few more in the first volley, boys. An' keep your goddamn heads low to the rocks. Don't want no more damn fools ending up like Tallis, you hear me?"

Tallis, who was lying back up the valley, unburied and now minus his hair, had been a popular member of the group. They would miss his cheerful good humor, his excellent camp-fire cooking and the stories that had grown a little more lurid and exaggerated with each telling; but most of all they would miss the fire-power of his Henry rifle and two Colt pistols.

Though Tate and his crew didn't know it yet, it had been Cheyenne Dog-Soldiers that killed him and scalped him, members of a band that formed, in effect, a tribe within a tribe. These were the very fiercest of Cheyenne warriors, and the valley Tate and his men had foolishly entered was considered sacred by them. Those who rode there uninvited had, in their eyes, insulted the Black Dog Lodge and declared war on the Cheyenne tribe. Unfortunately for Tate and the others, the band had been returning from a raid on a homestead when they spotted tracks and dust that indicated one group of white men being followed by another. When they saw the first group enter the valley, and the second one turn back, it had been a simple choice. They must defend their own land and kill the intruders. They divided into two groups to make their attack on the outlaws. By using a winding trail over the hills, one band maneuvered to get in front of the white men. The others had only to follow the five riders to complete their trap. Led by a warrior called Wapotsit, meaning 'White Wolf', they were in full war-paint and regalia and comprised a fighting group of thirty-three men. Well-motivated and formidable as they were, they had even stronger reasons to take their revenge on these white intruders upon finding that the son of their chief had been killed, along with two other men from their village.

Tate, a former Confederate army sergeant, with an eye for a defensive position, had his men tether their horses in the cave in the valley-side, and take cover on the slope next the entrance where rocks formed a shoulder-high mini-fortress to shield them. With horses spent after a day's hard riding, there was no chance of outrunning the braves. A fight to the death was the best they could do. One way or the other, the scrap was likely to be decisive.

Nor did the four outlaws have long to wait before an attempt to silence them for good was made. Barely a quarter-hour had passed, time enough only for a miserable late meal of a few hard biscuits, jerky and water. A patter of light, unshod hoof-beats on either side announced the arrival of the two war parties, hidden at first by a grove of pines on one side, a curve of the valley on the other. Without the four fugitives so much as sighting an Indian, a rifle bullet exploded on the rock next to Tate's head to announce the onset of the battle. Tate flinched as a fragment of lead cut the skin above his left eyebrow. Cursing, he dabbed his wound with his dusty red bandanna.

"Looks like they've got in behind us already," he said. "Won't be long 'fore they climb up above us, neither."

Brenner, next to him, turned to speak, then noticed the trickle of blood on Tate's forehead.

"Jesus, Tate," he said, "You hit... agin?"

Lozano and Croft turned, and took in the fact that Tate had escaped death by a narrow margin once again.

Croft glanced knowingly at Lozano.

Take more'n a bullet to get Rory Tate," he said. "He's a charmed 'un all right."

"Yeah," said Croft; "Spooky, ain't it? Reck'n that's eight times he's dodged a bullet like that."

Tate, a man not given to ruminate on such trivial matters, acknowledged his latest brush with death with a dismissive shrug.

"Bullet missed me by a mile," he said; "Just got me a scratch from the ricochet, gents – ain't nothin' in that."

Brenner winked at his leader.

"Any way you look at it, Tate," he said, "you're a lucky son – an' we'll need a little luck to get us out of this."

"Might need more'n just luck," said Tate. "Them Cheyenne won't give us no free pass. Anyone got any bright ideas, let's hear 'em."

"Mebbe send ol' Croft out there to kiss their red asses an' beg 'em to let us go," said Brenner, grinning widely at his own lame joke.

He wouldn't have laughed if he'd known that the nearest war-painted Cheyenne was now only six feet away, behind the very boulder that sheltered him from bullets and arrows. Like Tate, a few feet to his right, he cast his gun-sight over their eastern approach. Meanwhile, fifteen feet behind them, Lozano and Croft peered westward along the other reach of the valley, into the setting sun, which now glowed a brilliant vermillion color, like blood dripped into water.

"Purty sunset," said Croft gloomily. "Be dark in half an hour. Then we're in for it."

"If we last that long," said Lozano.

"Quit that sort o' talk," said Tate. "We ain't dead yet; and even if they get us, we'll go down fightin'."

"Yessir!" said Lozano, making a mock-salute toward Tate, "That's the spirit – we'll all die nobly."

Tate merely looked at him with contempt, and shrugged.

"Sure, why not? You boys can give up now an' go beg our Cheyenne friends for mercy if you like," he said, "but I tell you gents for free, this game ain't over till it's over."

"He's right," said Brenner. "They got to winkle us out first. I don't see them too eager to chew lead."

"Just wait," said Croft; "Them sons can see in the dark."

"Hey Tate," said Brenner, "I heard them Cheyenne won't fight at night... that true, Tate?"

"Don't count on it," said Tate, peering round the rock. Then he raised his carbine, took careful aim and fired.

"Well – that's one less," he said.

"That's just peachy then," said Lozano, "Only nine-hundred-ninety nine to go."

Again the dirty look from Tate.

"One more remark like that, Lozano," he said, "an' I'll be over there an' kick your ass, Injuns or no Injuns."

Lozano gave him a quick sidelong glance, decided that his boss might just do it, and buttoned his lip.

Brenner, looking eastwards out of the valley toward the pines, spotted movement high up on the precipitous slope. A few pebbles rolled down from a cluster of rocks, and he raised his Spencer carbine and waited. A warrior showed himself for no more than a second as he darted for better cover and the rifle roared. The Cheyenne let out a stifled yelp and fell, rolling down the valley before coming to rest on a jutting rock.

"Nice shot," said Tate, nodding in appreciation. "Keep your eyes up there. They're tryin' to get closer. I got the valley covered. Some of 'em think they're invisible – but they ain't."

In front of him, other braves were crawling forward through the fallen rocks and heaps of scree of the valley bottom. Though the slopes rose up steeply five hundred feet and more, with scrubby and stunted pines and thorn bushes amongst the boulders offering good cover, few of the braves wanted to climb up to shoot down on the white men. The reason was simple: thinking that the end of the battle was close, Dog Soldiers preferred to be ready for the final hand-to-hand battle when scalps would be taken. That was where a warrior's mettle was really tested, they believed, and where the real glory lay.

Croft's rifle crashed, and its echo resounded around the valley. A 56 Spencer is a noisy weapon with a large and deadly projectile.

"Got ya!" he shouted; "Come and show yourselves if you want the same, you bunch o' yeller bastards!"

"Stop that shoutin'," said Tate, "They ain't yeller or fatherless, Croft, but even if they were, I don't want you stirring 'em up even more."

"Why not?" said Croft, "You think they'll up an' leave us be if we're real polite?"

"No," said Tate; "but if you provoke 'em too much they'll take it as a dare an' rush us, and that's no good. Them's Cheyenne Dog-Soldiers – I can see the paint and markings on that one hung up above us – which means if they refuse a challenge they're shamed in the eyes of their tribe. Our best bet is to keep picking them off, till either they're all dead or they see the cost's too high and pull out."

"You ever known Dog Soldiers to give up on a scrap?" said Croft.

"Now you mention it – no," said Tate, "but then I don't rightly know all their fightin' habits since I tend to avoid rilin' up the biggest an' meanest damn tribe in the territory. I was just doing fine too, till some stupid son shot one of their kids who'd come to stare at us."

"If he'd only been *starin'* at me I wouldn't have fired," said Croft, "but that little devil loosed off an arrow that damn near took me off my horse. That's why I downed him."

"He was just a kid," said Tate, "I saw him."

"Yeah," said Brenner. "That was a dumb move, Croft. This is your damn fault. Could've been in Greenrock by now, drinkin' Dutch Tom's moonshine."

"That gutrot?" said Croft, wiping his brow with his bandanna; "Brenner, you're better off here! Last year a whole bunch of hombres went blind after drinkin' that evil stuff."

"I'd take my chances," said Brenner; "I'd rather die drinkin' his moonshine than havin' Cheyenne shoot goddamned arrows at me. That last 'un damn near took my hair off."

"Talkin' of 'em getting our hair lopped off, gents," said Lozano, "I got three bodies crawling through them-there bushes. You see 'em, Croft?"

"I see 'em," said Croft. "Surprised they didn't do it earlier."

He raised his rifle sights into the bushes. A thunderous report sent echoes through the valley once more.

"Ha!" said Croft, as he squinted over his gun-sight, "That one won't be firin' any more of them damn arrows, that's for sure."

Then he ducked just in time as an arrow from another Cheyenne flew at his face. It missed by a fraction, causing him to swear, and keep low. The others roared with laughter at Croft's lucky escape.

"Look out!" grinned Brenner, turning round, "That Dog Soldier's pals are really pissed now!"

Tate was about to warn Brenner to watch his front; but at that moment the Cheyenne behind the boulder sprang up and vaulted into the enclosure. He landed right on top of Brenner, knocking him to the ground. There were two simultaneous screams, one a blood-curdling battle-cry from the Indian as he swung his tomahawk, the other a yell of anguish from Brenner as he rolled on the ground and tried to draw his Colt. Brenner succeeded in pulling his gun, and tried to get his muzzle to bear on his assailant. He even got a finger in the trigger-guard – but the pistol was pointing at Tate rather than the Indian. Tate, for his part had his rifle-sights on the wrestling combatants, but held his fire for fear of hitting Brenner. Croft and Lozano looked on desperately, but dare not leave their own stations, lest another Indian leap at them from the west side.

Then Brenner's Colt went off. The hammer was not cocked but resting on a cap, but as it was struck against a rock, the thing discharged. Tate leapt in the air as the bullet passed through the leg of his chaps and pinged off a rock behind him. Meanwhile, the Cheyenne got in his blow with the hatchet, a swift stroke aimed at his opponents head. But the swing was deflected by a blocking forearm in front of its shaft, so that the blade chopped harmlessly into the ground. A second later, the combatants were rolling over and over in the dirt again, pistol and hatchet dropped as both reached for knives on their belts. The Indian drew his own first, and lunged at Brenner's belly - but the blade struck his gun-belt and failed to penetrate by more than a fraction of an inch. Brenner cried out in pain, and punched out at the painted face. The Indian, trying to press home his blade, screamed as another knife sunk deep in his own back. Instantly he dropped sideways off Brenner, writhing in his death agony.

Tate had finished him with his bowie knife, and followed up with a single, heavy kick to the man's shoulder to get him off Brenner. Tate bent down and snatched back his knife. He gave the dead man a look of respect, shook his head dismissively at Brenner, then returned to his position behind the boulder.

Brenner, panting, picked himself up, and stood there dazed for a few seconds.

"Thank, Tate," he said.

Tate, back in his position, aimed his rifle along the valley and fired.

"Now they're really stoked up, boys!" said Tate. Without turning his head he added: "Brenner, I'd pick up that goddamned gun and get back to your place if I were you."

Brenner, badly shaken, but recovering himself a little, snatched up his rifle and gamely returned to his position.

"Coming t'other way too!" yelled Croft.

All four rifles then began to fire in sequence. Shot after shot they fired; and slugs came whistling back at them, several of them ricocheting off the protecting rocks. Arrows came humming into the fortress. There were near misses, but none struck home on Tate and the others.

Then, as suddenly as the attack had begun, it stopped, and

there was no sign of the Cheyenne. Long minutes passed. The outlaws waited expectantly. Finally, Lozano broke the silence:

"What you think, Tate?" he hissed; "They gone, or what?"

"Reck'n not," said Tate. "They're just taking a breather. They'll try again. Hey boys, how many'd we get?"

"I got three, at least," said Croft.

"I downed five or six," said Lozano, "All dead."

"I got two," said Brenner, "and two winged. Plus that one down there." He indicted the dead man at his feet.

"That one was mine," said Tate, still scanning his front; "I dropped four. That makes seventeen. Not enough. They'll try again after dark."

"Let 'em try," said Lozano, snatching a Colt from its holster; "They know what they'll get if they come too close to me."

"Yeah," said Tate, "bet they're just terrified."

"Still, we got seventeen," said Croft, "Mebbe a few more. An' now they've hunkered down again. Mebbe they've had enough. Mebbe they'll light out."

"Naw," said Tate, "that's just wishful thinking. We already cost them dear – if they're Dog-Soldiers they'll want revenge for sure."

"Revenge?" said Brenner thumbing bullets into his magazine, "And it nearly dark? Well, ain't we just the lucky ones, boys."

CHAPTER TWO:
END GAME

For a half-hour all was quiet. The shadows lengthened, merged, and darkness fell. Still, the Cheyenne waited. A half-moon crossed the sky, obscured from time to time by wispy clouds. One or two of the braves began to make coyote calls, some of them unnervingly close to the beleaguered men. A couple of arrows struck rocks in the fortress. In their hideaway in the hillside, the neglected horses stamped their feet and snickered nervously.

Almost invisible in the darkness, Tate began to move. First he removed his jacket, hat and gun-belts. Then he checked his two pistols, and stuck one into his waist-band. The other he took in his left hand. In his right he brandished his bowie knife.

"What's up, Tate?" said Brenner, catching sight of Tate in a glimmer of moonlight. There was a note of desperation in his voice, which made Tate smile.

"Pipe down," said Tate, "I won't be long."

"You're not goin' out there?" gaped Brenner; "Surely not!"

"Surely, yes," mocked Tate; "You comin' too, Brenner?"

"What's got into you, Tate?" said Croft abandoning his post, "You ain't serious, are you?"

Tate, for his part, merely laughed. In the gloom the others could just about make out his gap-toothed grin. Or was it a snarl? At any rate his face had changed.

"Don't you go out there!" hissed Lozano, coming from the other side of the fortress; "Don't – don't leave us here, Tate!"

"I ain't leavin'," said Tate, checking the point of his knife; "Just gonna give 'em a taste o' their own medicine."

"Don't do it," said Lozano; "They'll kill you. Them Cheyenne can see in the dark."

"So can I!" whispered Tate, leaping up onto the parapet and disappearing into the night.

The others stiffened with fear, caught glimpses of each other's nervous faces in the moonlight. They seemed turned to stone for a few seconds. Brenner was the first to speak.

"Better get back to our places, boys," he said. "Check our weapons too – we gonna need 'em real soon."

It would be impossible to describe the fears and agonies of the three men left behind in the fortress. Night-fighting, or even the fear of it, is a terror re-lived a thousand times by those forced to endure it. Every sound, every shadow, every looming shape is imagined to be an omen of impending death. Panic is never far away. Every second seems an eternity.

Thus it was for Brenner, Croft and Lozano, trapped in their enclosure, facing out into the darkness, fingers tight on the triggers of their guns.

But not for Tate.

A sudden scream of pain tore through the darkness - a cry of pain from a Cheyenne. Then a pistol shot echoed through the valley, followed by another. Somewhere up on the hill, men were shouting. The racket caused a disturbance among their own horses, caused them to stamp and whinny. Most disturbing of all was a long peal of laughter – Rory Tate's laughter – followed by yet more pistol shots. Then there was silence.

The men looked at each other, showing the whites of their eyes, their mouths dry as dust; but they stuck to their posts. That silence was hard to bear. How long had it been since those sounds of a fight? Ten minutes? Half an hour?

Suddenly, there were more screams, gunshots and – shouts from the Cheyenne. Once, for a few seconds, the others heard Tate singing crazily at the top of his voice. This was followed by a flurry of shots, coyote calls, and, more screams of pain. Finally, all was silent again.

"Christ, boys," said Croft, "I can't stand much more of this! Mebbe they got him. Let's try for the horses while we can, and make a run for it. We got a chance. Mebbe if-"

"Button it, Croft!" said Brenner; "If he can stand goin' out there, we can stand waitin' in here. Keep your eyes skinned – I'm going to fire some pistol shots to distract them devils. Might keep them away from the horses, an' give Tate a chance."

From time to time he fired his Colt into the darkness. His bullets pinged off the rocks, rattled through the trees. It made him feel better, less at the mercy of unseen forces in the darkness. The others began doing the same.

Suddenly a voice hissed out of the darkness:

"Don't shoot, you jumpy bunch o' tenderfeet, I'm comin' in."

Tate dropped down off the parapet like a wolf – or the shadow of a wolf – into their midst.

"By the way you're shooting at nothing, I can tell you boys got a bit windy," he grinned.

"Who wouldn't?" said Croft. "This is one night I'll never forget. Almost wished I was back in the pen."

"That bad, eh?" jeered Tate, "You poor little thing."

Then the moon came out from behind a cloud and the others noticed that Tate stood upright, not crouching, and keeping low like his comrades, but leaning casually against a rock. He didn't even have a gun in his hand.

"Christ, Tate," whispered Lozano, "we thought you'd had your throat cut out there. Croft was just about to bolt for the horses!"

"Oh was he now?" said Tate, "Nice to know you bunch o' tenderfeet missed me."

He made no attempt to keep his voice low, nor conceal himself at all. Then, he took out his tobacco pouch and proceeded to roll a smoke. Taking out a match, he rasped it against a boulder. It did not ignite first time.

The others looked on, horrified.

"Hell, Tate," Brenner hissed, "Don't light that!"

Tate merely laughed, struck the match, which flared brightly to illuminate a devilishly red face for a second. Then the company was plunged in darkness once again, save for the glowing tip of the cigarette that gave away their leader's position.

"Tate!" gasped Croft, "You gone loco, or what?"

Brenner, Croft and Lorenzo watched in horror as Tate enjoyed his smoke, expecting him any second to get his head shot off, or an arrow in the neck. Tate, however, seemed amused by his companions' nervousness. Suddenly he shouted:

"C'mon Injuns!" he yelled at the top of his lungs, "Come and get it, you bunch of yeller Dog-Soldier bastards!"

"Christ, Tate," hissed Brenner aghast, "what you doin'? You told me not to cuss an' rile 'em up, an' now you look at you!"

"Yeah," said Tate, "but things is different now."

"What you mean?" said Brenner, "Different? How so?"

"Well," said Tate, "it turned out there were nine or ten of 'em left out there cussin' and plannin' how to get us."

He drew on the last little bit of his cigarette, exhaled and tossed aside the butt.

"Only now there ain't," he said.

"What're you tryin' to tell us?" said Croft, half standing up, "You tryin' to tell us they're all dead?"

"Dead or nearly dead," said Tate.

"How the hell could that be?" said Lozano. "There was a whole war party – Dog Soldiers they were, so you said..."

"Guess those boys made a little mistake," said Tate.

"What kind of mistake, Tate?" said Lozano.

"Oh, thinkin' they could see an' fight better in the dark," said Tate

He wiped his face with the back of his sleeve, before taking out his pouch for yet another smoke.

"Turns out," he said, "they was wrong."

The others stared at him in wonder for a few seconds.

"Hell, Tate," said Brenner, "we sure are thankful you're on our side!"

The others laughed nervously at the joke, while Tate built himself another cigarette. As the match flared to light his smoke, the others caught a better look at his face. It was bright red, and curiously luminous. When the match died, in the veiled moonlight and weak glow of the stars his face and clothes seemed to glisten, as if wet.

Lozano reached out and touched Tate's shoulder.

"Christ, Tate," he said, "you're soaked."

"That's funny – we ain't had no rain," said Croft.

Puzzled, the others drew closer, to get a closer look at Tate.

"That's blood," said Lozano; "Tate... you're covered in it!"

Tate, his gap-toothed grin in the darkness just visible in

the feeble light, seemed amused by this observation.

"Blood is there, gents?" he said; "Well – a little blood's to be expected in the circumstances. Reck'n they stuck me a couple o' times."

He paused, feeling his head and upper body for injuries. Again, the others saw the gap-toothed grin.

"Anyhow, they got the worse of it, boys," he said, "you can depend on that."

He slumped down to a sitting position, his back resting against a boulder.

"You all right, Tate?" said Lozano.

Tate ran his fingers over his head again, and examined his bloody fingers.

"Head's beginning to smart a little now," he said. "When a man gets all riled up in a bit of a fight, he generally don't feel no pain till he's out of it agin. Where's my canteen?"

"Get him some water," said Lozano.

"You sure are one tough son," said Brenner, handing him a canteen.

"Yeah," said Lozano; "What you did out there... well, it almost weren't human. If I hadn't been here, I wouldn't have believed it."

"Aw shucks," said Tate, taking the canteen, "Now I'm all choked up. Hey you tenderfeet, go check on them horses and tighten them cinches. We'll take us a little walk for an hour or two. We'll light a shuck an' get clean away from this-here spot before we make camp an' sleep. The thought of all them bodies lyin' around us starin' up at the stars is beginning to give me the shakes..."

THE END

BOOK SIX:

A FELLOWSHIP
OF DEATH

'It isn't how you die. It's what you live for.'
  -Daniel Boone

'Here was a royal fellowship of death!'
  -Shakespeare - Henry V
  ...after the battle of Agincourt

A FELLOWSHIP OF DEATH

CHAPTER ONE:
THE MEN WITH MASKS

On the edge of the cedar, aspen and lodgepole pine forest, Christie Henderson was sawing down saplings for corral railings when five mounted strangers appeared through the mist. When they were about forty paces away they divided into files of three and two, and rode slowly up either side of him in an encircling movement. Christie, a skinny lad of eighteen, of medium height, with dark hair and eyes, and skin tanned by long hours of toil in the open air, had been going about his work as usual, unarmed and unprepared for confrontation. In truth, he was no fighter.

But neither was he timid in nature. So when he straightened, and stood there staring, it was in fascination rather than fear. The men wore black masks. They slowly approached the spot where he was working. Then Christie started slightly, as he recognized the fore-most rider as Shaun Tranter, a neighbor. His long red beard with gray streaks that hung below his mask, and his big, iron-gray horse, were distinctive enough. The other four men would be his sons, thick-set men in their twenties and thirties, all with rifles over their saddle pommels. He had heard stories of this quarrelsome family putting on masks and venturing out on expeditions to rustle stock from other homesteads, but had thought these tales fictitious – until now.

"You boy," said the man with the red and gray beard, "are trespassin' on Tranter land."

Christie Henderson was puzzled by this statement. He looked about him into the woods, opened his palms toward the masked rider in honest bewilderment.

"You must've lost your bearins'," said Christie, "This land's been Pa's for nigh on thirty year."

"He got no claim on it," said Tranter.

"He's got more of a claim than you," said Christie, looking him in the eye.

The men all raised their rifles until their muzzles all pointed straight at Christie.

"One of my boys is filing a claim," said Tranter; "That's all you need to know. Now git. You got ten seconds."

"But that's just plumb crazy," muttered Christie, now with ill-concealed contempt. "This-here's Henderson land – an' you-all know it. We've been working it all our lives."

As yet Christie had not understood the danger he was in; he simply thought the masked riders were mistaken, or bluffing, and would let him be. So, shaking his head dismissively, he turned his back and went on with his sawing.

A gunshot made him leap into the air in alarm, its bullet putting a white gash in the pole he was attempting to fell. Recovering himself a little, he looked round slowly.

"Don't you disrespect me, boy," snarled Tranter. "Bodie, go teach that little weasel a lesson."

"Now hang on a minute-" said Christie, holding up his hands in outright surrender; but his words were cut short. One of the masked men slid down from his horse, walked up to Christie and punched him squarely on the mouth. The blow knocked him flying into the leaves and pine needles. As he tried to rise, Bodie Tranter kicked him in the ribs with all his strength, sending the boy back down to the forest floor. Two other men now got down from their mounts, and all three took turns hefting kicks as Christie writhed on the ground. After a minute they stopped, stepped back to their horses and mounted. Christie lay face down on the damp ground, only the slight rise and fall of his back indicating he was still alive.

The riders watched him for a while in silence, as if admiring the effect of their wanton act. Presently Christie raised himself up a little, so that his jaw was off the earth, enabling him to speak – at least after a fashion.

"Why, Mr Tranter, why?" groaned Christie. "An' them masks – you don't need to wear no masks round here-"

About four rifle shots kicked up the dirt next to his face.

"Tell your Pa," said Shaun Tranter, "the next time we see one o' you weasels stealin' our lumber, ketchin' our fish, or sniffin' round our stock, we'll shoot him dead. Savvy?"

Wisely, Christie lay still and held his tongue. He heard the jingle of bridles and thud of hooves as the five men spurred their horses and broke into a canter. He waited until the beats grew faint, and only then did he attempt to sit up; but the pain of his bruised body and cracked ribs was too great. He tried to call for help, but even that brought on more searing pain in his chest. All he could do was lay quietly, and wait.

CHAPTER TWO:
THE HOMESTEAD

On a moonless September night when the pine forests of the Cascade Mountains stirred not a leaf, the shapes of two men might have been seen lying flat on the ground, gazing across Henderson's Creek to the place of ill-omen on the other side. There was no sound but the distant soft rush and murmur of Little Elk River, which the creek, one of its many tributaries, joined it a quarter mile distant. The Little Elk flowed through the foothills of the mountains to Big Elk Lake, a lone stretch of fine trapping country skirted by towering forest.

This was a truly stunning and largely untouched part of the north-western country. Here and there the settlement of a nester who had faced immense difficulties in creating a home out of the wilderness was to be found, but for the most part, a great many miles separated one settlement from another. For these were the days when the lower foothills of the mountains were still largely passed over, at least by those of European ancestry, in favor of land easier to manage. Very often the men and women who achieved the great work of creating a homestead there were as happy as they were brave.

Two of this class of pioneers were Daniel and Elizabeth-Jane Henderson of the Little Elk Ranch, some mile or so south of the creek named after him. Though they called this land a ranch, it was something of a misnomer. Their forty head of cattle grazed on the natural meadows betwixt woods and craggy slopes, but their strength was in the variety of their agricultural enterprises. They had their tiny fields of corn, barley and potatoes, a vegetable patch, a milk-cow, hogs, goats and hens. There were four horses, a mule and a donkey, all of which had to serve as draft animals or mounts for the family according to need. Elizabeth-Jane was as hard-working as her husband, perhaps more so. They had three sons. Ben, with arms and chest as powerful any older man, was nineteen, and Kit, almost his equal in size and strength, eighteen. The pair were tireless and diligent in their labors, able to tackle any job required of them in field or farm. Christie, sixteen, was already as tall as his oldest brother, though skinny as a bean-pole. All three sons labored long hours, six days a week, to keep the spread running smoothly. Time away from the farm was generally employed in hunting for food and pelts, never in hunting for its own sake.

Both parents looked rather old for their ages, because life had been a tough business involving ceaseless work, constant strain. Therefore, Daniel Henderson, though still dauntless in spirit, was rather stiff of body, and his cigarette smoking wife was inclined to chest complaints at times of cold and foggy weather, which was an autumn speciality of this peculiar altitude of the mountains. Thus, a good deal of responsibility had fallen on the sons in recent years; this they accepted readily, all three being respectful of their parents, persevering, and steady.

In the case of Christie, perhaps a little too steady; for he, was, according to his father and brothers, a 'milksop', a 'mother's boy'. Perhaps this was an exaggeration. Certainly, he was hesitant and reluctant to do some of the more 'manly' tasks about the place, though he he worked as many hours in total as the others. But the other men regarded him, in fact, as something of an oddity. Christie wouldn't shoot a wolf on the hills, or a hawk near the yard. He hated guns in general. From an early age, he was afraid of the noise when his father's shotgun was discharged, and expressed sorrow and regret that turkeys or rabbits were shot to fill the cooking pot. Daniel Henderson was furious when Christie refused to set the traps. Nor would the boy take any part in the slaughter of a fattened cockerel, never mind a hog or goat! From the age of twelve, moreover, Christie had refused to eat meat, surviving on a diet of vegetables and cereals supplemented by eggs and milk. The other men blamed Christie's peculiar behavior on the adoption of this diet – that, and the molly-coddling of his mother, who would hear no criticism of her youngest son.

Ben and Kit were obliged to leave him out of many routine tasks that needed a bit of inner strength and resolve. Roping, branding, horse-breaking, stump-pulling, even plowing he would not attempt, these needing a firm hand on the horses and mule, which he was reluctant to give. Instead, he busied himself with gentler pursuits. Tending and milking the cow and goats, rearing and feeding fowls, weeding and watering the crops: these were things at which he excelled. In the vegetable garden he was happiest, taught all the skills required there by his mother. Sometimes she helped him sow, weed, hoe and harvest a variety of vegetables, not forgetting to nurture a few flowers with which to decorate the house. In the evenings the two of them conversed happily together in the kitchen, and on occasion he helped her cook, sew linen and brew beer. All but the latter drew frowns from Daniel and his older sons; but no amount of criticism and cajoling could persuade Christie to renounce any of his preferred activities.

As the youngest boy had advanced in years, the other men of the family grew ever more perplexed. Despite his slighter build, Christie was almost as strong as they were physically. He was not outwardly effeminate, nor was he timid, or the least afraid of encountering the displeasure of his father and brothers. In fact, he argued forcefully and fearlessly as to why it was not necessary to kill wild animals for food and skins, and even how the family might survive on a diet of vegetables alone – if only the others would help him expand the vegetable plots and grow more cereals. This did not go down at all well with the other men.

His brothers pointed out that at times of danger, he would have to show a little more backbone, and overcome his aversion to guns. There were Indians a-plenty in the region who, on occasion, attacked the settlers. Outlaws had been known to enter the area and threaten the owners of the sparse farmsteads of the foothills; and then there was their own problem with the Tranters.

This quarrelsome family were evidently taking advantage of their being no law enforcement agency close by, to steal and usurp the property of others. An extra gun, or pair of fists, might make all the difference when the inevitable clash came. More than for any other reason, Ben and Kit resented their brother for refusing to ready himself for a fight with the Tranters, despite what had happened to him not two months before. Pacifism would not help them survive if that clan came raiding; but vigilance and being prepared to meet force with force *might* just save them...

That is why Ben and Kit were crawling like Indians through the underbrush, as near as they could get to the crossing point at Henderson's Creek where the woods gave way to the muddy banks on the edge of the water. There, they could watch the movements of the family now living across the creek at 'Tranters' Reach', as the new arrivals called the land on 'their' side of the creek. The stronghold of Shaun

Tranter and his four sons was a log cabin and some wooden buildings beneath the edge of a cliff-like bank, and within the shelter of the woods. There was little cleared land on this side of the creek, only about two acres of felled trees, with patches of grass battling with thorny scrub for domination. Truly, Tranters' Reach was no working farm, nor did the place show much evidence of effort to improve their lot. Had it not been for a broad swathe of grassy land on either side of the creek, it is doubtful whether there would even have been enough fodder for the horses. One thing was evident, the Tranters' supplies of corn, grain, vegetables and meat did not originate on their own land.

Indeed, considering the number of people living on the Tranter side of the stream, and the ramshackle nature of the buildings and house, it was remarkable that man or beast could survive there at all. The small corral was made of poles and posts of all shapes and sizes, with bits of twig and knots still attached. A barn looked as if designed and put up by a half-wit, its base being an irregular rectangle, and its sides and door made of warped planks with many slits and gaps to let in the cold air. The hog-pen, from which the entire herd had long escaped, consisted of a circle of posts dug into the ground with lengths of briar and thorn woven in between. Hog shed, house and barn had the wonderful material of turf laid over planks on their roofs to repel the rain.

All in all, the chaotic lay-out and build Tranters' Reach spoke of a neglectful, untidy and slothful frame of mind. Small wonder that, when thinking of expanding his domain, old man Tranter could think only of usurping a neat, well-run farmstead, instead of constructing one of his own. But then, Shaun Tranter was a poor and twisted example of a pioneer.

Said to be the survivor of a feud back east in West Virginia, he had reputedly brought his family into the western wilderness to escape his many enemies. This was easy to believe, for the Tranters had revealed themselves as belligerent, suspicious and foul-tempered in their dealings with outsiders. The dwelling they occupied on the north side of Henderson Creek had originally belonged to two French trappers. While they were away hunting, the Tranters had moved in. It was a simple matter to drive the pair away with gunfire when they returned to assert their right to the cabin.

The Tranters had attempted to construct log extensions to this dwelling, but the crude result did not look very homely. Somehow, five sons, two daughters and the father survived in the hovel. The mother of the family was dead. She had been a big powerful woman, but had nevertheless died suddenly during a previous harsh winter. The daughters, as savage as the sons, did the housework, animal husbandry, trapping, or anything else they put their minds to, unrestrained by their gender. This included participating in raiding expeditions.

When old man Tranter took his clan into the surrounding countryside, they came back driving horses or cattle from other properties. If they needed stock, they simply put on their masks and took it. The masks, they rightly or wrongly believed, would cast doubt on the identity of the nocturnal raiders, making it more difficult for the law to say with certainty who was responsible for the spate of thieving. The masks might also, they thought, intimidate those who opposed them. Ironically, when out on a raid, the Tranter clan had, when challenged, claimed on more than one occasion to be 'vigilantes' looking for stolen stock!

Thus did that feral bunch of robbers brazenly ride out and

terrorize their neighbors, taking by force whatever they needed. Otherwise, they fished, hunted and trapped to feed themselves, and occasionally sold pelts and livestock at the Trading Post at Big Elk Lake to generate hard cash.

It was there, six months back, that old man Tranter had met Daniel and Ben Henderson and made them a startling proposition:

"Henderson," he said to Daniel, "I want to buy your spread. Name your price and I'll pay it. I won't take no for an answer."

The answer was not the one he wanted or expected. Daniel and Ben looked at each other uneasily. Then Dan Henderson stuck out his chin and spoke his mind.

"You ain't got enough money to buy Little Elk," said Dan Henderson, "an' even if that old cabin o' your'n were stacked from floor to ceiling with silver an' gold, I still wouldn't take it."

That was the first deadly insult. The second followed shortly, when the Hendersons turned their back on Shaun Tranter and walked away while he was still cursing them.

A few days after this episode the Tranters began to turn their full attention towards Little Elk and its occupants. Their activities were, for a time, fairly harmless, just hunting expeditions close to the Henderson's land, and animals stolen from snares and traps; but then more valuable items and livestock began to go missing from their property. Unbranded calves, a couple of piglets that strayed from the pens, even a goat had made their way across the creek. The hour before dawn was their favorite time to strike. The barking of the dogs had more than once roused the Henderson men, but by the time they had dressed and fetched guns, the thieves were long gone. Tracks inevitably led down to the creek.

That the Tranters had no scruples about rustling stock, nor emptying and stealing any traps they came across, was common knowledge in the region. But what were they to do about it? The Hendersons did not consider it sensible to accuse their neighbors outright of stealing, for such an accusation would doubtless lead to bloody confrontation. If the law were involved, there was the small matter of backing up their suit with solid proof; moreover, it would need armed defence to protect the Hendersons from the moment the Tranters were openly challenged.

The savage beating of Christie two months previously had taken things to a new level. Daniel had written to the new county sheriff, George Villiers, at Big Elk and described both the actions of the Tranters, and the suspicions he had that bigger crimes were likely to follow. Villiers was already aware of that notorious family, and was considering what he might do about them. He was also mindful of the fact that his predecessor, Frank Bowman, had disappeared on a trip to investigate the goings-on at Tranters' Reach some six months previously. Perhaps the Indians had got him, perhaps not; but it was a mystery that had put him in a cautious frame of mind. Furthermore, Villiers wondered what exactly he was expected to do when he finally caught up with eight extremely dangerous specimens way out in the wilderness.

The Tranters had only been three years at the cabin by the creek, but their increasing boldness, not least the undermining of the peace and prosperity of the Henderson family indicated they would stop at nothing to get what they wanted. The simple truth was that Sean Tranter coveted what Daniel Henderson already had, namely the pre-cleared land, the lush grazing meadows, and the house into which members of his own clan could be deposited to expand his domain; and by hook or by crook, he intended to have it.

One morning, upon opening his front door, Dan Henderson had found a square of white paper pinned to the outside of it. On it was written:

> YOU BIN STEALIN OUR STOCK
> WE'R COMIN TO GIT IT BACK.
> SIGNED THE VIGILANTEES

Across the yard in their corral, the oldest, scrawniest, meanest old mule they had ever seen had been planted. It would have been a laughable attempt at incriminating the Hendersons, had it not been done by so reckless and violent a clan. Clearly, the Tranters intended to escalate matters until they finally got the altercation they so desired...

CHAPTER THREE:
THE INJURED MAN

The Hendersons, who had never stolen so much as a bean in their lives, were outraged, for they were the ones being robbed of stock. Indeed, they had even considered visiting the Tranters to demand their own stolen animals be returned. This however, Elizabeth-Jane had talked them out of, reasoning that they would be lucky, if they did so, to return with their lives. Ben and Kit were furious about the note, and wanted to make a night visit to Tranters' Hill to return the mule. Daniel was willing enough, but again Mrs. Henderson wouldn't have it.

"If you go there like thieves in the night, they'll get you. Day or night, a trap awaits you. Oh, they'd like to get us fightin', all right," she said. "There's five of them men, and the daughters more like wildcats than women. There's only four of you – and they'll shoot you down the minute you turn up in their yard."

"Four of us, Ma?" said her husband gloomily," "You can't count Christie. He ain't disposed to fight."

Ben and Kit looked at each other knowingly and nodded in agreement.

"Christie," said Ben, "You gonna let us take 'em on without you? Are you a Henderson, or what?"

"I ain't fightin' them," said Christie, "'cos it's not needed. They're tryin' scarin' tactics. But if we let them be, they won't do us no harm, I'm sure of it."

"Just like the last time you met them?" said Kit without humor.

But Christie was not to be convinced; he went outside to

see to his fowls and rabbits. Afterwards, he led the old mule past their meadows, back through the woods towards the creek. Keeping within the cover of the trees, Christie released the mule from its collar and set it free. The beast wandered down to the creek, let out a terrific braying noise, then waded in and swam like an otter for home. By the time it reached the far bank, Christie was already on his way back to the farm.

Christie, who had never fought anyone in his life, not even his brothers, hated confrontations and quarrels, guns and knives, and all such horrible things. He loved the woods and the hills, the river, the beauty and peace. Most of all he loved his home. In his heart of hearts he simply couldn't understand why anyone would use violence to further an aim. But it was he who discovered the second note, and perhaps he begun to realize then, that the Tranters were not going to let them be. The note read:

UNLESS YOU ALL GON BY SUNDAY
ALL YOU'R GONNA GIT IT. YOU'R BIN
WARNED. THE VIGILANTEES ARE COMIN

The day this was found pinned to the door, Mrs. Henderson begged her husband to leave the hill, move the homestead and get out of the danger zone. At least, she said, make a temporary camp further into the hills. But Daniel Henderson and his sons knew that if they left, they would never come back. Even if they camped out, they would soon be pushed further away. Years of work had been put into the little farm and the fine, strong, log house with its outbuildings. The brothers knew that, if they wanted to hold on to their property, sooner or later they would have to fight;

and there would be bloodshed.

If Christie at last took the matter more seriously, he was not altered in his belief that it was still possible to talk to the Tranters and come to some agreement. As for Daniel Henderson, after the second demand, he took out and cleaned all the firearms they had in the house with care and precision. They had a muzzle-loading shotgun, a rifle, two pistols and a musket. After loading each of these, he selected the handguns, took Christie outside and pinned a piece of paper to a tree.

"Now, Christie," he said, "There's five shots in each of these-here Colt Patersons. See what you can do."

"I ain't firin' no guns," said Christie firmly.

"If you love your mama," said Dan, "You better learn to shoot. If them Tranters ever broke in and hurt her, you'd never forgive yourself. Do it for her."

Christie looked towards the house, saw his mother in the yard hanging out clothes. Without a word, he took the two old Colts, tore the paper from the tree and marched out to the woods. Presently, shots could be heard echoing through the forest. After ten shots, Christie returned, walked into the house and threw the guns back on the shelf.

"Can't hit a house," he said bitterly.

"Well," said his mother, "at least you tried. Ain't no shame in that."

"I hate the noise of them things," said Christie, "and the stink o' that powder. They scare the birds and stop their singin'. There was a chipmunk got a home in the split pine, but he lit out and charged up the forest. Guns are cruel things, Ma; why can't people talk things over to keep the peace?"

"Because," said his mother, "men are beasts, and beasts love to fight. But listen, Christie, if you don't want to end up like that chipmunk, practise and shoot them guns from time to time. Reck'n the more noise we make, the less likely it is them Tranters will come a-callin' one day, you hear me?"

Christie fired two or three shots each day, but always returned to the house despondent and shame-faced. Ben and Kit exchanged glances and shook their heads doubtfully.

"Reck'n he's more likely to shoot one o' us in a fight than hit a Tranter," said Ben.

"'Least he's made an effort to learn shootin' at last," said Kit.

"Too little, too late," said Ben; "He'll cave in at the first sign o' trouble."

"I'm not so sure," said Kit; "He's tough an' stubborn as hell when he wants to be."

"Yeah," said Ben, "but will he stand up an' shoot a man if them Tranters come at us with guns blazin'? I mean, he can't even wring the neck of a chicken."

"Well," said Kit, "come to that, ain't one of us ever drew a bead on a man before. But I've a feelin' we soon will – if we wanna stay put, that is."

The two older brothers increased their scouting expeditions by the creek to watch for any suspicious movements of the Tranters. On the very Sunday of the second note's ultimatum, when Ben and Kit were doing their observations, they crawled to the edge of the low hill opposite Tranter's Reach and surveyed the land below. From their position overlooking the creek, they could see the place was quiet, with nobody visible.

"I guess they ain't home," whispered Kit.

"Look," said Ben, pointing to the bank on their own side of the creek. There, three canoes were moored, indicating that the Tranters had crossed to the Henderson side some time earlier.

"I don't like the look of it," said Kit, "they've come over on foot and made themselves scarce – but why?"

"They may have gone over to our place by a roundabout route," said Ben, "Otherwise we'd have seen them on our way here. We better go back..."

Suddenly his brother gripped his arm, pinched it hard, and made a sign towards the woods below them. Forty yards distant, a path led down to the river. Both of these young men had the hearing of forest-dwellers, and in the moment that Ben touched him, Kit knew someone was approaching. Motionless they lay, eyes fixed on the patch of dusky woodland from whence the sound came.

"It's them," Kit whispered in his brother's ear. In a moment each of them had drawn from his pocket a pistol. They pulled their hats low, and waited.

It was already evening, and the setting sun threw a pale light on the woods. Through a long gap in the undergrowth they saw a shape move past, then another and another. There was no noise, other than the faintest snap of a dead twig, or the rustle of leaves, sounds that might be caused by the gentlest of breezes. It was just possible to see that each figure carried a gun, and over each head, instead of a hat, was a hood, with two holes for eyesight in the front. Their masks were black, and covered their heads and necks. The effect of seeing this parade of masked men was disturbing, not least because it suggested the wearers might already have carried out some outrage. Even in the wilderness close to home the Tranters had taken the usual precaution of hiding their faces, always mindful that this might one day save them from the law.

As the sons of Henderson watched, they saw the file of men go down to the creek. A formidable bunch they were too, for most were tall and well-built. They made for the base of the creek, embarked in their canoes and paddled the few feet over to the other side. Before they reached the far bank, all masks were off, and Ben and Kit could hear their murmurs of laughter and praise and congratulation for each other. But what had they done to earn those sinister accolades? That was the question that perplexed the brothers. They did not wait to see the Tranters finally reach their cabin, but made for home immediately.

"The whole lot of them," whispered Ben as they strode on, "came from the direction of home. I got a horrible feeling in the pit of my stomach."

"Me too," said his brother, breaking into a lope; "Let's get back quick. Those masks – nobody dresses up like that 'less he's up to no good."

"Dad was out by himself with the steers this afternoon," panted Ben as they hurried.

"He'll be all right," answered Kit, "I hope..."

As they ran, their moccasins made little sound on the moss and pine needles of the forest. About half a mile from the homestead, on the track that led from the cattle grazing down to the yard, their worst fears were realized when they came upon a prone body by the side of the trail.

To all appearances Daniel Henderson was dead. His sons thought so at first, and they looked for a bullet wound when they found him covered in blood. In a few seconds they learned that he still breathed and that he was not shot. He was beaten nearly to death. His arm was broken and his head terribly cut. Between them they carried him home, and vowed a terrible revenge on the Tranters, though they had no idea how they might ever carry it out. They took the unconscious man into the house and laid him on the quilt of his own bed. At first their mother cried in anguish, but soon recovered and set about tending to his wounds.

"They half-killed him with fists and rifle-butts," muttered Ben in a voice that was savage with anger. "It's that Tranter lot, Ma. Our Pa never done harm to a living soul, an' look what they done. But we'll get them for it, Ma."

"That's a promise, Ma" said Kit.

But as the brothers were vowing how they'd visit the Tranters and take the rifle and shotgun to level the score, their mother suddenly turned on them.

"Ben! Kit!" she cried, "Your father here is bad sick, an' all you can talk about is gettin' yourselves hurt – or worse. Just look!"

She stepped aside and pulled back the blanket so that Daniel Henderson's face and upper body was visible. The man was covered in bruises, and his breathing was labored and fast.

"Boys, talk sense," she said more quietly. "Our first task is to get your father a doctor. One of you must go to Big Elk first thing in the morning. I won't have either of you away from the house tonight, nor do I want you riding off into the dark. One injured man is enough for me today."

Neither Kit nor Ben so much as spoke to Christie. When it came to protecting the farm, and their parents, he simply did not count. The way they saw things, a brother who was yellow was no good to anyone.

Their mother, as courageous as her type needs to be in times of serious danger, sat up all night watching her husband, holding his hand and attending to his every need. She said nothing, her face gray with anguish. Early in the morning she bathed him again with warm water, and covered him in more ointment for his welts and bruises. Then, she waited by his side patiently.

Just as she closed her eyes to sleep, Daniel woke with a start and began to speak. He was surprisingly lucid.

"Lizzie," he said, "They got me. They busted my arm an' collar-bone, I can feel it. Help me get to my feet."

"Oh Dan," she wept out of relief, "Don't try to move – you're hurt bad. You need a doctor."

"My legs are all right, I think," he said, "but I need this arm set quick. The bone's bust."

"Ben'll go for the doctor, at the trading post," said Elizabeth-Jane; "He'll come an' fix you, you'll see."

"No," said Dan firmly, "he won't. Their policy is for the physician there to stay put, except in the case of company men that get in trouble. He'll not come all this way."

"Oh Dan!" wept Elizabeth-Jane, just as the three sons came in the room.

"Listen," said Dan gamely, "I ain't hurt so bad – only this arm's bust, and you gotta get me to Big Elk. I need the doc there, an' it won't wait. I'm bleedin' under my skin."

"Pa," said Ben, "we can't move you in your condition, You'd never make it."

"Listen," said Daniel Henderson through gritted teeth, "I've made the trip before, that time young Christie busted his ankle. I carried him over to the creek, then paddled him down to the lake an' over to the company surgeon. Now you boys gotta do the same for me."

"But Pa," protested Kit, "you'll be in terrible pain-"

"No arguments," said Dan, "My mind is made up. If you don't take me, I'm a-walkin' there myself."

He set his jaw tight and stared defiantly at the sons, who in turn looked at their mother for support.

"He's right," she said. "I don't like it neither, but that break will fester if he don't get to Big Elk. If the doc won't come here, well then boys, we've got no choice."

After giving him a modest breakfast of broth, the family managed to get Daniel dressed and prepared for the journey. Though they were able to get him in his baggiest corduroy pants, his upper body had to be covered in two thick blankets, his head protruding through holes cut poncho-style to keep him warm.

"Now boys," he said, "Christie an' Kit carry me down to the river. Ben, get the rifle to guard us in case them Tranters show up. If you see hide nor hair of 'em, shoot on sight. You got that Ben?"

"Sure, Pa," said Ben. "Ma, you stay here, keep the shotgun close by, and we'll be back soon's we can."

"Don't worry about me, boys," said Ma Henderson picking up the shotgun. "Your pa must have a doctor. Now go."

"We sure hate to leave you, Ma," said Kit.

"I got me a musket, too," said his mother. "You boys take the pistols and rifle. Here's money to pay for the doctor, and a good nurse too. Christie, you stay there with your pa for a couple of days till he's ready to travel. Ben an' Kit, you hurry back home. So long, boys."

The plan was that they should carry their father down to the river, make him as easy as could be managed in the largest canoe, and paddle him down to the settlement at the trading post some forty miles distant. The route was along Little Elk

River to Big Elk Lake, then to Ravens Point as it was called, a thriving hamlet on its northern shore. There they would find the company headquarters and a doctor or person skilled in medicine, whose job it was to tend to the medical needs of the trading staff and those who trapped for them. Anybody else in need might also find assistance, at the discretion of the doctor.

It was a chance, a bold venture, but they believed their father would die unless he had skilled treatment. They must risk the autumn cold and a long journey. First they would carry him down to where the creek joined Little Elk River. Their trail would be a diagonal one that avoided the area opposite Tranter's Reach.

Once embarked in their canoe, they would go upstream into Big Elk Lake, and then follow the shore to Ravens Point. Though the boat journey would be easier and quicker than the jolting of a ride on horseback, it was still an arduous undertaking for a man risen from his sick bed, with terrible bruising and a broken arm. But all members of the family were in agreement that the thing must be done; and so they set about their labor of love.

While Christie and Kit carried him down in a blanket, Ben went ahead to reconnoiter and ready the big canoe they kept hidden in the trees for fishing trips.

"We shan't camp, nor sleep, Pa," said Ben, "but it'll take us ten hours solid to get there."

"Sure," agreed Dan Henderson, wincing in pain as they traveled, "I'll doze on the way, just press on, boys, press on, and I'll be just fine."

He took the devotion of his sons for granted. They would get him through. The preparations had been swift, with the three brothers working together. They had even thought to give their father the last of their laudanum to deaden his pain on this first part of the journey.

Before the sun had risen too high, he had been borne down the well-worn trail, and made as comfortable as possible in the large birch-bark canoe. In the gray mist of morning, Dan Henderson lay in his blanket bed, covered with pelts, with Ben at his head, and Kit by his feet.

"Push off, Christie, and get in my end," said Ben, there's just room; "We'll take turns with the paddles, we only got two of 'em."

"I ain't coming," was the answer, as Christie pushed the long craft out into the stream. "I'm going home to Ma. She got to see to all the stock alone, an' it's too much for her on her own. 'Sides, if them Tranters come, an' Ma's all alone..."

"He's right boys," said a weak voice from under the blankets. "Give him the pistols, Ben. If anyone's gonna need them now, it's him."

Ben and Kit exchanged anxious glances.

"Pa's right," said Kit; "Ma needs him – though what use he'd be in a fight I don't know."

"I can shoot," shrugged Christie, "if I have to."

"No sense arguing," muttered Ben; "Give him your gun, Kit, an' let's go."

CHAPTER FOUR:
THE SIEGE

The long craft slid away into the mist, and Christie set off on the mile or so walk back. When he reached the yard, it looked strangely lonely and desolate, with no one to be seen. The only living thing that came to meet him was Mazie the dog, who had two fat puppies sleeping in the woodshed. She ran, tail wagging, to see the return of her beloved master. Christie touched her muzzle in greeting, then looked about him for his mother.

"Ma!" he called, "Ma! Where you at, Ma? It's me Christie..."

"Christie! I almost shot you," said a voice from behind the henhouse; "You came back – an' I'm mighty glad of it."

Christie walked over to his mother, who was carrying the old shotgun, and gave her a quick embrace. The old dog Bruno was with her. He flapped his tail lazily at the sight of Christie.

"It'll be all right, Ma," he said; "Pa's on his way in the canoe. We'll work the farm together today."

Then, seeing her glance at the path behind him nervously, he added:

"Don't worry, Ma – I got the Patersons."

He was referring to the ancient Colt .44's, relics of a bygone era, though they still worked perfectly well, at least the last times they'd been used. The Colt Paterson was a curious gun, a five shot revolver with a concealed trigger that dropped down when the hammer was cocked. There was no guard over the trigger, so that, once readied, the guns had to be handled with care. Furthermore, the hammer rested over a cap, so that a slight tap might set the thing off. To all these oddities, Christie gave never a thought, only noting how heavy the weapons were, tucked into his belt all day.

Mother and son were kept busy with the milking, feeding, and tending as required; and then fetching and storing wood and water within the house. They hardly knew whether to expect a siege or not, but they were cautious and prepared for the worst. Christie thought it wise to take certain precautions. With that in mind, he looked at all the locks and bolts, tried them for fastness. He closed and secured the windows, and drew curtains, which were left open as a rule. Most of the windows were too small to admit a human figure, with the exception of one in the kitchen and one in the living room.

As the evening came on, Elizabeth-Jane brought a simple meal into the living room and put the two dishes on the table. Then she leaned her shotgun next her chair and called Christie in to eat. She had decided already that this central position would be her post if it became necessary to defend the house. She could watch the big window, which gave a view of the rear fields; meanwhile, Christie could guard the kitchen, which had the main entrance door to the porch as well its own big window, which overlooked the yard.

With all other windows closed and bolted from the inside, including the parents' bedroom on the ground floor, and the loft room overhead with the three beds for the sons, the house was pretty much inaccessible from outside, unless something as formidable as an axe was employed.

At the last of twilight, Christie asked of his mother that the dogs be allowed in the house. Elizabeth-Jane, though she feigned annoyance, agreed to his request, for she was secretly pleased to have the dogs close by. Mazie and Bruno were excellent guard dogs that would warn them of danger. When 'strangers' such as the preacher or a friendly neighbor called round, they would refrain from getting down from their horse or buggy until they had called out: 'Is that ol' devil Bruno locked up?' Mazie, like Bruno, was a formidable animal when her blood was up, and her hackles raised. She would be assigned a box for her and her puppies, the latter making her extra vigilant. So, Elizabeth-Jane reasoned, if any stranger was to get into the house that night, there would be serious consequences.

It was a strange sensation, with chores and meals completed, as evening stars came out, for Christie and his mother to be sat in the house, with the quiet ticking of the family clock, the snoring of the dogs on the floor, and the stirring of the leaves on the trees outside. The signs suggested all was peaceful and well in the world. Yet, if the Tranters were serious about ousting their neighbors from Little Elk – and they were – this was the time they would strike.

"You think they'll come, Ma?" said Christie.

"They'll come," said Elizabeth-Jane.

"When, Ma?" he asked, knowing the answer already.

"Soon," she said; "There's a big ol' moon tonight for them to see by. The boys will be back tomorrow, and you can bet those cowards have found out by now. And those Tranters have already shown their true intentions. If it were any other family, I'd say they'd be ashamed to do what they're doin'. But they ain't right in the head... so they'll come. An' they'll either kill us or run us off the place. "

"They can try," said Christie.

"They might do more'n that," said Elizabeth-Jane, making herself a cigarette.

"I ain't leavin', Ma," said Christie.

"Nor am I, son," said his mother.

"I'm sorry, Ma," said Christie.

"What for, son?" she said.

"Bein' kinda odd, I guess," he said.

"You ain't nothin' out o' the ordinary," she laughed, lighting her cigarette and puffing away happily. "Lots of men are kind and gentle like you, son," she said; "It's just that most folks have fixed notions of how you should, you know, carry yourself, work, fight – all that ol' nonsense."

"I guess," he said.

"Lots of men, too," she said bitterly, "feel the need to go upsettin' their neighbors an' fellow man, an' take what ain't rightly theirs."

"But why, Ma?" he said, "Why can't all men get on, without fightin', an' cheatin', an' stealin' each other's land? Why?"

Elizabeth-Jane blew a big cloud of smoke in the room and laughed. She went to a cupboard and brought out a brown bottle. Christie recognized it as the 'medicinal' whiskey she kept there to ease her chest when the cold, damp weather got the better of her. She poured two fair-sized measures into glasses and handed one to her son.

"Drink it," she said.

"Ma!" said Christie, "You know I don't drink."

"Drink it, anyway," she said, "and then listen."

Christie drank a big gulp, screwed up his face and listened.

"I got a premonition," she said; "It's only a feeling, but I reck'n them Tranters are gonna kill me tonight."

"Ma!" he said, shocked; "That's nonsense! They won't harm you, I won't let 'em."

"T'ain't in your power," she said, "to save me from five or more of them; so I want you to listen. If they get me, I want you to bury me under that big apple tree out yonder – you know the one, in the middle of the orchard – an' every time you pass by, you'll know I'm sleepin' peaceful, an' that I'm happy there in my own little orchard. Can you do that, son?"

"Ma!" said Christie, with tears in his eyes, "I ain't listenin' to your nonsense. You ain't gonna die, Ma, I won't let you. We'll be all right – maybe they won't even come, an' the others'll be back an', an'-"

Bruno stood up and began to growl. He had been fast asleep on a rug, but now he was wide awake and facing the door. Mazie, too, was on her feet, hackles raised, lips drawn back in a prolonged snarl.

"It's time, son," said Elizabeth-Jane, picking up her shotgun; "You go in the kitchen now. You know what to do?"

Christie nodded to his mother, blew out the oil-lamp, then walked into the other room with his two pistols.

Christie laid the Colt Patersons on an empty chair next the window and peered out into the yard. The guns were heavy, well oiled and clean. They had been carefully loaded. He regarded them with mixed feelings. Had his father been armed with one of these, he might have escaped last night. Yet, though they were necessary, they were instruments of death, and he was not sure he could use them, even in anger.

"Nothin' but killing, everywhere you look in this ol' world," he muttered.

"Don't talk like that, Christie," said his mother, who had heard him through the open door. "We only kill when it's strictly necessary, you know that."

"Sorry, Ma," said Christie in a low voice; "It's just that after all that's happened, I got to thinking how everyone'd be better off without these darned guns at all."

"Well," said Elizabeth-Jane; "since them crazies out there is very likely armed to the teeth, tonight we got to meet fire with fire. Be strong, son, we're gonna need to use them irons before this night is through."

"I won't let them kill you, Ma," said Christie. "But why can't them Tranters be content with their own side of the Creek? It's land enough for the likes o' them, with grass an' lumber, an' good huntin'..."

"Hush your foolish talk now, son," said Elizabeth-Jane, "We got business to attend to. Watch that yard – them horses are stampin' fit to raise the devil."

Even as Christie saw the first shadowy figure out by the stables, his thoughts were racing, unable to focus on the approaching danger. Instead of coldly calculating how his guns might protect his mother and the house, he began to think of days he had spent with her making soda bread, flapjacks, cookies and stew. He thought of the two of them gardening, gathering fruit, feeding the hens and rabbits...

A masked man crossed the yard in front of him, and Christie carefully and quietly unlatched the two hinged frames of the window and pushed them apart. He saw a man trying to get into the stable to his right. Another was standing with his gun pointed at Bruno's empty kennel.

Christie raised a pistol and tried to aim at the man by the kennel, but he couldn't bring himself to hold the sights on a human form, no matter what the man intended to do.

"Though shalt not kill," be muttered to himself. Mazie, in the other room, heard him speak, and came to his side. From her throat rolled one continuous growl of protest. Christie

247

caressed her head with his free hand, whispered some nonsense to her, but she ignored his fussing and kept up the steady grumbling and growling. In its box, a puppy cried pitifully for milk, but Mazie stayed next to Christie, her nose sniffing the chill air coming in from outside.

Standing by the window, Christie looked out at the place he loved, the dark sheds, the barn and stables, the shine of the moon on the harvested corn and barley fields.

Somewhere across the yard, hens cackled in alarm, and a faint noise reached Christie as if someone or something had come up against the outside of the house not ten feet away. He peered out into the moonlit yard. When nothing caught his eye, he lowered his gun, hoping that what he had heard was only a bush or plant touching against the side of the house as the breeze blew it to and fro.

But his worst fears were confirmed when the door-latch was lifted and the bolted door creaked as somebody outside tried to push it open. Mazie flew snarling towards it, and the latch dropped back into its bracket. Then, Christie saw two masked men boldly walking toward him, rifles in one hand, axes from the woodshed in another.

"It don't have to be this way!" he shouted.

The moving figures both seemed to disappear at once.

For a minute there was dead silence. Then came the harsh voice of Shaun Tranter:

"We don't aim to kill you, boy;" he said, "Not 'less we have to. If you light out, now, we'll do ye no harm. But if you choose to fight us – I won't answer for the consequences."

"My brother Ben's gone for the law," said Christie, trying a different tack; "He'll be back with the sheriff any minute."

Loud and raucous laughter greeted this comment.

248

"I hope not," said another voice, "We buried the sheriff o' this neck o' the woods six month ago."

Despite this last statement, Christie persisted:

"They got a new one," he shouted; "He's poison, so they say."

More laughter.

"So's we, boy," said one of the men.

Again, Christy tried to engage them, thinking something might come of it.

"An' what you did to my pa," he said. "That was a terrible thing to do to an old man. Ain't you ashamed?"

"Oh sure," said a voice, "We's all cut up 'bout the old goat!"

"My pa ain't no goat," protested Christie.

"We won't stand for no more cackle," broke in Shaun Tranter. "I'll level with you kid. We saw your brothers paddlin' up Little Elk with your ol' man. That means you'n your ma are alone. If you take her out o' here an' git, we'll give you the mule an' that burro. If you say no, we're comin' in shootin'. That's your last chance, boy. Take it or leave it."

Just then, Elizabeth-Jane came stomping over to the kitchen window, pushed Christie to one side and stuck out the muzzle of her old double-barreled gun. Two of the sons in their masks walked into view, and she pulled her first trigger. The gun went off with a terrific roar, sending her backwards a step with the recoil.

Outside, as the smoke cleared, two men could be seen writhing on the ground, both plastered with buckshot from the same charge. A figure ran forward to help them, and she took aim and fired again. There was a loud scream, and the man lurched sideways, dragging a leg.

Christie, his hands over his ears, was horrified.

"Go home!" he shouted out the window, "We don't want to kill ya!"

"Speak for yourself!" cursed his mother. "Damn – I shot too low – now the varmint's run off to join the others."

She grounded the stock of the gun and began her re-load from the powder and shot flasks she'd hung around her neck.

"This is crazy," hissed Christie, looking out into the gloom. He was about to try words of peace again, when he caught a glimpse of another shape in the moonlight.

"Get away from the window, Ma!" he said, reaching out to push her aside. But his arms didn't make contact. Shots rang out from the darkness, and his mother staggered backwards as if she were going to fall. Christie stepped over to help her, but she recovered herself, and pushed him away.

"Let me be, I'm all right," she said. "Christie, they're running out the back. Go cover the parlor window!"

At that moment Bruno in the other room let out a terrific snarl, and pounced. A man had leapt in through the window. It was a brave move on the part of one of the Tranters – and a foolish one. The big, wolf-like dog soon had the man on the floor. But two other sinister figures dropped down into the room to help him. Seeing the dog, they drew their knives and advanced.

Mazie flew at them and joined in the fight. Christie went to the doorway and peered inside at the commotion. It was dark, but enough moonlight streamed in through the big window to see at least the outlines of the men. At first, Christie dared not shoot for fear of hitting the dogs, but one of the men had heard his footsteps, and fired twice in his direction. Christie felt one bullet graze his cheek, before the other thumped him squarely on the left shoulder, sending him reeling back into the kitchen. A dog yelped in terrible agony, as a knife found its mark. Then, a shot rang out, followed by another, and the snarls ceased abruptly.

For a few seconds Christie froze, unsure what to do next. His left arm was numb, useless. Over by the window the shotgun roared again, to be answered by another flurry of shots. Then, he heard his mother fall. In a few strides he was by her side. There was blood all over her clothes, and her eyes were half-closed in pain. Christie raised her head off the floor and held one of her hands.

"Christie," she whispered, "Is that you?"

"Yes, Ma," he said.

Her hand gripped his with a surprising force, her nails digging into his skin, and then, with a little sigh, her eyes flickered and she was gone.

Christie's face grew hot and red, a buzzing filled his ears, and he stood up. In an instant the nagging feeling that had kept him from hitting back at his tormentors had vanished. Instinct and rage took over. He would go on living, and the only way to do that was to strike out at those who deserved no mercy.

Without consciously thinking about it, he took up one of the old Patersons in his right hand and pulled back the hammer with his thumb. The trigger clicked into position and he turned to the window just as a masked man appeared there. He poked the muzzle in the chest of the man and the gun kicked in his hand, sending the man flying backwards. There were no others in view outside, so he turned his attention to the living room. Gruff voices were urging each other to enter the kitchen.

"You go!" said one.

"Hell no!" said another, "You do it."

"Step back," said a third, "and let a man do it!" and he stepped toward the door.

Christie appeared in the door-frame, fired once. The three intruders were lit up in the flash. As he loosed off his remaining three shots the Tranter boys let rip too. Bullets criss-crossed the room, smashed crockery, rent woodwork – and flesh. The air became filled with thick, acrid gun-smoke, and the floor slippery with blood.

CHAPTER FIVE:
THE FELLOWSHIP

When Christie awoke, it was still dark, and he was lying on the boards of the porch. He had no idea how he had got there. A bearded man was lying next to him, his face grinning in mockery, sinister in the moonlight. As Christie's senses came back to him, he realized the man, Shaun Tranter, was not moving. In fact, he had a large knife – Christie's own pocket knife – sticking out of his ribs. A mask lay beside him. With a start, Christie remembered the gunfight, the dogs in the kitchen... his mother. He tried to rise, but he could not move. He began to weep, quietly, almost silently. The only comfort came from the puppy noises within the house. He could hear both of them – they would be all right. He was glad he had thought to bring the critters inside. But they were young, not yet weaned – who would feed and look after them now?

When a gray veil covered the moon, and nothing was to be seen outside the cabin, nor through its open door, he grew dizzy, weak, and became unconscious. He awoke to find Mazie prodding him with a cold nose. She had a deep gash in her side, but her tail was wagging, and she stood easily on her bloody legs. It was dawn. A new day had begun.

The dog persisted in its nuzzling, as if to say 'Come on, get up and fetch me my breakfast, then feed those fowls an' critters, they're hungry like me,' and Christie smiled. Then Mazie, hearing her pups, limped off into the kitchen to suckle them.

Christie lay back, heard the hungry note of the pups give way to contented silence as their mother suckled them. He closed his eyes again, and listened to the singing of the birds high up in the trees.

Ben and Kit appeared in the yard just before sun-down. They brought with them George Villiers the new sheriff, whom they'd met at Big Elk. He was a small, tough fellow clad in buckskins and a trapper's fur hat. He had a Sharps rifle, a Colt Walker and a large, antler-handled knife on his belt. Two weeks into the job, conscious that his predecessor had disappeared in mysterious circumstances, he was somewhat wary of meeting the notorious Tranters. But he could hardly refuse the request of the two Henderson boys, namely, that he go back with them and offer their family some kind of protection; and so he went in their canoe, not quite sure what he might find at Little Elk Ranch.

The first thing the three men saw were a pair of twisted bodies peppered with buckshot next the stable door. One of them was a woman, wearing men's breeches and a gun-belt, a rusty pistol still clutched in her hand. A trail of blood led to a third body behind the dog kennel. Elizabeth-Jane had been wrong: her second target hadn't got away when she shot low after all.

"Lord Almighty!" said Villiers, "Who done all this?"

Then they turned toward the house and saw Christie and the body of Shaun Tranter on the porch. Christie was in a bad way by this time, but he still breathed. Badly in need of water, he would live and his many scars would heal, given time. But first, his shoulder, through which a slug had passed, required some attention, and his knife-wounds cleaning and stitching. For sure, a large measure of Ma's old whiskey would be needed to deaden the pain during those activities.

While Ben and Kit examined Christie, George Villiers stepped over old man Tranter and went gingerly into the kitchen.

"Good Lord Almighty!" his voice exclaimed from within, "Good Lord Almighty!"

"I had to do it," whispered Christie to his brothers. "They wouldn't listen to no reasonable talk."

"Good ol' Christie," muttered Kit, "You downed 'em all, eh?"

"Me an' Ma," said Christie.

"Ma?" said Kit with a start, "Where is she Christie? Where's she hiding?"

Christie closed his eyes and let out a stifled sob. The two older brothers looked at each other with trepidation, then stood up and walked like automatons into the blood-washed house.

Villiers was already on the way out. With ashen face he stepped back out onto the porch, fumbled in a pocket for his tobacco, and began to roll himself a smoke with unsteady hands.

"Well, here was a royal fellowship of death!" said Villiers, who knew his Shakespeare, in a low voice; "I come expectin' to talk to old man Tranter and his kin about a few serious matters, an' find the lot of 'em dead – wiped out by a skinny kid and an old woman. Heck, is this a homestead or a battlefield? Men, women, even a dog, all shot to death or cut to ribbons. A royal fellowship of death, indeed."

THE END

WESTERNS: WARPATHS & PEACEMAKERS

Six novellas, including the tense drama of *'Cross-Gun Cairns!'* in which Sheriff Stevie Fitzpatrick goes gunning for the most dangerous man in the territory...

WESTERNS 2: WILD AS THE WIND!

Seven novellas of the old West & Civil War... check out THE PLAINS OF ARIZONA in which outlaw Matty McCray is recruited as a law enforcer – with tragic consequences.

WESTERNS 4: YARNS OF THE OPEN RANGE

Cow-punchers stuck in a cabin in a storm share curious tales of life in cattle country, including encounters with Wild Bill Hickok, a killer hiding out in a cabin, and a man named 'Hookey Cross' who sells guns to the Apaches...

WILDCARD WESTERNS
In association with the DERNFORD PRESS

Made in the USA
Columbia, SC
10 June 2024